REPROBATE LORD, RUNAWAY LADY

To the friends who listened.

'A maidservant who speaks French as well as having a French name! It becomes more and more intriguing.' Gareth looked searchingly at Amelie.

'I'd hardly say that I spoke French,' she said, desperately seeking a way of moving the conversation onto less dangerous ground.

'Still, it's an unusual maid who knows any French. And you *are* an unusual maid, aren't you? You're proud and independent, you speak genteelly and hold yourself like a lady. If it weren't for your clothes I would take you for a lady.'

Isabelle Goddard was born into an army family and spent her childhood moving around the UK and abroad. Unsurprisingly it gave her itchy feet, and in her twenties she escaped from an unloved secretarial career to work as cabin crew and see the world.

The arrival of marriage, children and cats meant a more settled life in the south of England, where she's lived ever since. It also gave her the opportunity to go back to 'school' and eventually teach at university. Isabelle loves the nineteenth century and grew up reading Georgette Heyer, so when she plucked up the courage to begin writing herself the novels had to be Regency romances.

REPROBATE LORD, RUNAWAY LADY is Isabelle Goddard's debut novel for Mills & Boon® Historical.

REPROBATE LORD, RUNAWAY LADY

Isabelle Goddard

First published in Great Britain 2010
Harlequin Mills & Boon Limited,
Eton House, 18-24 Paradise Road, Richmond, Surrey TW9 1SR

© Isabelle Goddard 2010

ISBN: 978 0 263 21474 1

Harlequin Mills & Boon policy is to use papers that are natural,
renewable and recyclable products and made from wood grown in
sustainable forests. The logging and manufacturing process conform
to the legal environmental regulations of the country of origin.

Printed and bound in Great Britain
by CPI Antony Rowe, Chippenham, Wiltshire

Chapter One

London, 1817

'Amelie, you will do this for me, for the family.' It was a command rather than a question.

The young woman held her head high and blinked back the tears. Despite her resolution, there was a stricken look in the soft brown eyes.

'Papa, I cannot. Ask anything else of me, but I cannot marry that man.'

Her father, pacing agitatedly back and forth across the worn library carpet, stopped suddenly opposite her and raked her with a piercing glare. 'Sir Rufus Glyde is a respected nobleman, one who will give you an elegant home and a secure future. And one who will save this family from disaster.'

She looked past her father to the open window, but hardly saw the mass of roses filling the garden with a riot of colour in the late afternoon sun.

'Surely, Papa,' she pleaded, 'the situation cannot be that desperate.'

Lord Silverdale was silent. His face, though still handsome, appeared haggard and drawn. He carefully brushed the snuff from a velvet sleeve and spoke quietly but insistently.

'The family is virtually ruined. Over the past few months I have had to sell my entire stable of horses and rent out Nethercott Place to a wealthy cit. Generations of Silverdales dishonoured by the taint of city money! And now Robert's addiction to gambling is likely to lose us our last piece of security—our house here in Grosvenor Square.'

'In that case,' she responded sharply, 'why doesn't Robert find a way of repaying what he owes?' Her brother's decadent lifestyle was something she could not forgive. 'Why doesn't *he* marry for money?'

Lord Silverdale looked at his daughter, breathtakingly lovely even in simple sprig muslin, and said gently, 'Amelie, you know that it isn't possible. What does he have to offer except debt and unsteadiness? Certainly nothing the matchmaking mamas at Almack's want. You, on the other hand, have youth, beauty and a steadfast character. Rufus Glyde admires you and wants to make you his wife.'

'But he is nearly twice my age.'

'He is no more than fourteen years older than you. That is no great age. It is well for a husband to be more experienced than his wife. Then he may teach her how to go on in society.'

An image of Rufus Glyde's dissolute eyes and thin, sneering lips swam into her vision and made her shudder. She would not wish to be taught anything by such a man. In her revulsion she twisted the cambric handkerchief she held into a vicious knot.

'I can never care for him,' she declared hotly.

'But do you care for anyone else? You have had an entire Season to find someone to your taste, a Season I could ill afford. And look what has happened. You have been distant and unapproachable to the young men you've met. Only one was willing to brave your coldness and actually offer for you, and you dismissed his proposal out of hand. So what do you want?'

'I want to remain single, Papa. I'm grateful for my introduction to society, but the men I've met have been either shallow or profligate. I shall never marry unless I find a man I truly love and respect—and that seems unlikely.'

'You will be lucky to find any man in the future. There will be no more Seasons—and no home, either, if Sir Rufus forecloses on our mortgage,' her father added bitterly.

She caught her breath. 'What do you mean?'

'I had not meant to tell you, but you should know the truth of the situation. Your brother has lost this house to Rufus Glyde. In a fit of madness he used it as a stake for his gambling. Either you marry Sir Rufus or we are homeless.'

'How can you allow him to threaten us like this?'

'Come, come, child, the man is willing to make a generous settlement on you, apart from returning the mortgage. He will, I am sure, always treat you with respect and you will have ample money and time to pursue your own interests. Such marriages of convenience are common among our class. You know that.' Lord Silverdale paused, thinking of his own love marriage, its first intoxicating passion barely surviving a year. 'They can often work far better than marrying for love.'

Amelie turned away, unwilling to show the disgust she felt.

'I have no choice,' her father said heavily. 'This is a debt of honour and must be paid, one way or another.'

'And I am to pay the debt,' she cried, her anger bursting forth. 'I am to be the family sacrifice, am I?' She strode furiously up and down the room between the dusty book-filled shelves, chestnut curls tumbling free and framing her lovely face.

With an exasperated mutter, Lord Silverdale walked swiftly towards her and grasped her hands. 'Enough. You forget yourself. You are beautiful and clever, my dear, but you are far too independent. It puts men off and those it doesn't, you will not have. Think yourself lucky that Sir Rufus values high spirits as well as being a connoisseur of beauty. He has very properly asked me for permission to pay his addresses to you, and I have agreed.'

'No, no, I cannot do it,' she uttered a strangled cry. 'Anything but that! I'll go out and earn my own bread rather.'

'Earn your own bread? What is this? Your taste for the dramatic is regrettable and too reminiscent of your French relations,' he said disdainfully, walking away from her towards the tall windows.

When he turned again, his face wore an implacable expression and he spoke in a voice that brooked no further disagreement.

'You have been made a highly advantageous offer, Amelie, which will secure this family's future and your own. You will go to your room immediately and stay there. In the morning you will make yourself presentable. Sir Rufus will be with us at noon and you will accept his offer. Do I make myself clear?'

The interview was at an end. Lord Silverdale sank wearily down at his desk, and began listlessly to leaf through his scattered papers. His daughter, overcome with angry tears, turned on her heel and noisily banged the oak-panelled door behind her.

Once in her room, she cast herself down on to the damask bedspread and wept. Her grief was intense and though her tears soon subsided, her fury remained. To be forced into a repugnant marriage because of her brother's stupidity! And by her own father! She knew him to be autocratic, but never so unfeeling that he would contemplate selling her to the highest bidder. He might try to wrap it up in clean linen, but that's what it came down to.

When she was a child he'd been an indulgent parent, reading with her, schooling her on her first pony, bringing surprises each birthday. Yet, if crossed, he could be unrelenting.

Until now she'd been spared this side of his character, but she knew the suffering it had caused his wife. Her heart ached for her dead mother. Louise St Clair's life had not been a happy one: an *émigrée* from France, an unhappy marriage to an English aristocrat and then an early death.

Lord Miles Silverdale must have seemed like a white knight when Louise first met him, just months after her dangerous journey from the outskirts of Paris to exile in England. The Bastille would not be stormed for another year, but revolution was already in the air. Signs of dissent and rebellion were everywhere and when the St Clair family home was ransacked without any attempt by the servants to prevent it, Brielle St Clair had decided it was no longer safe for the family to stay. She and her eighteen-year-old daughter, disguised as servants themselves, were forced to steal away under cover of darkness and embark on a slow and tortuous journey to the Channel coast. They had travelled by night, resting beneath hedges in the daytime, and ever fearful of discovery.

To a refugee in a foreign land, Lord Silverdale's offer of marriage must have seemed like a miracle. He promised happiness and security, a new future for the young, homeless girl. Happiness, though, had lasted only a year until the birth of Robert. Louise was sickly for months afterwards, needing constant nursing, and unable to share in the social flurry of her husband's life. Miles Silverdale, having fallen violently in love with a youthful form and a beautiful face, found himself without either as a companion.

The constant miscarriages that followed year after year pushed them yet further apart. Amelie's birth and her unexpected survival had brought a brief reconciliation only. Even as a child she'd understood the pain written on her mother's face, as her husband left for yet another lengthy stay at a friend's country house, knowing that most of his time would be spent enjoying the company of other women.

But that was not going to happen to her! She had her mother's beauty, certainly, but also her grandmother's spirit. Louise might have been scared half out of her wits by that flight across France, but Brielle St Clair had exalted in it. Her tales of their adventures had enthralled Amelie as a child. Brielle's subsequent life would always be a shadow of the excitement she'd known. Understanding this, it seemed, she had deliberately made her new home amid the dull gentility of Bath. Amelie smiled wryly as she imagined her mettlesome grandmother exchanging vapid gossip at the Pump Room every day. She'd visited Bath as a young child, but the last time she'd seen Brielle was five years ago at her mother's funeral, a sombre and painful affair.

She stiffened. That was it. She would go to her grandmother. Brielle would be her refuge and would be sure to defend her from the man she blamed for her own daughter's decline and early death. She had warned Louise not to marry Lord Silverdale, but, desperate for stability, her daughter had not listened.

Amelie got to her feet and straightened the green satin ribbons that encircled her waist. Her grandmother would be her champion, she was certain. But how to get to her, how to get to Bath? Deep in thought, she didn't hear the bedroom door open until a tentative voice disturbed her meditations. Her maidservant, pale and concerned, white cap slightly askew, hovered in the doorway.

'Oh, miss, is it true? Are you really going to marry Sir Rufus Glyde?'

'No, Fanny, it's not true.' Her voice was sharp but adamant. 'I've no intention of marrying. And I detest Rufus Glyde. He's twice my age and not a fit husband.'

'But, miss, he's very wealthy, or so Cook says, and moves in the best circles.'

Amelie shook her head in frustration. 'He may be invited everywhere, but there are whispers that he is a vicious and degenerate man. He repels me.'

Fanny shut the door carefully behind her and said in a conspiratorial voice, 'Mr Simmonds told Cook that Sir Rufus was coming here tomorrow to make you an offer of marriage.'

'You shouldn't listen to gossip,' Amelie chided her. 'He may be coming to the house, but I shan't be meeting him.'

'But, Miss Amelie, how can this be?' In her abstraction the maid picked up a stray hairbrush and began to rearrange her mistress's locks.

'I'm going to escape—I'm going to Bath to my grandmother. But mind, not a word to anyone.'

Her maid, brushing Amelie's chestnut curls in long, rhythmic strokes, gaped at her open-mouthed. 'However will you get there?'

'I'm not sure at the moment. How would *you* get there, Fanny?'

'On the stage, I suppose, miss, though I wouldn't want to travel all that way on my own. It's sure to take a whole day. Master's old valet used to visit his daughter in Bath sometimes and there was always a fuss about how long he was away.'

'Do you know where he caught the stagecoach?'

'It was an inn in Fetter Lane. The White Horse, I believe. He used to leave first thing in the morning.'

'Then that's what I shall do. You'll need to call me early.'

'You're never thinking of taking the common stage, Miss Amelie?'

'Why ever not, it's a public conveyance. What harm can I come to?'

'But it's not right. All sorts of vulgar people take the stage—you'll be squashed in with the likes of clerks and pedlars and I don't know what. And I've heard it's dangerous. There are highwaymen on Hounslow Heath and they'll slit your throat for a necklace. And if *they* don't get you, then the coachman will get drunk and land you in a ditch.' Fanny shook her head ominously.

'Nonsense. If other people travel on the stage, I can, too.'

'But, miss, you're Quality,' Fanny maintained stubbornly. 'Quality don't travel on the stage. And you mustn't go alone.'

'I have to, and no one must know where I've gone. I need time to reach Lady St Clair and explain the situation to her before my father realises where I am.'

'But you can't have thought.' Fanny's voice sank low. 'You'll be unchaperoned, you'll receive Unwanted Attentions,' she whispered in a horrified voice, emphasising the last two words.

'Well then, I must do something to blend into my surroundings,' her mistress said practically.

She was thoughtful for a moment. 'Who wouldn't be noticed on a stagecoach, I wonder? A maidservant such as yourself? I'll go as a maidservant and you can lend me the clothes.'

'No, miss, that I won't.'

'Fanny, you're the only friend I have in this house. You must help me. No one will know and once I'm established at my grandmother's, I'll send for you. Now, we must plan. First we need a ticket.'

She went to the bottom drawer of the walnut chest that had been her mother's and brought out a small tin box. How lucky it was she still had most of her quarterly allowance. She pulled out a roll of bills and thrust them into Fanny's reluctant hand.

'Here, use this to buy a ticket for the stage tomorrow.'

'But, miss, even if I can buy a ticket, how will you find your way to Fetter Lane?'

'I'm sure I'll manage. I'll walk until I find a hackney carriage. That can take me to the inn, and once there I'll take care to stay concealed until the coach is ready to leave. There's bound to be crowds of people and a lot of activity—I imagine the Bath stage isn't the only one leaving the White Horse in the morning. It should be easy to find a hiding place.'

Her maid still looked unconvinced and Amelie put her arms around her and sought to soothe her worries. 'Don't fret, it's going to work. When you return, get some suitable clothes ready for me, but keep them in your own room. And then stay away from me for the rest of the day so that no one will suspect anything.'

Fanny seemed rooted to the spot. 'Go on,' her mistress urged, 'do it quickly before supper and then you won't be missed. Bring me the clothes and ticket at dawn tomorrow. I wouldn't ask you to do this for me, Fanny, if I were not truly desperate. But I must escape this nightmare.'

In the City some miles from Grosvenor Square, Gareth Denville was also contemplating escape. He sat uncomfortably in the shabby offices which housed Messrs Harben, Wrigley and Spence, solicitors, and wished himself elsewhere. But his demeanour betrayed nothing of his emotions. His straight black brows and hard blue eyes kept the world at bay. He could be accounted a handsome man, thought Mr Spence, who sat opposite him, but for the harshness of that gaze. And the decided lack of fashion he exhibited. He was a well-built man slightly above average height with good shoulders and an excellent form for the prevailing fashion of skin-tight pantaloons. But instead he wore buckskins, his coat fitted far too easily across his broad shoulders to be modish and his necktie was negligently arranged. Rather than the gleaming Hessians of *ton*nish fashion, he wore topboots, still dusty from his long journey.

Mr Spence gathered together the papers scattered across the huge oak desk and sighed inwardly. The new Lord Denville was likely to find it difficult to adjust to life in the capital. He looked up and encountered Gareth's austere gaze and quickly began the task at hand. Over the next quarter of an hour, Mr Spence carefully enumerated the full extent of Gareth Denville's inheritance while the beneficiary remained unnervingly silent.

The news of his grandfather's death several weeks ago had been accompanied by a polite request from the solicitors for his immediate return to England. His first reaction to their letter had been to shrug indifferently and carry on with his life, but his grandfather's man of business was nothing if not persistent, and after several summons of increasing urgency, he had bowed to the inevitable. He had been travelling a night and a day now without pause, but his powerful frame appeared not greatly fatigued and his air of cool detachment never left him.

The situation was not without its humour, of course, but that did not prevent a slow burning anger eating him from within. He'd known as he travelled to England after seven years' absence that he was now the Earl of Denville whether he wished it or not. But as Mr Spence drily read the pages of his grandfather's will, the size of his inheritance astounded him. Infuriated him, too, when he recalled the shifts he'd been forced to adopt simply to maintain the appearance of a gentleman. Charles Denville had husbanded his estate well. How ironic that such care and duty should ultimately benefit him, the black sheep, the grandson who could never be spoken of again. His grandfather could not deny him the title, but he must have tried and failed to leave his estate elsewhere. Gareth could imagine the old man's fury that such an unworthy successor was about to be crowned.

'Are you sure, Mr Spence, that there are no other legitimate heirs to the estate?' he asked crisply.

'None whatsoever, Lord Denville. We have done our searches very carefully, particularly…' and here he coughed delicately '…in the light of the peculiar circumstances surrounding your lordship's inheritance.'

The solicitor was far too circumspect to mention details, but Gareth knew well that Mr Spence referred to his banishment as a young man for the gravest of sins in *ton* circles. He had cheated at cards, or so it was alleged, a transgression that had brought instant shame to him and to his family. His grandfather had bundled him out of the country overnight, refusing to listen to his version of events.

'Like father, like son,' Lord Denville had said grimly. 'I was stupid enough to let your father stay in the hope that he would reform his way of life, but he died in the gutter where he belonged. I'll make sure that you at least cannot disgrace the family name further.' And what, thought Gareth, had the family name come to after all?

It had all once been so different. He'd been everything to his grandfather, an unexpected light after the black years of his own father's ruin. He remembered his childhood at Wendover Hall, his grandfather teaching him to ride and to shoot, watching over his progress to manhood with pleasure and anticipation. And then disaster, just three months on the town and accused of marking his cards.

That night was etched on his brain. The heat of the room, the guttering candles, the disarray of empty glasses. And the four other men who sat round the table: his dearest friend, Lucas Avery, General Tilney, an old ally of his grandfather's, the languid form of Lord Petersham, whose customary lethargy belied a sharp intelligence, and Rufus Glyde, playing recklessly that night, his spiteful tongue unusually stilled. It was the General who had first seen the mark on the card and raised the alarm. He remembered the incredulous stares of his companions as it became obvious to all who had cheated.

But he hadn't cheated. Someone there had done so, but why and how remained impenetrable. The men he played with were wealthy and had no need to cheat. But he was on a tight allowance and awaiting the next quarter's in some desperation. It was common knowledge that he was short of money. He had vehemently protested his innocence, but his grandfather had been deaf to him and to Lucas's staunch pleas that his friend was an honourable man; Lord Denville had listened in stiff silence and remained unmoved. General Tilney's embarrassed account of the evening was the only one his grandfather was willing to countenance. Gareth's disgrace was instant and so was banishment.

'My lord, if you would be so kind, we will need to go through a number of documents for which I need signatures.'

The solicitor was trying to regain his attention. His mind left that shadowed room in Watier's, and returned to the attorney's untidy office. He felt he was suffocating, yet the window was wide open.

'I need to take a walk,' he said. 'I need to clear my head.'

'Of course, your lordship.' The solicitor rose and bowed politely. 'I will await your lordship's pleasure.'

'I'm staying at Crillon's. I'll send from there when I'm ready to go through the papers.'

'Certainly, my lord.'

He walked quickly out of the room and down the stairs. The fresh air hit him with welcome relief. Waving away the proffered services of a jarvey, he began to make his way towards the West End of the city. He walked swiftly, street after street, hardly heeding where he went. Inside, he was seething with anger. His fortunes had changed, but his sense of betrayal remained acute. He had no wish to inherit anything that had belonged to his grandfather. Pride made it impossible that he would ever accustom himself to being the Earl of Denville or ever seek to become part of a society he deemed rotten to the core.

Without a glance, he passed the turning for St James's, a thoroughfare housing some of the most famous gentlemen's clubs in London, and continued as if by instinct towards Piccadilly. He came to a halt outside No. 81, Watier's, the Great-Go as it was fondly known to its members. Somehow he'd returned to the scene of his disgrace. He walked slowly up the stairs and prepared to confront his demons.

The doorman, resplendent in black grosgrain and scarlet silk sash, bowed low.

'Good evening, Lord Denville,' he intoned, 'on behalf of Watier's, may I offer you sincere condolences on your grandfather's death, and say how very glad we are to see you again.'

Gareth made no reply, reflecting cynically that commerce knew no moral shades. The doorman handed him on to a footman hovering by the doorway of the salon. He remembered the room immediately. The Aubusson carpet, the straw-coloured silk hangings and the endless line of chandeliers blazing light had not changed.

A group of men nearest the door looked up. They were engaged in a companionable game of faro, but at the sight of him the game stopped and for an instant their conversation withered. A man he did not know, and who was evidently in charge of the day's bank, said something in an undervoice which caused a ripple of amusement around the table. Lord Petersham, looking a little thinner and older now, hushed the man and play continued. The incident was over in a moment, but to Gareth it was as though time had stood still. His newly acquired title and wealth might open the doors of society to him, but he would never be allowed to forget the scandal. His grim reluctance to return to England, even for a few weeks, had been prescient. He had no place here and wanted none.

He blundered down the steps and headed towards the river. The grey waters flowed bleakly by the embankment, an echo of his harsh mood. Defiantly, he decided to drink to the day he would shake the soil of England from his feet for ever and sought out a boozing-ken in a poor area of Vauxhall, known to him from his days of youthful indiscretion. He ordered a brandy and the drink was rough but fiery. He ordered another and tossed it back quickly. He wanted to sink into oblivion. Over the next hours he drank steadily, as though each drink took him one step further from a hated homeland. It was just short of dawn when he finally lurched to his feet and sought his hotel room. His brain, befuddled by brandy, was treacherous and led him in the wrong direction. Very soon he was lost in a labyrinth of unknown streets.

* * *

Fanny woke her mistress at four in the morning. She carried in her arms a set of her own clothes and clutched the stage-coach ticket tightly. She appeared nervous, her hands trembling as she gently shook her mistress awake. Her agitation was soon explained.

'Miss Amelie, I don't think you can go. Mr Simmonds is in the hall and he's been sitting there all night. I was so worried I'd oversleep that I woke really early and crept downstairs to see the time. And there he was. You'll have to stay, miss, you'll have to meet Sir Rufus. But maybe it won't be too bad. You'll be rich and have your own house to manage and plenty of fine clothes and carriages and—'

'Do you mean my father has actually set the butler to spy on me?' Amelie was now sitting bolt upright.

'Not exactly spy, miss. But he's there in the hall as right as nine-pence and there's no way you're going to get past him unseen.'

'I have to get that coach, Fanny. I must find another way out—the back door?'

'The scullery maids are already up and working in the kitchen. They would be bound to report it to Cook and she'll carry it to Mr Simmonds. You'd have to get over the garden wall into the alley behind and they would know of your escape before you'd even got halfway.'

'Then I must go out of the front—maybe you can distract Simmonds?'

Fanny looked doubtful.

'I have it, I'll go out of the window—we're only on the first floor and we should be able to fashion a ladder from the sheets, long enough for me to reach the ground.'

'You'll never climb out of the window on sheets, Miss Amelie. It's too dangerous. They could give way at any moment.'

'Not if we knot them very carefully. In any case, it's far more dangerous for me to stay. Quick, let's hurry.'

With that she hastily dressed herself in the clothes Fanny had brought. Then, sweeping the sheets from the bed, she began to knot them urgently, calling on the maid to help. More sheets were pulled from the large linen chest, which lined the bedroom wall, and very soon they had put together an impressive rope.

'We must make sure we've knotted the sheets as tightly as possible. I don't weigh much, but it's quite a way down.'

'It's as safe as I can make it…' Fanny paused in her labours and looked anxiously at her mistress '…safer than for you to be travelling alone all the way to Bath.'

'I don't have a choice. I have to get to my grandmother's. I promise I'll take care. Don't forget,' Amelie tried to reassure her, 'I'll be travelling in disguise and nobody will think of looking twice at a maidservant.'

'But you'll still be a very beautiful maidservant, miss, and people are bound to look at you. You must wear my cloak and make sure you pull the hood over your head whenever you're in public.'

Her mistress fingered the black velvet robe. 'This is your best cloak, Fanny, I can't take it.'

'You must, it will make people think you're a very superior lady's maid and they won't bother you! And it will keep you warm. You've never travelled in a stagecoach before, Miss Amelie, but I'm told they're the draughtiest vehicles out and you'll be travelling for hours.'

'Fanny, you're the best friend anyone ever had.' The maid blushed with pleasure. 'As soon as I get to Lady St Clair's, I'll make sure she sends for you. Then we'll both be safe. My father will never dare to follow us there.'

She quickly slipped the cloak over the borrowed dress, pulling the hood well down over her tangled curls. A small cloak bag lay ready with just a few of her most treasured possessions. She could take hardly anything with her, but she had no regrets. Once this room had been a beloved haven, but now it was a prison, a prison leading only to betrothal with a detested man. Sir Rufus Glyde would arrive at noon, but by then she would be miles away and her family confounded. She knew that Fanny would keep her secret, even on pain of dismissal.

She turned quickly to her. 'I must be gone. Give me the ticket for the stage.'

'When you get to the inn, miss, be sure to hide yourself away until it's time for the coach to leave.'

'I will. Once I've gone, you must go back to your room immediately and don't discover my absence until the last possible moment. Please God they won't find out that it was you who helped me.'

'You're not to worry, Miss Amelie. I'll make sure they won't know from me where you've gone.' Fanny was suffused with tears, her voice cracking. 'Now go, quickly, miss.'

She deftly tied one end of the sheet ladder to the bedpost and opened the window wide. The sash cord groaned ominously and they both held their breath. But the house was silent except for the distant sounds from the kitchen. They breathed again. Fanny played out the sheets over the window sill and helped her mistress on to the ledge. The dawn was spreading a grey light over the quiet streets. A fresh breeze fanned Amelie's cheeks as she climbed nimbly over the ledge and began lowering herself down the improvised ladder. The descent wasn't easy. She had to lower herself one movement at a time and the cloak bag, though light, impeded her progress. She wondered if she dared to throw it down into the cellar area below the railings. But Simmonds might well hear the noise and come to see what had caused it. So she continued to edge her way carefully downwards, the bag slung over one arm.

Fanny's pale face was at the open window, whispering encouragement. 'You're doing fine, miss. Don't look down, not far to go now.'

But her estimation proved to be optimistic. The sheets, which had seemed so prolific in the bedroom, suddenly appeared scanty and far too short. They had both forgotten the deep well below the front door steps and had calculated only to the pavement. Amelie was now at the bottom of the ladder, but still at least fifteen feet above solid ground.

She looked up at the imposing Georgian facade and then down to the terrifying black-and-gold railings that marched along the pavement. What a horrible fate that would be. She suddenly felt very sick. How on earth was she going to reach the ground? She could jump into the well, but she was more than likely to break a leg or worse. Then all chance of escape would be gone. She would have to endure her father's fierce recriminations. She could see him now, his brow creased in red furrows and his prominent eyes glowering.

As she hung there, her light form bracing itself against the cream stucco of the house, the noise of whistling broke the stillness. Tuneless and somewhat melancholy, the whistling was coming nearer. A late reveller, perhaps, on his way home? He was almost sure to see her. Fanny had heard the noise too and began desperately to try to haul in the sheets.

'It's no good,' Amelie whispered hoarsely, 'you'll never have the strength to get me back.'

She could only hope that the unknown figure meandering towards her would be too inebriated to notice a young female hanging from a window. That was wishful thinking. The reveller drew near and stood gazing at her for some time, seemingly trying to work out just what he was viewing.

Amelie looked down and pulled her cloak tighter. She didn't recognise him and he didn't look like any of the fashionable bloods who often ended a riotous evening by staggering home at dawn. But he had an indefinable air of authority about him and she worried that by chance he might remember seeing her at one of the many gatherings of the *ton* this Season. She must avoid discovery at all costs.

Despite having drunk far too much, he seemed alert. His face slowly broke into a derisive smile.

'What have we here then? A mystery indeed. Plainly an escape, but what are you escaping from? What do maidservants escape from before the household is awake? Have you been stealing and now you're trying to make off with your ill-gotten gains? Should I knock and instantly let your employers know of your wickedness?'

'No, sir, indeed I am no thief.'

'Well, if you're not a thief, what are you doing climbing out of the window? The house has a door, you know.'

She answered with as much dignity as she could muster, 'There are circumstances that make it vital for me to escape in this manner. I must not be seen.'

She hoped that he would ask no more questions and be on his way. But the brandy fumes still wreathed around Gareth Denville's brain. He was indifferent to the fact that he was miles from his hotel and had no idea in which direction it lay. He felt reckless and pleasurably detached from a world he hated. He had no intention of walking away—he was in the mood to enjoy this ridiculous imbroglio.

'But why must you leave unseen? It seems unnecessarily dramatic,' he offered provocatively.

'I have my reasons,' she replied stiffly. 'Please leave me.'

'By all means, but is that wise? It might be more sensible to ask for a little help. Of course I would need to know just who I'm aiding and why.'

'My name is Amelie and I'm maid to the young mistress of this house. I'm escaping to avoid the attentions of her brother.'

Gareth caught sight of a chestnut curl and looked intently at the heart-shaped face trying to cower deeper into the enveloping cloak. 'He has good taste,' he admitted. 'But then so do I.'

He swayed slightly on his heels and finally pronounced, 'We'll make a bargain, shall we? I'll rescue you on one condition.'

'Anything, sir,' she said recklessly. Her arms felt as if they were being torn from their sockets and she knew she would not be able to hold on much longer. The sharp sword points of the railings seemed already to be coming nearer.

'A rather rash promise, but one I shall keep you to. I'll help you to the ground, but in exchange you'll come with me—as entertainment, shall we say.'

'Dear sir, I cannot. I have a journey to make. I'm on my way to—Bristol,' she amended, thinking it best not to reveal her plans in their entirety. 'I have to get to the White Horse Inn in Fetter Lane to catch the stage.'

'Excellent. Bristol, why not? There are boats aplenty there,' he added obscurely. 'We'll go together.'

He needed to get away and he was intrigued by the glimpse

of the beautiful face beneath the cloak. Mr Spence would have to wait for his papers to be signed. Perhaps he would never sign them, never avail himself of his newfound wealth. If so, he would manage—he had for the last seven years.

'A perfect solution, then,' he said swiftly. 'I extricate you from your difficulties and we travel to Bristol together.'

He saw her dismayed face. 'You won't have to know me very long—a few hours only. You might even get to like me,' he added harshly. 'I'll bespeak a private parlour when we get to the inn. You can have a good breakfast and I can have—well, let's say, I can have the pleasure of your company.'

Amelie heard her maid moan. Fanny had her head below the window sill, but could hear all that was being said. This was her worst fear come true, but she was powerless to intervene. If she made herself known, the man, whoever he was, would discover Amelie's deception. He might spread rumours about her mistress and Amelie would be shunned by society. Then she would never find a husband, not even a degenerate twice her age. As Fanny fidgeted in despair, the decision was made for her.

Her arms breaking, Amelie gasped out, 'Yes, I'll come with you. Just get me down from here, please, immediately!'

'At your service, madam.' Her knight errant leapt over the railings and down the stairs to the cellar area. Amelie, her hands now nerveless, fell into his arms. He held her to his chest, enjoying for a moment the softness of her young body.

'Let me introduce myself,' he said, putting her down abruptly, and quickly casting around in his mind for a name. 'I am Gareth Wendover.'

Chapter Two

She allowed herself to be led up the area steps and away from the house. Instead of letting her go once they reached the pavement, her rescuer kept a tight grip on her arm as if to prevent any flight. She noticed that his hands were strong and shapely, but tanned as though they were used to outdoor work. He appeared an enigma, a gentleman, presumably, but one acquainted with manual labour. His earlier nonchalance had disappeared and with it his good humour. Glancing up at him from beneath her eyelashes, she saw that his expression had grown forbidding. A black mood seemed to have descended on him as he strode rapidly along the street, pulling her along in his wake. His chin jutted aggressively and his black hair fell across his brow. When he finally turned to her, his eyes were blue steel.

'Why are you dawdling?' he demanded brusquely. 'I thought you were desperate to escape.'

'I am,' she countered indignantly. 'I'm walking as fast as I can and you're hurting my arm. I'm not a sack to be dragged along the street.'

Ignoring her complaint, he continued to tow her along the

road at breakneck speed. 'Come on, Amelia—that *was* your name?—try harder. We need to move more quickly.'

He must be drunker than I supposed, she thought ruefully. His voice was cultured and his clothes, though shabby, were genteel. But his conduct was erratic. One minute he appeared to find her situation a source of laughter, the next he behaved in this surly fashion. He thought she was a maidservant and had doubtless helped her to escape because of her pretty face. But he'd hardly glanced at her since that unfortunate moment when she'd landed in his arms and now he was sweeping her away from the house as if his life depended on it, propelling her along the pavement until she was breathless.

Incensed by this treatment, she came to an abrupt halt, almost tripping him up. 'Perhaps you didn't hear what I said. I cannot walk any faster than I'm doing already. And,' she added coldly, 'my name is Amelie, *not* Amelia.'

'However fancy your name, you're still a fugitive,' he responded drily, 'and a fugitive under my command. And my command is to make haste.'

'I will certainly make haste, but at a more seemly rate.'

'Seemly—that's a strange word for a girl who escapes through windows.'

She looked mutinous, but was too tired to argue any further and submitted again to being led at a spanking pace through a maze of streets until they came across a hackney carriage waiting for business.

'In you go,' her persecutor said shortly and pushed her into the ill-smelling interior. He uttered a few words to the jarvey and they were off.

Keeping company with a drunken man, who looked as though he'd known better days, was not part of her plans, but she decided that she would not try to escape just yet. She would stay with this Mr Wendover while it suited her purpose. He'd been useful so far and if he could deliver her to the White Horse Inn, then she would be set for her journey to Bath. Once in the inn's courtyard, it should be easy to give him the slip and hide away until the stage departed.

They sat opposite in the dingy cab, silently weighing each other up. It was the first time she'd been able fully to see her rescuer. He was a powerfully built man, carelessly dressed, but exuding strength. She was acutely conscious of his form as he lay back against the worn swabs. She had no idea who he was, other than the name he'd given, and he was evidently not going to volunteer further information. Instead, he sat silently, gazing at her, assessing her almost as though she were a piece of merchandise he'd just purchased, she thought wrathfully. But he would discover that she had other plans; she would leave him as soon as she was able. Doubtless he would start to drink again at the inn and, once fuddled, would not care what happened to her.

In this she was wrong. Despite his dazed state, Gareth had been watching her closely and had seen her recoil as she sat down on the stained seat of the cab. A trifle fastidious for a maidservant, he thought. The hood of her cloak obscured much of her face, but what he could see was very beautiful, from the glinting chestnut curls to the fine cheekbones and flawless complexion. A strange maidservant, indeed, and a strange situation.

As the brandy fumes began to dissolve, he was left with an aching head and a confused mind. What on earth was he doing miles from his hotel, his solicitor and legal papers all but forgotten? How had he embarked on this mad adventure with a woman he didn't know and one who could well be a thief? Perhaps the hue and cry to apprehend her had already started. And he'd been the one to make sure she escaped pursuit, rushing her along the streets away from any possible danger. He must be very drunk. He would need to keep her close until he worked out what to do. In the meantime there must be a few hours before the Bristol stage left, and he would remind her of her promise. She'd provide a pleasant interlude.

The hackney bounced over the cobbles at considerable speed. There was little traffic at this time of the morning and they were soon at the White Horse. He helped her down with one hand while paying the jarvey with the other. No escape, she reflected. Never mind, her opportunity would come, she would just have to be a little cleverer.

'I suggest we repair indoors and find some breakfast. A private parlour should give us some respite from this din.'

He had to bend down and speak directly into her ear, the noise coming from the inn courtyard was so great. She could hardly believe how many people were gathered into such a small space. There was luggage scattered everywhere: trunks, cloak bags, sacks of produce, bird cages heaped up pell-mell. Ostlers ran back and forth leading out teams of fresh horses, coachmen took final draughts of their beer before blowing the horn for departure. Everywhere people shouted instructions and were not heard. It was bedlam, and the relative quiet of the inn taproom seemed like sanctuary.

The landlord came bustling out, rubbing his hands with pleasure as there was normally little hope of trade at this time of the morning. All anyone usually bought was a quick cup of scalding coffee. But here was a gentleman and his companion, surely more substantial customers, even if the man did look a little the worse for wear and the woman kept her face shrouded.

'A beautiful morning.' The landlord beamed ingratiatingly. 'And how can I help you, sir?'

Gareth frowned. 'Prepare a private parlour for myself and the lady,' he said curtly. 'We leave on the Bristol coach, but wish to take some breakfast first.'

'Of course, sir. Right away. If you would care to come with me.'

The room the landlord led them to was small and poky with a low window that looked out over the back garden, but it was mercifully quiet. The curtains were grimy and the furniture looked faded and uninviting. Amelie plumped one of the chair cushions and sent up a cloud of dust. Her rescuer glanced across at her, his expression mocking. 'The housekeeping can wait.'

She glared at him. 'If you don't mind, Mr Wendover, I would prefer to be outside.'

'I'm sure you would, but here we'll stay. I can keep an eye on you and we can eat breakfast together. Won't that be companionable?'

His voice was light and his tone ironic, but somehow he made the phrase sound like a caress. Yet the look on his face was calculating. *Weighing me up again*, she thought, *deciding whether or not he made a good bargain when he rescued me.* She was beginning to feel unusually vulnerable, confined to this isolated room with an unknown and unpredictable man. But indignation at her imprisonment gave her courage.

'I'm unsure what you mean by companionable, Mr Wendover. I certainly thank you for the service you've rendered me this morning, but I've no need of food and would prefer to wait for my coach in the courtyard. If you allow me to pass, you may enjoy your meal undisturbed.'

'Not so fast. I have no wish to be left undisturbed. On the contrary, I very much desire to be disturbed.'

He smiled derisively as he spoke, but his eyes were hard and measuring. 'You are mighty proud for a maidservant, are you not?' he asked. 'But then a challenge is always welcome.'

She made no reply, for the first time conscious of a shadowy fear. The ancient clock in the corner of the room ticked out the minutes loudly in the gulf of silence that stretched between them. She felt bruised by his scrutiny. Then, without warning, he began to walk slowly towards her, his dark blue eyes intent. He no longer seemed a harmless reveller. She was very aware of his close physical presence and the way he was looking at her was disquieting. His hard gaze seemed to drink her in. She was angry that he dared to stare at her so, but at the same time the pit of her stomach fluttered uncomfortably.

Desperately she strove to exert control over the situation. 'I don't understand what exactly you want of me.' Even to her ears, she sounded faint and foolish.

'Really? I'm surprised. Do they make maidservants that innocent these days? Perhaps I should remind you that we had a bargain. I helped you from your predicament and you promised to stay with me until your—sorry, our—coach left the inn.'

'But why?'

'Come, you can't be that naive. Why would any man want a beautiful young woman to stay with him?'

She stepped back hurriedly and collided with the threadbare sofa. 'You surely cannot pretend any feelings for me.' Her voice was hoarse with alarm. 'You know nothing of me.'

'True, but do I have to? You'll be a charming diversion just when I need one. Here, pull your hood back.'

Before she could stop him, Gareth had flung her cloak back to reveal her face fully. He looked at her wonderingly. A tangle of silken curls tumbled down around her shoulders. Her eyes, the colour of autumn, were wide and frightened and the soft cream of her cheeks delicately flushed. It seemed an age that he stood looking at her.

When he finally spoke, his voice was thick with desire. 'You *are* beautiful,' he said. She flinched and wrapped her cloak more tightly around her body.

'There's no need to be scared,' he murmured smoothly. 'I'm sure we'll deal well together.'

'Indeed, no, sir, we will not,' she protested. 'I'm an honest woman and you shall not touch me.'

'Honest,' he mused. 'An interesting word. Honest women hardly choose to escape from their homes at four in the morning. Nor do they come away with men they don't know. Don't play your tricks off on me. Instead, let's be truthful with each other. I'm in need of amusement and you, I imagine, are a little adventuress who will take whatever comes her way.'

He grabbed her hand and pulled her towards him. In a moment his arms were round her waist, a gesture shocking in its intimacy. She shrank from him, but his nearness was making her senses falter. He pressed closer and she felt her body begin to tingle. For a moment they stayed body to body, then quickly she sprang away.

Her face was pink with vexation. 'How dare you touch me!'

'Very easily, I'll think you'll find. Women are made for pleasure and you'll provide it amply.'

He made as if to recapture her in his arms, but was interrupted by the door opening. The landlord arrived bearing a ham, eggs, some devilled kidneys and toast. A servant followed with a large pot of steaming coffee.

'There we are, sir,' the innkeeper sang out, determinedly ignoring what he had seen as he came in the door. 'Just the job for a chilly May morning. But good travelling weather, I'll be bound.' He continued to spill out words while Amelie retreated to a corner of the room, trying hard to quell her jumping heart.

When the landlord had left, Gareth sat down at the table and began calmly to carve slices of ham and place them carefully on the two plates.

'Come to the table, Amelie, you must eat,' he coaxed. 'No point in starving yourself—you have a long road ahead.'

The glorious sense of irresponsibility that he'd known earlier had gone, but he was still enjoying himself. He had no idea who he was with or what would happen. But this beautiful girl had felt warm and tremulous when he pulled her close and he looked forward to repeating the sensation. It was escape that he needed right now and she had literally dropped into his arms, ready to furnish it.

Amelie resolutely refused even to look at the food.

'Come to the table!' His tone was now peremptory.

She remained sitting in the corner of the room. 'I'm not hungry,' she said in a freezing voice.

'Don't be silly. Of course you're hungry. Come, I wish to eat the ham, not you. Sit down—or I'll make you.'

Alarmed at any further physical contact, she abandoned her station and went with as much dignity as she could muster towards the table. Perching at the corner, as far away as possible, she nibbled at the ham and a slice of bread. The coffee was mercifully strong and hot and she gratefully downed two cups. He ate more leisurely as though he had the entire morning to finish his breakfast. *And when he's eaten his fill*, she thought, *I'll be next on the menu.*

She was going to have to make her getaway fast if she were to avoid another dreadful scene. She couldn't rely on the landlord to come in so opportunely again. Indeed, he'd had an unpleasantly knowing look in his eye as he'd laid the food down in front of his patron. He would do nothing to help her; she would have to save herself.

She cleared her throat. 'Why do you wish to go to Bristol, Mr Wendover?'

'Why should that concern you?'

'If we are to be travelling companions today, it might be sensible to get to know each other a little.' She wondered anxiously if he would take the bait and relax his guard.

'A change of tune? When I tried to get to know *you*, you weren't too keen,' Gareth said caustically.

'I'm sorry for that, but I find this room a little overheated and when you pulled me towards you…' her voice wavered at the thought '…I felt faint.'

'Ah, that's how it was. Well, I certainly don't want a fainting woman on my hands, so I'll open this window a little and then we can be comfortable. Come here, Amelie, and let me look at my prize.'

Steeling herself, she walked slowly towards him. He stood up, facing her, and smiled. She realised with a jolt that when he smiled, his whole face was transformed from a threatening harshness to engaging warmth. His blue eyes had lost their steeliness and smiled, too, suggesting humour and good nature. His white teeth were even and his lips full. She stared at him, enjoying the picture he presented.

'I'm not surprised you've had trouble from your employers,' he broke into her rapt contemplation. 'You're far too lovely ever to be let near the average young man.' He laughed softly. 'But

I'm hardly the average man, so we need have no fears on that score.'

She woke abruptly from her dreamlike state and realised the danger she was in. Picking up her reticule, she fanned herself energetically. 'I'm sorry, sir, but I'm still very warm in here. And I wonder if the ham was all it should be?'

'And what exactly do you mean by that?' he exploded. The moment was gone.

'Just that the ham had a slight taint, I thought. But ham never really agrees with me, so perhaps it was fine.'

'If it doesn't agree with you, what the devil do you mean by eating it?'

'You insisted, Mr Wendover. I was scared of you, so I ate it. But now I don't feel at all well.' She pressed her handkerchief artistically to her mouth and closed her eyes. 'I think I might really faint this time.'

Gareth cursed under his breath and shouted for the landlord, who came suspiciously quickly. She was sure the salacious old man had been lurking outside the door, waiting to see what would occur.

'My companion is unwell, landlord, your ham seems to be to blame,' Gareth said tersely.

'That can't be right, sir, the ham was freshly cured. Mrs Fawley would be very upset to think that aspersions had been cast on her ham. It's the best in the city. You won't get better anywhere.'

'Yes, yes,' said Gareth irascibly, 'that's as may be. My friend here is feeling ill and needs to lie down. Do you have a bedchamber where she can be accommodated?'

'Yes, sir, of course, I'll call my wife immediately.'

Mrs Fawley soon appeared on the doorstep with a martial look in her eyes. It was obvious she had overheard the conversation and was ready to defend her ham. But when she saw Amelie, small and white, and looking decidedly unwell, she took pity on her.

'I've got my own opinion as to what's made the young miss faint,' she sniffed, and escorted Amelie to a small but clean bedchamber on the next floor, overlooking the courtyard.

Once on her own, she locked the door and laid herself on the bed. She was exhausted by the morning's adventures. It seemed that she'd thwarted one persecutor only to fall into the hands of another; she'd only very narrowly eluded her would-be ravisher. It was second nature for her to mistrust any man and she wondered at her stupidity in imagining that Gareth Wendover would be no threat to her.

When she'd first seen him he'd appeared no more harmful than a lively reveller returning from a night of pleasure—untidy and unfashionable and probably a little the worse for drink—but for some reason she'd trusted him. Only after he'd used her so roughly, dragging her along the street, throwing her into the hackney and then—certainly best forgotten—pulling her into his arms, had she realised what a foolish mistake she'd made.

And yet even then, she admitted shamefacedly, there'd been temptation to remain in his embrace, to let those strong arms encircle her. Of course that was simply a reaction to the alarms of the last few days, but thank goodness the landlord had come in when he had. And now her pretence of illness had saved her again, although for a short while only. She was sure that Gareth would be knocking on the door very soon and demanding admittance. And a bedchamber was an even worse place to meet him than the parlour downstairs. She had to be gone by the time he arrived.

She quickly washed her hands and face and tidied her hair in the tarnished mirror, which hung lopsidedly on one wall. She'd noticed as the landlady escorted her up to this floor that there was a second stairway leading downwards. It was much smaller and far less grand, obviously the stair used by the servants. She was sure it would lead out to the garden; if she could reach that, she would easily be able to creep unnoticed to the front courtyard.

She glanced at the clock and could hardly believe the time. The coach for Bath left in just five minutes. Carefully, she unlocked the door and peered out. All was quiet and she tiptoed as swiftly as she could to the head of the small staircase and listened again. The only noise wafting up to her was the convivial banter from the taproom. No strong footsteps mounted towards her door. Gareth Wendover thought she was travelling to Bristol and would not know the Bath stage was about to leave. This was her chance.

Regretfully, she would have to leave her cloak bag behind in the parlour below, but at least she had her reticule and in it the precious ticket. In a minute she was down the stairs and lifting the latch on the door leading to the garden. A woman servant suddenly appeared from the kitchen quarters and stared at her uncomprehendingly. Amelie whisked through the door and quickly took the path to the front of the inn.

The scene was a little less chaotic than when she'd arrived in the hackney as many of the morning coaches had already departed. She was easily able to identify the coach to Bath, and once she'd shown her ticket to the guard, she was helped aboard. She chose one of the middle seats of the bank of four that lined either side. It was likely to be the most uncomfortable, but it would shield her from anyone looking in from outside. A large burly farmer sat to one side and a rotund country woman with an enormous basket on her lap on the other. There was very little room, but she could almost disappear between them.

It seemed a lifetime before the guard blew the signal to leave and the coach was pulling out of the yard. There was no sign of her tormentor. By now he was sure to have begun drinking again and would hardly miss her absence. Strangely, she didn't feel as elated at her escape as she should. It was ridiculous, but she almost fancied that she'd let him down in some way. After all, he'd shown some care for her. If it weren't for him, she would still be dangling on the rope of sheets or, even worse, impaled on the front railings. He'd helped her down, found a cab and escorted her to the inn. He'd offered her shelter and refreshment. He'd pulled her into his arms. He'd held her in a crushing embrace. Her mind stopped. That was an image she must be sure to leave behind.

They were already passing through Belgravia and turning out on to the highway that ran westwards. She hoped her family had no idea yet that she was gone. Fanny would be worrying frantically and the sooner she could let her maidservant know that all was well, the better. And all was well, she convinced herself. She'd had a gruelling experience, but she'd achieved her aim. She would not be there to greet Rufus Glyde this morning. Instead, she was on her way to her grandmother's and to safety.

Gareth drained the last of the coffee pot and decided to go in search of his reluctant travelling companion. He'd been unsure whether she was telling the truth about the ham, but she'd certainly begun to look very white and he'd not wanted to risk any unpleasantness. Truth to tell, she'd looked so small and vulnerable he'd felt a wish to protect her rather than pursue her. He shook his head at his stupidity. She was as mercenary as the rest of the world, no doubt. Her story about escaping from an importuning son probably had a grain of truth in it, given her undeniable beauty, but he was quite sure there was another tale to tell. Perhaps she really was a thief. Perhaps she'd allowed the son too much licence and was now scared to tell her mistress of the inevitable result.

Thanks to the very strong coffee, he'd sobered up completely in the hour that she'd been gone. He still didn't know what had possessed him to get involved with the girl. A sense of the ridiculous, perhaps? Or a whiff of intrigue—a maid with a French name, finicky manners and a keenness to hide her face. He felt too weary to puzzle any further. Two sleepless nights had begun to take their toll and he was now eager to wash his hands of her. He would simply put her on the Bristol coach and go back to his hotel. It had been stupid of him to think that he could flee his obligations. Tomorrow he would send a message to the solicitor and sign whatever papers that worthy presented.

He glanced at the cloak bag Amelie had left on the bench. He'd better restore it to its owner and assure her that she had nothing further to fear from him. He made his way upstairs to the front bedchamber, but it was empty. Thinking he'd got the wrong room, he looked into another and surprised the chambermaid who was making up the bed.

'I'm looking for a young lady,' he excused himself, 'she was feeling unwell and came up to rest.'

The maid looked at him blankly. 'She's not 'ere.'

'I can see she's not here,' Gareth returned shortly, 'but have you seen her?'

'I shouldn't think so.' The maid continued smoothing out the bedspread with a bored expression on her face. 'Not many people come up 'ere.' She paused and looked vacantly out of the window. 'There wus a stranger on the stairs a while ago.'

'A young woman?'

'I couldn't rightly say.'

'Why ever not?' he asked impatiently.

''Cos of the cloak.'

'A black velvet cloak?' The maid nodded absently.

'That's her. Where is she?'

'How would I know? She went down the stairs and out the door.'

'What door?' Gareth was suddenly alert.

'The back door, of course.' The maid shook her head at his obtuseness. ''Appen she's in the garden taking the air,' she said helpfully.

He swore softly to himself and ran down the stairs two at a time. The garden was empty as he knew it would be, but he saw the path that led around the inn and followed it into the courtyard. The yard was also nearly empty. The last coach of the morning had departed and the inn servants were clearing up the mess the passengers and drivers had left behind.

He accosted a thin, gangling youth who was mournfully sweeping the last of the straw from the cobbles.

'The stage to Bristol?' he enquired curtly.

'There ain't no stages to Bristol today,' the boy confided happily, leaning on his broom and glad for an excuse to stop work. 'Bath now, mebbe. And you can allus go on from Bath.'

'Where's the stage to Bath?'

'Where? Somewhere near 'Ounslow, I reckon.' The boy grinned cheekily. 'What d'you think, Jem?'

Jem staggered to a halt, bent double under the weight of the saddle he was carrying. 'With ole Tranter driving, probably not yet clear of Kensington,' he jeered.

The other men stopped their work and joined in a chorus of raucous laughter. An elderly ostler leaned lazily against the inn wall and chewed a straw. He smiled widely, enjoying Gareth's discomfort.

'Next one's tomorrow, sir. That's if you don't mind a little wait,' he sniggered.

'Move yourself and get me a horse immediately,' Gareth snapped in response and ran back into the inn. He threw money onto the table in payment and snatched up Amelie's cloak bag. He'd been willing to let her go when he could play the benefactor. But how dare she play him false? A bargain was a bargain and he was going to make her pay.

He stormed back into the inn courtyard and tapped his foot impatiently.

It took nearly fifteen minutes to make the horse ready and by that time he was in a towering rage. He threw the cloak bag across the saddle, then leapt onto the horse's back and wheeled her round to face the courtyard entrance.

''Appen you might catch 'em up,' opined the old ostler, still chewing his straw vigorously, 'but I ain't anyways too sure on it.'

Gareth's reply was to spur his mount forwards and out of the courtyard in one bound.

Chapter Three

Wedged uncomfortably between her fellow passengers, Amelie endured the miles as they rolled wearily on. By now her escape must have been discovered. Her father would be spreading tempest through the house; he would find it impossible to explain her absence to Rufus Glyde when the latter came calling. For a moment the thought of Glyde's likely retribution made her feel a little sick, but she resolutely pushed it from her mind. Lord Silverdale would have to find another way of saving the family.

She had no clear idea of the time, but it had to be around noon. Any moment now Sir Rufus would be stepping up to the front door of the house in Grosvenor Square, expecting to have acquired a bride before he left again. A wave of revulsion passed through her. Anything was better than that, even the harassment she'd suffered from Mr Gareth Wendover.

She was glad to be free of him, too, yet she couldn't quite subdue a twinge of regret. He'd behaved abominably, but then her conduct had hardly been that of a delicately raised young woman. If he'd realised her true situation, he wouldn't have attempted to make love to her. But that was a nonsense. It would have made no difference to him if she were maid or mistress. From the outset he'd shown a predilection for seizing her in as close an embrace as possible. Whether she was the daughter of Lord Silverdale or the daughter's maid would be immaterial.

And shamefully, it hadn't mattered to her either whether he was Mr Wendover, gentleman, or a choice spirit of dubious origins. She'd enjoyed the feeling of being held against his powerful frame. Eyes closed, she thought reminiscently of the strength that had encompassed her, the masculine warmth that promised as much excitement as security. But how foolish! She had no intention of being at the mercy of any man—ever. She'd just escaped from one threatened entanglement and she must preserve herself from any other, particularly with a man who by the look of him could bring her nothing but trouble.

She shifted her position, trying to get more comfortable, but in such a crowded carriage it was difficult. Her feet were already numb from inactivity and her left arm ached with the weight of the portly farmer bunched in beside her. A thin-faced clerk in the corner scowled at her attempts to move, but the country woman smiled in motherly sympathy.

'There ain't much room in these coaches, miss, and we large 'uns don't make it any easier.'

The farmer snorted at this and shifted his bulk again, trapping Amelie's arm even more heavily than before. As well as aching from head to toe, she was beginning to feel very hungry. She'd hardly eaten a crumb at the inn, so intent had she been on eluding Gareth. The motherly lady, sensing her thoughts, reached down to the basket, which now nestled on the floor between her feet. She drew out some slices of pie and cheese and apples and smilingly offered to share her fare. Natural politeness would normally have made Amelie refuse, but her hunger was tormenting and the morning's events had somehow dispensed with normality. She plunged her teeth into the succulent pie just as they left Hounslow Heath.

Her benefactor adjusted her white cotton cap and sighed with relief. 'I'm certain glad we've left that Heath. Terrible things happen there. Just last week my neighbour told me her son was held up in broad daylight and robbed of everything, including his horse. He'd to walk all the way to the City and never a chance of catching the man who robbed him.'

Amelie, too, was relieved, for Fanny's words still echoed in her mind; that at least was one danger she'd evaded. Once replete with food, it was easy to slip into a doze. She knew it must be another eight hours or so before she reached her destination and if she could catnap at least some of the time, the journey would not be so wearisome. She started to rehearse what she would say to her grandmother when she finally reached her and was in the middle of a masterly speech in which she painted a frightening picture of what her life would be like with Rufus Glyde, when her head began to droop and she drifted gently into a deep sleep. The red-faced farmer beside her also slept, his snores keeping time with the rhythm of the coach, but Amelie heard nothing. Even when the stage came to rest at its designated stops, she remained undisturbed.

She slept on, mile after mile, until suddenly just past the Chippenham turn-off the coach lurched to an abrupt halt. She was jolted awake and thought at first that they must have reached the small town of Wroxhall, which she'd noticed was just twenty miles short of Bath. Hopefully some of the passengers would alight there and leave those remaining a little more room. Craning her neck round the still-sleeping farmer to look out of the window, she received a shock that sent her senses spinning.

Gareth Wendover wrenched open the doorway of the coach. He was smiling grimly and in his hand was her forlorn cloak bag. 'You seem to have forgotten something, Amelie.'

The coachman at that moment appeared at his shoulder. ''Ere, 'ere, you can't stop a coach on the King's 'ighway to give back a bag,' he blustered.

'Oh, but indeed I can,' Gareth said smoothly. 'You see, this isn't any old cloak bag and I'm not giving it back. In fact, I have every intention of keeping it—it is evidence!'

Her fellow passengers were now all wide awake and taking interested note of the proceedings. She heard the word *evidence* being bandied around between them and turned to face her pursuer.

Gareth's smile turned positively fiendish. 'It contains some very expensive trinkets filched by this young woman from her employers. In her haste to escape justice, she left the bag behind. But I'll make sure that she answers for her crime. I intend to deliver her immediately to the local magistrate. He is sure to have strong views on dishonest servants.'

There was a gasp from the stout woman who had befriended Amelie. 'Surely not, sir. This young woman can't be a thief.'

'One would not think so, I confess, but appearances can be deceptive. Unfortunately, the young and supposedly innocent may harbour evil impulses.'

'How dare you,' spluttered Amelie. 'You know you're telling a pack of lies. That bag is certainly mine, but it contains only a few personal items.'

'Is that so?' Gareth was maddeningly calm. 'Then I suggest, ladies and gentlemen,' addressing the inhabitants of the coach who were now all craning forward, intent on the play being enacted before them, 'that you decide whether or not a maid is likely to be carrying these particular personal items.'

And with a flourish he emptied the contents of the bag onto the ground. To her embarrassment a few of her garments spilled out, but her consternation was vastly increased when she spied along with them a diamond brooch, a jewelled tiepin and a battered but expensive gentleman's timepiece.

'Now what do you think of that?' her tormentor goaded. 'Do they look the sort of things a lady's maid would own? I really don't think so. They do, however, look the sort of items she might purloin from her employer's bedroom.'

Amelie found her voice at last. 'This is all lies. I've never seen these things before in my life,' she cried indignantly.

'And yet somehow they are in your bag. You did say it was your bag, didn't you?'

Her fellow passengers were muttering to themselves, the motherly lady still swearing that she was sure there was some mistake, but the acidic clerk in the corner talked darkly about the falling morals of servants these days. Even the farmer had woken up and was giving his pointed opinion that they were wasting time, and if they didn't get moving soon it would be dark before they could get anywhere near their homes. The rest of the coach nodded in agreement and seemed to lose interest in Amelie's plight.

Gareth reached into the carriage and grasped her arm. 'Now, my dear, I think you will come with me.'

He pulled her down from the coach as the driver started to put his horses into motion once more. Smiling, he waved the stage on its way. 'Don't worry, I'll make sure this young woman gets her just deserts.'

It was all over in seconds. One minute the coach was still there, the next she was standing in the middle of a deserted country road, Gareth Wendover at her arm and his horse placidly grazing by the roadside.

'You are abominable!' she exploded. 'What have I ever done to you to serve me so ill?'

'Desertion, perhaps,' he queried. 'Have you never been told it's dishonourable to make a bargain and not keep it? I thought you needed a lesson.'

'I need no lesson on how to conduct myself, particularly from you,' she raged. 'The last time I had the misfortune to be in your company, you behaved intolerably even for someone who was clearly not in their right senses.'

His smile faded. 'I may have been a trifle disguised,' he conceded, 'but my senses were working fine. You're a very beautiful young woman, Amelie, but too spirited by far. As a maidservant, you're in need of some schooling.'

She ignored the implied threat. 'How dare you make me out to be a thief? Every feeling is offended.'

'Who's to say you're not a thief? You've behaved most suspiciously.'

She stood erect and looked him squarely in the eyes. 'I have never stolen in my life and I have never seen those articles you tipped out of my cloak bag.'

'No, of course you haven't,' he agreed amiably. 'The watch and tiepin are mine and the brooch is one that belonged to my mother and that happened to be in my pocket.'

She gaped at him. 'Then why did you make up such a wicked story?'

'To get you off the coach, of course,' he replied blandly. 'What else? I could hardly hold the stage up and request you to dismount. You would have refused and your fellow passengers would have supported you, but thinking you might be a thief, they just wanted to get on their way.'

'You are insufferable. You've stranded me in the middle of nowhere because I didn't keep some shameful bargain. Rest assured that I still won't be keeping it.'

'Now that's where we might disagree.' His tone was unyielding. 'After all, what else can you do? As you so rightly point out, you're stranded in the middle of nowhere, and the only possible transport looks to be that horse over there, and that horse belongs to me. So I think perhaps you might be persuaded to keep your bargain after all.'

'Then you think wrongly. I would rather walk for the rest of the day than be anywhere near you.' With that, she stuffed her few belongings back into her bag and began marching rapidly along the road.

'It's at least six miles to the nearest village,' he called after her.

'Then I'll walk six miles,' she responded angrily.

He swung himself into the saddle and sidled his horse up to her. 'I always get my way, you know. You might as well give in gracefully and enjoy our splendid isolation together. The shoes you're wearing hardly seem to be made for rural walking.' The steel had given way to wry mockery.

She looked down at the dainty pumps she still wore, annoyed that she'd not thought to change them for some of Fanny's much stouter shoes. With compressed lips, she marched onwards, Gareth Wendover walking his horse just a pace behind. *We must look like a carnival show*, she reflected bitterly.

'Come, Amelie, this is stupid. Get up on the horse and I'll engage to take you to the nearest inn.'

'Thank you, sir, but your offer is declined. I'm well aware of my likely fate there. I've had experience of what you consider fitting conduct for an inn.'

'You're an obstinate young woman, but I shall win. You might as well resign yourself to accompanying me and be saved a good deal of discomfort.'

His manner was relaxed and he seemed to have all the time in the world, confident that she would eventually capitulate. Her feet were already pinching badly and she knew that the soles of her shoes would hardly stand up to six miles of rough road, but her anger drove her on. The earlier vision of his smile and the remembered pleasure of his embrace had evaporated without trace. He was a persecutor, there was no doubt. He was as bad in his own way as Rufus Glyde and, just as she'd defeated Glyde, she would defeat him, too.

Still incensed, she trudged on and now both were silent. Gareth saved his breath. He could see it was pointless trying to persuade her otherwise. He'd been seized by fury when he discovered she'd disappeared without a word and had made a snap decision to go after her and wreak his revenge. It was a stupid thing to do, but he was unused to a female besting him. From the moment he'd met her, he'd behaved irrationally; she'd somehow got under his skin and it was a new sensation. Women were for dalliance, passing fancies to be enjoyed lightly before moving on. They were not to be taken seriously. Now he was landed with this ridiculous situation.

He was willing to concede that she had cause to be angry. He'd behaved badly, but *her* conduct was hardly blameless. She'd been lying to him ever since they met, he was certain. And she'd made use of him when it suited her. He would show her that no one, least of all a chit of a girl, treated him in that way and emerged unscathed. Let her walk off her temper and destroy her shoes. She would be all the more acquiescent when he made his next move.

Musing in this way, he was unaware of the sounds of an approaching coach. Amelie, far more alert, heard in the distance the clatter of wheels before a curricle and four swept round the corner at breakneck speed. She had a terrifying vision of four magnificent greys thundering down on her before she made a dive for cover. Lost in his thoughts, Gareth could only take avoiding action when it was too late. His startled mount reared into the air, and he was flung over the horse's head, landing heavily in the ditch. The curricle swept by, its driver, clad in a caped overcoat, according them not a glance.

Cowering in the shelter of the grassy bank, Amelie thought she spied a crest on the side of the coach panel. Surely it could not be Rufus Glyde. But she knew that it was. She was all too familiar with that crest. Her flight must have been discovered earlier than she'd hoped and he'd been sent for, or most probably had taken it on himself to hunt her down. Fanny would never have given her away; her father must have guessed that she'd fled to Bath and her grandmother. Terrified that Glyde might turn the coach and come back to inspect his handiwork, she remained in hiding. There she stayed silent and unmoving for a long time before finding the courage to crawl up the bank to the roadside.

Gareth Wendover was nowhere to be seen. His mount was once more quietly cropping the grass, but there was no sign of the master. A perfect opportunity to escape. The horse was close by and looked biddable. If she led him to the nearest field gate she could manage to clamber into the saddle, then ride to Wroxall, and from there catch the next stagecoach westwards wherever it was going. The sooner she was out of this part of the country, the better. She knew Glyde was not travelling here for his own enjoyment. He was searching for her and he would be back.

A groan sounded from the ditch a few yards away. Tiptoeing to the grass edge, she peered downwards. Gareth was lying on his back, but his foot was at a sickening angle. He had his eyes closed and his face was ashen.

'Are you all right?' She knew it to be an ill-advised question even as she asked.

He opened his eyes and looked directly up into hers. 'Does it look like it? No, I'm not all right, but it's hardly your problem.'

'What's happened to your foot?'

'It appears I may have broken my ankle—I'm not sure. In any case, I can't move more than a few inches. There's no way I'll be able to walk on it.'

She remained silent and he rasped out, 'Don't mind me, rejoice all you wish. You're free to go now. Take the horse and make your escape while you can.'

'But what will you do?'

'Do you really care? I can't imagine so. I shall stay here—I don't have much choice. Someone will come by sooner or later.'

'Let me try to help you up.' She half clambered down the ditch and put her hand under the shoulder that was nearest. At the same time he tried to raise himself to a standing position with his other hand, but the effort was too great. His face turned even whiter.

'I can't do it,' he said, sinking back onto the damp bed of grass once more, 'but thank you for trying. I probably don't deserve your help.'

'No, you don't,' she said shortly, 'and this could be just punishment for your behaviour.'

'Spare me the lecture on my morals and go.'

She hesitated, but then walked down the road and led the horse forwards to the nearby gate. Gareth's last glimpse of her was a mass of chestnut curls flying in the breeze as she disappeared into the distance.

She was an accomplished rider and the few miles to the nearest inn took her only a short time to cover. She rode into the deserted courtyard of the George and called out for help. No one came. She had to dismount and walk into the taproom before she found anyone. An angular woman with a sharp-featured countenance confronted her. Her worn pinafore and rolled-up sleeves suggested that this was the landlord's wife.

She barred Amelie's passage, her arms folded pugnaciously, and her eyes snapping. 'And what do you want, missy?' she asked in an ill-tempered voice as she looked Amelie up and down with a thinly veiled disgust. 'We ain't that sort of place. Off with you. The Cross Keys is where you need to be.'

Amelie was startled. She'd never before been spoken to in that fashion. She supposed she must look a fright; she was certainly dishevelled from the long coach journey and her tumble down the bank. The hem of her dress was muddy and her shoes practically falling apart. She rather thought her face was smudged, too. It was true she looked an unlikely member of the *ton*, but to judge her a lightskirt!

However, she couldn't afford to alienate the woman further and so pinned on her most appealing smile. 'Dear, ma'am, I'm sorry to disturb you. I'm afraid there's been a riding accident and my present state is due to having been thrown from my horse.'

The landlady's wife looked unimpressed. Her arms stayed folded and her expression was grim.

'We, my brother and I, were on a pleasure ride, you see,' Amelie extemporised wildly, 'and my horse went lame, so we had to leave her behind at a farm we passed and we decided to continue home on Gareth's horse. Only then a coach came along at a tremendous speed and the horse reared up and flung us both into the ditch.'

That, at least, was partly truthful. The woman began to look a little more interested, but her arms remained in their fixed position.

'Gareth, my brother, has hurt his ankle—I fear he may have broken it—and I've had to leave him lying in the ditch. I said I would ride to seek help.' She gave a nervous laugh and finished lamely, 'And here I am. Yours was the first inn I came to.'

The landlady continued to maintain her unnerving silence and Amelie cast round for something that would penetrate the woman's iron reserve. Her eye caught the garish design of what looked to be new curtains.

'Oh, how wonderful!' she exclaimed. 'Such beautiful curtains. I know my mother has been looking everywhere for colours like these, but hasn't been able to find just the right shades.'

She prayed fervently for her dead mother's forgiveness. The praise seemed to be welcome and Mrs Skinner unbent slightly, but it was the thought that she had stolen a march on Amelie's unknown mother that really sealed the matter.

'Where d'you say your brother wus?' she enquired roughly.

'Just a few miles along the road going west,' Amelie said hopefully. 'If we could send an able-bodied man with a horse and cart, we could carry him back here.'

'*We,*' said the landlady with emphasis, 'can't do nuthin'. You'll 'ave to wait till Mr Skinner gets back from Wroxhall, then we'll see.'

'Yes, of course,' Amelie said placatingly, wondering with anxiety just how long that would be.

* * *

In the event it was two very long hours before she heard the horse and cart pull up in the yard. Two hours of nervously keeping watch at the parlour window, ready to run should Rufus Glyde reappear. And two hours of thinking of Gareth, alone and cold, lying in that ditch. He might be spotted by a labourer returning home from work, but it was unlikely that a passer-by would search the gully without reason. And by now he probably lacked the strength to attract attention. Perhaps she shouldn't have left him? What if he caught a fever or, even worse, died? It would be all her fault. No, that isn't fair, she countered angrily—it would be *his* fault. If he hadn't stopped the coach, told such appalling lies about her and forced her to go with him, the accident would never have happened. He wouldn't be lying badly injured and she'd be safe with her grandmother instead of stranded in this dreary inn.

'I heerd you had an accident.' Mr Skinner was as stout as his wife was thin and by good fortune lacked her chronic ill temper. He smiled pleasantly at Amelie, 'I'm sorry I weren't home to help, but I've told Will to pack up the cart with blankets and brandy and then go arsk the doctor to come quickly. When the horse is fed, Will and me will be off sharp to look for your brother.'

'Thank you truly, Mr Skinner. I'm very worried about him.' And to her own astonishment, she shed genuine tears.

'Don't you fret, miss. It'll be all right. It's May and the weather ain't too bad. Happen he'll be a little cold and mebbe in pain, but he'll come off fine.'

'Can I come with you?'

'No, m'dear—best stay here. It's getting dark and we don't want another accident.'

She had docilely to agree. But now that dusk had fallen, she thought it would prove difficult to locate the injured man by lantern light. If she'd been allowed to accompany the rescuers, she was sure she would have found the place easily. Instead she was forced to remain at her post by the window, scanning the darkness with such intensity that it seemed she might cut a path to Gareth through the gloom and herself bring help.

In the first hour after Amelie left, Gareth remained cheerful. She'd had the chance to break free and he'd expected her to desert him. He was surprised that she'd even hesitated. He thought of her attempts to help him. It had been excruciatingly painful, but he'd borne with it because she'd cared enough to try and because she was near. What was it about this girl that led him to behave so rashly? She seemed to exercise a malignant charm over him. By rights he should be at ease in his London hotel, sending a message to his lawyer and planning his escape to the Continent. He supposed wryly that this was a kind of escape although hardly one he would have chosen.

The minutes ticked slowly by and he grew colder as the sun waned and the chill of dusk settled around him. He began to fall into a troubled dream in which a card table and a chandelier swam around the periphery of his vision while a beautiful, chestnut-haired girl danced in front of him. Gradually, he lapsed into a feverish state, the dreams becoming more vivid and frightening. The girl had disappeared and the chandelier was burning his eyes. The cards rose from the table and smacked him hard around the face. Blearily he swam back into consciousness as a hand gently slapped his cheek and a homely country voice encouraged him. 'Come on, sir, time to go. We'll have you in the cart in a twinkling and get you back to a warm bed.'

Mr Skinner's plump build belied a strength that was needed

to raise Gareth from the depths of the gully. Only then could Will reach down to help them both up the steep bank. Gareth was now as weak as a kitten; though he tried manfully to aid their struggle, he had to allow himself to be pulled, pushed and finally lifted from his mossy bed onto the rough boards of the cart. A twinkling had been an exaggeration, he thought, in the throes of extreme pain. At some point he must have passed out. He came to, choking on the brandy that Mr Skinner trickled down his throat. The blankets wrapping him smelt slightly fetid and the jolting of the cart sent shock pains through his leg. At last when he felt he could bear it no longer, they turned into the yard of the George Inn.

The first face he saw was Amelie's. He could hardly believe she was there. He'd been too dazed to think how his rescuers had found him, but now he saw he had her to thank.

'You've found my *brother*,' cried Amelie, running forwards and gratefully squeezing Mr Skinner by the hand. She hoped that Gareth was alert enough to grasp his supposed relationship. The innkeeper lifted him carefully down from the cart and, with Will's help, carried him up to the spare room. Gareth was no lightweight and Will could only gasp between breaths that the doctor would be with them presently. Once in the room, Gareth sank, pallid-faced, onto the bed.

With difficulty, he turned to Mr Skinner, and murmured in a faint voice, 'My sister and I are most grateful for your kindness in coming to our aid.'

She was thankful for his quick thinking. If he'd repudiated the relationship, she was sure that Mrs Skinner would have instantly ejected her from the inn, darkness or no darkness.

* * *

After the doctor had visited his new patient and made his examination, she crept quietly back into Gareth's room.

'What's the verdict?' she asked anxiously.

He looked up slowly and smiled. It was the warm smile she'd seen in the London inn. That seemed a million miles away now.

'I haven't broken the ankle, thank the lord, but I've sprained it badly and I'm likely to be laid up for a good few days. The doctor's left me a draught for the pain and he'll come back the day after tomorrow to change the bandages.'

She could only smile in response. She felt tongue tied, badly shaken by how intense her relief had been when Gareth was carried into the inn courtyard and how sharp her distress at seeing him in pain. Powerful feelings had surfaced despite her effort to control them. There was an awkward silence. The painkilling draught was already having its effects and Gareth lay dozing. She was about to tiptoe out of the room, when his voice stopped her in her tracks.

'I should say thank-you.'

'There's no need,' she said quickly.

'You could have taken your revenge by leaving me to my fate.'

'I am not dishonest,' she said squarely, 'and neither am I heartless. You'd suffered a misfortune and needed help. I would have done the same for anyone.'

'You could have told them here of the accident and then gone on your way. You need not have stayed.'

His smile had vanished and his voice was almost brusque. It was as if he resented her help, resented being put in a situation where he was beholden.

'Don't worry, I won't be staying long,' she said in a cool voice, 'just tonight and then I'll be gone.'

'Where will you sleep? This seems to be the only spare room.'

'I'm to share a chamber with Betsy—the kitchen maid.'

'Good,' he said mysteriously.

She couldn't see anything good about it. She'd never shared a bedroom in her life and a kitchen maid would not have been her chosen companion. A more worldly-wise Gareth was satisfied. If she were indeed the innocent young woman she claimed to be, then Betsy's chaperonage would be invaluable.

'No doubt I'll see you in the morning before you leave?' His tone was indifferent; it was clear that he was dismissing her and preferred to be alone.

'If you wish,' she replied distantly.

He closed his eyes in weariness, looking so ill and worn that she instantly regretted her coldness. She would have to leave on the morrow as she'd promised, but a small inner voice was urging her to stay and make sure that he recovered fully. The thought was dismissed even as it occurred. It was impossible to remain at the inn; she'd spent the entire day evading his unwelcome attentions, so what on earth would he think if she continued by his bedside?

Chapter Four

She stirred restlessly as the bedroom door shut. There was a thin streak of daylight showing between the badly hung curtain and the window sill, but otherwise the attic room remained dark. Narrowing her eyes, she tried to read the battered clock face on the table beside her and saw that it was only five-thirty. She must have been woken by the maid, leaving for her unenviable duties downstairs. She supposed she ought to rise herself and be on the road to Wroxall as early as possible. There'd be no way of getting to the town at this time of day other than by walking and it would take many hours. She'd have to beg a strong pair of shoes from Betsy.

She tried to work out what time she would reach Wroxhall and if it would be possible to board a coach that afternoon for Bath. It might be that mail coaches also stopped in the town. They were much faster than the lumbering stage and would get her to Bath before nightfall. But the cost of a ticket was also much higher and her remaining funds were modest. She might even miss whatever coaches were passing through the town and be forced to spend a night there. That was something she dared not contemplate.

She'd embarked on this adventure nervous, but confident, that she would succeed in reaching her grandmother within hours. Complications such as Gareth Wendover had never entered her head. And he was a complication. By any measure he'd treated her callously and yet she felt a strong thread connecting them, a thread she was finding difficult to break. But there was no doubt he'd brought added danger into her life and she was well advised to be leaving him. Between them, the landlord and the doctor would do all that was necessary to guarantee his well-being; such a vigorous man would not be laid low for long. And if she left the inn this early in the morning, she could forgo a farewell visit. It would be unmannerly, but much easier to walk out of the door right now. If she saw him again, she might be tempted to stay. Her thoughts went round and round in circles until her tired brain gave up the struggle and she once more slept.

'Miss Wendover, can you hear me?' The landlord's voice penetrated her slumbers. It had a note of urgency and she wondered for an instant who he was calling and why, when she realised it must be herself. She was the mysterious Miss Wendover!

'Miss Wendover, can you come quickly, please?'

She hurried out of bed and hastily donned her travelling clothes from yesterday. At the door Mr Skinner looked apologetic, but very worried.

'Sorry to wake you betimes, miss, but Mr Wendover do seem bad. He's feverish for sure and don't respond. Will and me have tried to give him the doctor's medicine, but he won't let us near.'

She forgot her resolution to leave the inn as soon as possible and ran down the stairs to Gareth's bedroom. The scene before her struck her with dismay. A smoky candle still spluttered on the bedside table, but the curtains remained drawn. In the half-light she could see the bedcovers in disarray, half of them trailing on the floor and the other half heaped untidily on the bed. As for the patient, he was tossing and turning constantly, unable to get comfortable, first throwing off the sheets and then grabbing at them with hot dry hands while all the time muttering incoherently. She went forwards to the bed and laid her hand fleetingly on his forehead. It was burning to the touch and his eyes, glancing unrecognisingly at her, were blurred with fever.

'Have you sent for the doctor?' Amelie questioned, thoroughly alarmed.

'Not yet, miss, we weren't sure to do it, without your say so.'

'Why ever didn't you call me earlier?'

'We did think to,' Mr Skinner conceded, 'but he weren't too bad seemingly.'

'He's certainly bad now.' Her voice was sharp with anxiety.

'Ah, mortal bad.' The landlord looked gloomily down at the threshing figure and shook his head.

She tried to keep the irritation out of her voice. It looked as though she would need all the help she could get.

'Please send Will for the doctor immediately and ask Mrs Skinner to bring a sponge and some lavender water.'

'T'would be best if I get it for you, miss.'

'I really don't care who gets it, just bring it please,' she snapped, her nerves frayed by this frightening turn of events.

There was no help for it—she would have to stay. The Skinners believed her to be Gareth's sister and there was no way she could simply up and leave. And seeing him lying ill and alone, she knew that she wouldn't abandon him. When Mr Skinner returned with the bowl of lavender water, she asked him to raise the patient up while she attempted to plump the lumpy pillows into a more comfortable resting place. Then she sat down by the bedside and gently sponged his face. This seemed to soothe the fretting man and for a while he became calmer. But when she rose to move away from the bed, his hand, which had been aimlessly brushing the sheet, shot out and grasped her wrist.

'Don't leave me,' he muttered fiercely.

The doctor was not long in coming and did not seem overly surprised that his patient had developed a fever. He had, after all, been lying in a wet ditch for a number of hours and, by the look of him, Dr Fennimore thought, he'd probably already travelled a considerable distance and spent much of his strength. But his agitation appeared extreme.

The doctor rose from the bedside and looked thoughtfully at Amelie, his face shrewd and enquiring. 'His fever is unusually severe. Apart from his physical ills, he seems unquiet in his mind. You wouldn't know, I suppose, if there is something disturbing him?'

She avoided his question. She could not imagine that the events of the previous day had seriously bothered such a cool, audacious man. But Gareth Wendover was certainly a mystery and she sensed that there were dark shadows in his life which might complicate his recovery. She sat down by the rickety table, troubled and very pale.

The doctor clasped her hand warmly. 'Don't worry, Miss Wendover. I'm sure this fever is only temporary. Your brother looks a tough man, certainly not one that a few hours in a ditch will finish off.'

He continued bluffly, 'I'll leave you with a stronger remedy. Give it to him every three hours. If his condition worsens, send for me immediately. Hopefully, he should be back to his normal strength within a few days. His ankle is already showing signs of improvement.'

As Gareth's supposed sister, Amelie had also to be his nurse. Pitchforked into intimacy with a man she hardly knew, she could not protest without drawing attention to their false relationship. Fanny's horror would know no bounds, she reflected, but this was no time to be missish. Gareth needed her constant attention.

Throughout the next two days she bathed his forehead, administered medicine and kept his bedclothes as comfortable as possible. All the time his fevered ramblings punctuated the endless routine. He seemed greatly exercised about escaping from a room and needing to find a boat, but none of it made any sense to Amelie and she was too busy to worry over his words.

Mrs Skinner was invariably difficult, grumbling incessantly about the additional work Gareth occasioned. At times Amelie nearly came to blows with her. Fortunately, her husband was of a different disposition. He took Amelie's place by the bedside at nuncheon and dinner to allow her to eat and to stretch her limbs; at night he insisted on taking over Gareth's care and sent her to bed in the early hours of each morning. By then she was too tired to protest and retired gratefully to her little attic room, not caring that Betsy beside her was snoring heavily. She was so weary that she could have slept in Gareth's ditch.

On the third morning Mr Skinner reported that the fever had broken around dawn and that the patient was at last sleeping peacefully. After a hasty breakfast, she tiptoed quietly into Gareth's room with a bowl of chicken broth that the formidable Mrs Skinner had been persuaded to make. He lay supine, a stillpowerful figure, but the days fighting fever had taken their toll.

She felt a sudden surge of tenderness as she saw the leanness of his face and the pallor beneath the tanned skin.

At her approach, he opened his eyes and a puzzled look flitted across his face. He appeared to be in a bedroom, but it was certainly nowhere he recognised. He felt amazingly tired and cursed himself for his weakness. The events of recent days slowly began to filter through his brain—a nightmarish ride, exquisite pain and a pair of gentle, soothing hands in the midst of the threatened inferno. He recalled some kind of accident an age ago, or so it seemed; this ravishing girl had been there, she'd ridden away on his horse. So what was she doing in this room? For a while he considered the matter dispassionately but it remained inexplicable.

'You're still here,' he murmured.

She bent over him, gently arranging the pillows to support his shoulders. He was sharply aware of her soft warmth so close to him and her fragrance drifting on the air.

'Take some of this excellent broth Mrs Skinner has made for you. You haven't eaten for days.'

He gave up the challenge of trying to make sense of the world and meekly sipped from the spoon she held out to him.

A few days later he was well enough to leave the stuffy bed-chamber and make his way with Will's help down the stairs to the inn garden. Amelie brought up the rear of the procession with a stool and blankets in case it was chilly. But the sun shone blithely from a cloudless blue sky and Gareth, his ankle supported by the stool, lay back in his chair and gratefully soaked up the warmth. Beside him Amelie savoured the perfume of apple blossom and the rich smell of new grass.

He looked disparagingly at the glass she handed him.

'The doctor said you should drink as much milk as you can,' she chided. 'It will help you regain your strength.'

'You need strength to drink the stuff,' he protested. 'I think I'll settle for my present state of health.'

'You're a stubborn man.'

'And you're a stubborn woman. Why are you still here? I seem to remember sending you on your way.'

'You did and more than once—but it would be strange behaviour for a sister to abandon her brother.'

'Ah, yes, I'd forgotten that I'd acquired a new relative. Quite a surprise for me—though entirely beneficial.'

His blue eyes held the warm glow that she found so unsettling, but instinctively she returned his smile.

'It can't have been pleasant for you, forced to tend a sick man you barely knew and with no help from that bracket-faced termagant.'

She wanted to say that she knew him a great deal better now, but instead limited herself to murmuring neutrally, 'Even less pleasant for you, I fear. But Mr Skinner has been so very helpful. He's watched over you constantly and even persuaded his wife to cook for us.'

'Has she been very tiresome?'

'Shall we say she's not best pleased to be entertaining two vagrants.' Amelie grinned, remembering the skirmishes she'd endured while Gareth lay helpless above.

'One thing does occur to me,' he said thoughtfully. 'The Skinners must be wondering why no one has come from our supposed home to look for us.'

'I told them that I'd sent the local carrier with a message when he passed here the day before yesterday.'

'And they believed you?'

'Mrs Skinner probably didn't, but then she wouldn't believe anything. She decided from the outset that we were impostors, and of course she's right.'

For a moment he was startled, wondering how she could possibly have guessed that he was not the man he appeared.

'I mean,' she explained seeing the surprise on his face, 'that we're playing this charade of being brother and sister.' She looked at him enquiringly. 'Do you have a sister, in fact?'

'No.'

'Do you have any family—won't they be wondering where you are?'

'No and no,' he said shortly, then added in a more conciliatory tone, 'My only relation was my grandfather and he's now dead.'

'I'm sorry.' The compassion in her voice touched him on the raw.

'Don't be,' he said roughly, 'it's a matter of indifference to me.'

But she was not to be deterred. 'If you have no family in Bristol, why do you want to go there?'

He shifted his position, but remained sitting in silence.

'While you were suffering from the fever you mentioned taking a boat and escaping,' she persevered. 'What did you mean?'

'I've no idea. When people are feverish, they talk a lot of nonsense,' he retorted.

She had the distinct impression of an iron gate being swiftly clanged shut; she would learn no more. And in a trice he'd deftly turned the tables on her and begun to probe her own story.

'And why were *you* determined on travelling to Bristol?'

He must know that she'd been less than honest with him, at the very least that she'd lied about her destination.

'A family there are advertising for a lady's maid and I intended to apply for the position.'

'They must have advertised days ago. The situation might already be filled.' He'd evidently decided to maintain the pretence.

'I daresay you're right,' she replied airily. 'They're sure to have hired another girl by now.'

'So when you get to Bristol, what will you do?'

'I think,' she said carefully, 'I shall try my luck in Bath. There's any number of retired dowagers living there and one of them is bound to need assistance.'

'I wish you luck. Would you like a testimonial from me?' he joked. Then his face took on a more serious air. 'Without a reference from your previous family, you'll find it difficult to get work.'

'I shall manage. I've no reason to feel ashamed. I shall tell the truth about why I had to leave.'

'Will they believe you, though? As an employer I might find it difficult to accept your situation was so desperate that you had to climb out of the window on knotted sheets. Things like that only happen in novels. If you'd simply told your mistress what her son was up to, she would have intervened.'

'No, she wouldn't. He's spoilt and pampered and no one gainsays him, least of all his adoring mother. She'd never have believed me. She'd have accused me of plotting to ensnare him and I'd have been turned off without notice.'

'How has your situation improved? You're still without a job and still without references.'

'But I haven't had to endure lies and false accusations.'

He looked a little conscious at this. 'Until you met me, I suppose.'

'Yes, until I met you.'

She was looking directly at him and he was caught by her gaze. How could a pair of eyes sparkle with such militancy and yet drown a man in their allure?

'Was there nobody else in the family that you could turn to?' he said quickly. 'What about your young mistress?'

'She was a good friend to me,' Amelie admitted, happily weaving her fantasy, 'but she's to be married to a wealthy man against her wishes. She's powerless to offer me protection.'

'*You* could always marry. You'd receive ample protection then. You must have enjoyed plenty of attention from your fellows—beautiful and intelligent maidservants aren't two a penny.'

'I will never marry,' she declared resolutely.

Gareth smiled indulgently. 'You're not much more than a child—far too young to know how you'll feel in the future.'

Nettled by his mocking tone, her response was sharp. 'On the contrary, I shall feel in the future just as I do now. I intend to stay a single woman if I can.'

'Then you are vastly unlike the rest of your sex. Why so definite?'

'I don't wish to be subject to any man.'

'The right man can be a powerful defender.'

'Not those I've known—they've been either dissolute or vain and shallow.'

'There are men who are none of those things.'

She raised her eyebrows sceptically. 'You, for instance?'

Damn her, he thought, why was she forever putting him in the wrong? He'd behaved appallingly, he knew, and for no other reason than a desire to master her, to ruffle that beautiful surface. She was just too lovely.

Aloud he admitted to his offence. 'I behaved stupidly when we first met, more than stupidly.' He shook his head at his folly. 'I made a bad situation worse by getting extremely drunk.'

She looked enquiringly at him, but it was evident he had no intention of disclosing the cause of his erratic behaviour. She wondered if it had anything to do with the grandfather for whom he'd just professed the utmost indifference.

Trying another tack, she said quietly, 'You may not have relatives in England, but what about friends?'

'None of those, either,' he muttered roughly. 'I'm a wanderer, Amelie, and friends and family play no part in my life.'

She sensed that beneath his grim detachment, there lurked a vulnerability he would not admit. Her eyes clouded with sympathy and without thinking she reached out towards him, gently stroking the tanned forearm that showed beneath his rolled-up sleeves.

His hand closed over hers and held it tightly. He looked directly into her concerned face, hard blue eyes meeting soft brown, his gaze intent, wondering. For a long moment they sat thus. Then he reached out and slowly caressed her cheek. Her pulse began an erratic dance as his touch warmed her face. He let his hand slide from her cheek to tangle itself in the glossy curls which tumbled to her shoulders. Turning his body towards her, he cupped her face in both his hands and tilted it upwards. She watched as his mouth came closer and without thinking offered up her lips. His kiss was hard and warm and lingered long.

How long they would have kissed she had no idea, if Mr Skinner had not suddenly appeared from the depths of the inn leading the doctor behind him. She jumped back, flushed. Gareth looked annoyed. If Mr Skinner had seen that embrace, they would be in trouble. How to explain now that they were brother and sister! Jumping up from her seat, she nodded briefly to Dr Fennimore and quickly ran up the stairs to her bedroom in the eaves. She poured water from the jug into the chipped white basin and bathed her heated cheeks. She must truly have run mad. What on earth was she doing kissing a man of whom she knew nothing or at least nothing creditable? She sat down on her bed and stayed there for a very long time, trying hard to still her racing heart and erase the feeling of Gareth's hard, warm mouth on hers.

The doctor's visit was brief. He was evidently well satisfied with his patient and needed to come no more. She heard him call out his farewells followed by the sound of Will helping Gareth up the stairs from the garden to his room. Until she could leave the inn, she must make sure that they were rarely alone together. He could not be trusted; she'd allowed herself to show sympathy and his response had been immediate—an assault, an assault that she'd made no attempt to escape. She could not trust herself either. His gaze had sent her heart racing, a simple touch had left her breathless. And that kiss. No, she would not think of that kiss.

As the sun slipped from the sky, Mr Skinner appeared at her door with a message. 'Your brother would like to know if you will dine with him tonight. He's feeling a good deal better and would like to celebrate his recovery.' The landlord enunciated the phrases painstakingly, relieved that he'd remembered Gareth's precise words.

I'm sure he would, she thought crossly, *and I can imagine the kind of celebration he intends.*

'Tell my brother that I regret I have the headache and I will not be dining tonight,' she said, adding diffidently, 'It would be very kind of you, Mr Skinner, if you could bring a bowl of soup to my room.'

For the first time since she'd come to the George, she found it difficult to sleep that night, her mind endlessly roaming the day's events, but finding no peace. She could not banish the attraction she felt for Gareth Wendover. Her heart was forever pulling her towards a man with whom it was madness to embroil herself. He was arrogant and capricious. He was reserved and unforthcoming and she strongly suspected that unfortunate secrets lay hidden in the depths of his past. Yet she, too, was equally guilty of dissembling. From the outset she'd told him a pack of lies and ever since had spent considerable effort in embroidering them.

What was certain was that she must leave for Bath as soon as she could. She must not become any further entangled; she must not fall in love with him. If ever she were forced to marry, Lord Silverdale's daughter would be expected to look a great deal higher than a mere Mr Wendover of unknown and possibly disreputable lineage. And she *wasn't* going to be forced to marry. She would not emulate her mother's sad fate; her security and peace of mind lay in an unmarried life and that meant eschewing dalliance, no matter how attractive the man.

After breakfast she repaired to Gareth's bedroom to tell him she was leaving. It was another beautiful May morning and the leaded windows were flung wide to welcome the sun. A warm breeze gently lifted the curtains. He was sitting by the window fully dressed and smiled mockingly as she came through the door.

'I hope I find you recovered?'

She looked blank for a moment.

'The headache? I understand it was so painful that you could manage only a bowl of soup for dinner.' His tone was ironic.

'I'm well, thank you,' she replied, not meeting his eyes. 'And you?'

'I'm well, too—my old self, in fact. Does that strike terror into your heart?'

'Indeed no, why should it? I'm well able to take care of myself.'

He shook his head in some irritation. 'Let's stop sparring, Amelie. Come and sit with me instead.'

She moved towards the window and the empty chair. For the first time she met his eyes directly and her body warmed instantly beneath his gaze. But she ignored the answering pull and disregarded his welcoming hand; she was still on dangerous territory and must step carefully.

'When do you intend to leave for Bristol?' she asked. 'I presume you're still going there.'

'Maybe,' he uttered shortly. 'I haven't yet made up my mind.'

'If you don't continue to Bristol, where else will you go? Back to London?'

'Possibly.'

'So you're as free as a bird?'

'It would appear so.'

Frustrated at his stonewalling, she went on the offensive. 'Are you saying that nobody in the entire world will miss you, if you don't soon put in an appearance?'

'That about sums it up.'

She didn't understand him. Her questions were innocent enough and his bald refusal to answer demonstrated clearly that he didn't trust her. She was good enough to kiss but not to confide in. Sensing her anger, he smiled that warm, entrancing smile.

'Why don't we just enjoy this morning? I imagine you've come to tell me you're leaving soon.'

'Now that your ankle's better, I must be on my way.' She was annoyed with herself that she sounded almost apologetic.

'Of course you must, and I can't detain you. You've kept your bargain, after all.'

For a moment she looked uncomprehending; she'd completely forgotten their old quarrel. Then she gave a half smile. 'Yes, I've kept it—but not quite as you planned.'

'Better, in fact. You've seen me through some very trying days, so don't let's spend our last few hours arguing.'

She remained mute and stared fixedly through the window at the untended orchard beyond. When he spoke again his voice was tender and caught at her heart.

'I have you to thank for the good shape I'm in. You must know that I'm deeply grateful.'

'I don't want your gratitude.'

'What do you want?' he asked quizzically and once again reached out for her hand.

Mindful of her overnight resolution, she jumped up quickly and said, 'What I want is to leave tomorrow. But in the meantime I'm sure the George can supply us with some entertainment. I'll go downstairs and see what they have to offer.'

And with that she disappeared rapidly from view. Gareth looked after her, a slight flush creeping into his lean cheek. Tendering his hand in friendship to a woman was a new experience for him and being rejected was equally novel.

She returned half an hour later, having searched high and low for dominoes or Chinese chequers. Will had helped her for a while until Mrs Skinner, catching sight of the two of them, had ordered him angrily to fetch water from the pump. Then she'd stood coldly over Amelie and demanded just what Miss Wendover might be wanting. Her attitude was one of unconcealed hostility. Amelie was sure now that the landlord had seen her spring back from Gareth's kiss yesterday and had confided this unsettling news to his wife. She blushed deeply at the thought of their conversation.

'I'm looking for dominoes or chequers,' she said as calmly as she could. 'My brother is feeling a good deal better and it will be a way of passing the hours.'

Mrs Skinner snorted as though she knew well enough how they intended to pass the hours, but reluctantly led the way into an inner sanctum, opened a tall oak dresser in the corner of the room and shuffled around inside. The reek of mothballs floated out into the already malodorous room.

'There's some cards and a game of spillikins.' The landlady thrust the items roughly at Amelie and stood glaring at her.

Understanding that she was dismissed, Amelie made to leave. She couldn't picture Gareth playing the child's game, but she could always leave the spillikins in her bedroom. With hurried thanks, she gathered up the games and ran up the stairs.

'I've found something,' she called out gaily. 'A pack of cards! Or rather Mrs Skinner found them, tucked at the back of an enormous dresser, which I don't think has been opened for at least thirty years. Unfortunately, they smell of mothballs, but then this room isn't exactly fresh, even with the window wide open.'

As she was speaking, she cleared the small table between them of empty glasses and medicine bottles. 'There, a perfect card table. What shall we play? I know very few games, but I imagine you can teach me.'

'No.' The brusque monosyllable startled her.

'I beg your pardon?'

'I said no. I can't teach you any card games, nor do I wish to play.'

She looked puzzled. 'How difficult am I to understand?' he said sharply. 'I don't wish to play.'

'But it's only a game of cards—an amusing diversion,' she protested.

'For the last time, I don't wish to play.'

The familiar bleak expression had returned to Gareth's face. His eyes were once more stony and the straight night-black brows threatening. He leaned back in his chair, detaching himself from the proceedings and refusing to meet her earnest look.

'That's all right,' she said a little uncertainly. 'I didn't mean to upset you.'

'You didn't. Just learn to take a refusal when it's given.'

She bit back a retort. After tomorrow she would never see Gareth Wendover again. It was hardly worth quarrelling with him despite his extraordinary rudeness. But it was difficult to accept that he was the same man who had kissed her with such ardour only yesterday. He was transformed and she felt deeply wounded by the change.

'I'll find something else to play,' she stammered a little shakily.

Minutes later she returned with the spillikins. The hard look on Gareth's face had disappeared and when he saw the spillikins he laughed out loud.

'I know you've been my nursemaid these past few days, but

have I regressed that badly that you need to play a child's game with me?'

'That's all they have downstairs, and we must make the best of it.'

She held upright the bunch of thin sticks and allowed them to fall at will. They scattered wildly across the table top.

'The sticks coloured blue score most highly, red next, then yellow, and green are the most lowly,' she explained.

'I shall be lucky to pick up one stick cleanly, never mind its colour. I've suffered an accident, after all.'

'You've sprained your ankle, not your wrist.'

'But women are so much more dextrous, it's hardly fair.'

'Surely, Mr Wendover, you're not saying that a woman can outdo you.'

'Gareth, please. If we're to be serious competitors, we must use first names. That way our insults, when they start flying, will be nicely personal.'

'I've no intention of trading insults. It's just a game, not a competition,' she said carelessly.

Nevertheless, she tried very hard to win. When it came to her turn she took minutes to weigh up the arrangement of sticks before deciding which one she would try to extricate from its place without dislodging the others. Gareth had gone first and could begin with the easiest stick to lift, but once into the thick of the game, they were both forced to concentrate intently when their several turns came round. At one point, he appeared to disturb one of the sticks he was trying to avoid and she called foul.

'I merely breathed on the stick and it moved of its own accord,' he disputed, shaking his head in bewilderment.

She burst out laughing. 'That's certainly original. I'll give you the excuse if only for sheer invention.'

He laughed back at her, his heart filled with a strange happiness. So the game went on until there was just a small pile of sticks left in the middle of the table, all thickly entangled. They were neck and neck in the number they'd managed to acquire and, faced now with the most difficult moves, they both studied the table keenly, trying to decide their best approach. In the event it was Gareth who managed to extricate his last spill without disturbing the one other that was left.

'Voilà!' he exclaimed.

'Magnifique,' she unconsciously rejoined, responding spontaneously to his skilful play.

'A maidservant who speaks French as well as having a French name! It becomes more and more intriguing.' He looked searchingly at her.

'I'd hardly say that I spoke French,' she said, desperately seeking a way of moving the conversation on to less dangerous ground.

'Still, it's an unusual maid who knows any French. And you *are* an unusual maid, aren't you? You're proud and independent, you speak genteelly and hold yourself like a lady. If it weren't for your clothes, I would take you for a lady.'

From the bottom of her heart, she thanked the absent Fanny for donating her wardrobe, then set about allaying his suspicions.

'My young mistress made a great friend of me and I learned from her how to go on.'

He considered this for a while. 'You may have learned conduct from her but not, I think, your courage.'

'What do you mean?' She was disconcerted.

'Didn't you say that your mistress was being married off against her will?'

'She is, but courage won't help her. Her brother has gambled away the family's fortune and marriage is the only way to restore it. She's expected to make this sacrifice for her family.'

'Quite a sacrifice! Would you make it, I wonder?'

'I would not,' she declared ringingly and with a vehemence that surprised him.

He looked at her as she sat across the table. Her creamy skin glowed translucent in the shadowed sunlight that filled the room and the velvet brown of her eyes blazed a fiery spirit. She had never looked more enchanting.

'Nor should you,' he said, his voice husky with feeling.

The atmosphere was suddenly charged with tension, their bantering mood dissipated. He should defuse the moment, he thought, make a joke, turn away. She'd already chosen to put distance between them and she was right. Instead, he rose quickly from his chair, taking no heed of the damaged ankle, and took both her hands in his. Slowly he raised her up and encircled her in his arms.

Crushed against his hard frame, she felt the same foolish impulse to melt into him; she began to tremble beneath his hands. He touched her face, her arms, and brushed across the warm silk of her breast. He gently kissed her hair, her ears, her cheek. In a moment his tongue had parted her lips and was slowly exploring the softness of her mouth. His body moved against her and she groaned softly with pleasure. She wanted to dissolve into this nameless delight, yet some voice of wisdom pulled her back to consciousness. This was a man who had come from nowhere and would go to nowhere. She would never see him again once they parted. He'd made her vulnerable, created a desire in her that she'd never before known. And desire meant weakness; she had only to think of her mother's fate to know that. Impelled by a new urgency, she hastily pushed him away and began to tidy the scattered sticks, barely able to see them for the emotions churning within her.

'That shouldn't have happened.'

He was still standing close to her, his breathing ragged and his voice rough. He seemed furious with himself.

'After yesterday I vowed I'd never again touch you.'

Distractedly, she smoothed her tumbled hair and then began to pack the last of the spillikins in their box.

'Forgive me if I've distressed you.' His harsh tones grated, breaking through her silence.

'It's of no importance. I don't wish to talk of it,' she managed. Her outward calm belied the turmoil within. 'It must be time for nuncheon,' she continued smoothly. 'I'll fetch some refreshment from the kitchen.'

She glanced fleetingly out of the window, as she turned to leave. A carriage had pulled up outside. In itself this was unusual but this was not any carriage. It was a lightly built curricle drawn by four high-stepping greys and the curricle door had a well-known crest on its panel. It had to be Rufus Glyde. He had traced her after all. He was here. She turned sheet-white and the box dropped from her suddenly lifeless hand.

'Excuse me,' she gasped, 'I have to go.'

And with that she dashed from the room, leaving Gareth baffled and infuriated.

Chapter Five

Rufus Glyde was in no pleasant mood. He'd been driving almost continuously for days without once ever sighting his quarry. In addition he'd had to endure the sharp tongue of Brielle St Clair when he'd dared to enquire for her granddaughter at the Bath house. It had been a terse encounter on both sides, but he'd definitely come off worse, told in no uncertain terms that his intervention in family affairs was not welcome. It had been the first intimation for Brielle that all was not well with her granddaughter. She was furious that Lord Silverdale had not come himself to tell her of Amelie's flight, but instead left it to this sneering and patronising stranger to break the news. Most of all she was desperately worried. She felt sick when she thought of what might have befallen the young girl. Her dread fuelled a naturally acerbic tongue and Glyde was still smarting from his dismissal.

As he entered the George the idea that he was on a wild goose chase became insistent. For a while he'd thought that he might be on Amelie's trail. At Reading where he'd stopped for the night, he'd overheard a conversation between two travellers that gave him pause. One of them had told the strange story of a stage held up on the Bath road, not for jewellery or money, but for a young woman travelling in the coach. It had caused something of a sensation when the passengers had disembarked at Bath and begun to tell their tale.

He'd been sufficiently intrigued by the news to abandon his return to London and head once more in the direction of Bath. By dint of questioning everyone he met—and most of these he castigated as ignorant bumpkins—he'd managed to discover the district in which the hold-up had occurred and then begun to cast around at various inns for news of the errant Amelie. So far it had proved a fruitless task and the George looked no more promising.

Entering the taproom, he was greeted by drab, outmoded furnishings and the stale odour of old beer and tobacco. He turned round full circle. The afternoon sunlight in its attempt to pierce the dirty windows only served to emphasise the dilapidation within. Surely Amelie Silverdale would not be residing here. The inhabitants, if there were any, were either dead or asleep. Nothing stirred. Irritably, he rang the bell on the counter and when there was no response, rang it again more loudly. Mrs Skinner appeared from the top of the cellar steps and scowled at him.

'Did you want somethin'?'

Her voice was not encouraging. Glyde looked the woman up and down. She was gaunt, badly dressed and with a face marked by ill temper.

'It would appear so since I rang the bell,' he countered acidly.

'Well, what is it, then? I'm busy.'

He tried to keep the rising anger from his voice; he needed this woman's help. He told the same story as he'd told at the other dozen inns he'd visited. He'd been travelling with a friend, but they'd become separated. He carefully avoided mentioning the

sex of his companion. His friend had not appeared at the rendez-
vous they'd agreed on and he, Glyde, feared that his comrade had
met with an accident. Did the good lady have anyone staying at
the inn who might be his friend?

'Nobody you'd know,' she sniffed.

'But you do have someone staying?' he persisted.

Mrs Skinner grudgingly admitted the fact but added, ''E ain't
your friend, 'e ain't a top-lofty gent like you.'

'My friend is hardly top-lofty. May I ask who this person
is?'

'You can arsk, but mebbe I ain't of a mind to tell you.'

Again he had visibly to control his anger. 'I'm sure we can
remedy your lack of memory.'

A sneer slashed his thin white face as he took out his bill folder
and extracted a note of some considerable value. Mrs Skinner
blinked at this unexpected largesse and thought of extending her
prize curtains to the rooms above.

''Is name's Wendover and I've told you 'e ain't a gent, not with
'is scruffy clothes.'

Glyde's hopes withered. For a moment he'd thought he might
finally be close to success, but a male resident who wore scruffy
clothes and wasn't a 'gent' as Mrs Skinner put it, was not someone who could be of any interest.

'And he is your only guest?'

'You're a nosy one, ain't you?' Mrs Skinner's hand closed over
the tantalising money bill. 'As it 'appens, 'is sister's staying with
him. They 'ad an accident, too. Funny, the number of accidents
round 'ere these days.'

Glyde ignored the witticism, but his mind was working rapidly.
A sister of Mr Wendover might mean a young woman, and this
young woman could just be the prey he sought. It was a chance

in a thousand, but he had to know. He cast around for a way of distracting Mrs Skinner, who appeared to have taken root in front of her benefactor. His luck suddenly took a turn for the better. Will, who had been working in the cellar alongside his mistress, appeared at that moment at the top of the stairs.

'Mrs Skinner, ma'am, where d'you want the new barrels put?'

'Where d'you think, you numbskull?' was Mrs Skinner's pleasant reply.

'There's not enough room behind the old barrels,' Will bravely continued.

'Dratted men,' she muttered, 'can't be relied on to do anythin'.' Giving Glyde a last withering glance, she disappeared back down the cellar steps.

Her head had hardly faded from view before he made his move. In a few seconds he'd reached the stairway leading to the top of the house and made ready to search out Mr Wendover and his mysterious sister for himself.

Gareth stared blankly through the window at the curricle as it disappeared towards the stables. From the rear it looked to be a nobleman's carriage, but he had no idea who it belonged to or why it was at the George. Amelie had evidently gained a better view and she *had* recognised it. The thought came to him that this might be her previous employer, enraged by her dubious departure. He realised with a jolt that his initial suspicions had been completely lulled and now his mind could no longer consider the possibility that she was a deceiver. He dismissed the idea even as it came into his head. And common sense soon reasserted itself. If she were a dishonest maidservant, whatever she might have done and however furious her noble employer, the possibility of his seeking her out in a rundown country inn was extremely unlikely.

Annoyance at Amelie's abrupt departure mingled with feelings of self-reproach. He'd spoiled the warm companionship of the morning. One minute they'd been laughing, joking, funning with each other. And then everything had changed. He'd touched her and he shouldn't have. She was irresistible, but he should have resisted. God knew he'd had enough experience in escaping amorous situations, so why was this so different? He couldn't account for it. Indignation at the notion of sacrificing herself to family duty had rendered her beauty overwhelming, her eyes a molten brown and the sheen of her skin glowing fire. But it was more than physical beauty that had shattered his restraint. In that moment it seemed her very soul had been laid bare and spoken unmistakably to his. He gave himself a mental shake: such fanciful nonsense! Whatever the reason, he'd not been able to stop himself. Even now he could feel her mouth, soft but eager, opening delicately to his.

When he heard the bedroom door open he turned, a contrite expression on his face, but instead of Amelie he was confronted by Rufus Glyde, a man he'd not seen for seven long years. Both men stared at each other in amazement. Glyde was the first to find his voice.

'Surely,' he jeered, 'it cannot be Gareth Denville. Aren't you supposed to be resting on the Continent? Surely you haven't returned to claim the earldom? Even the blackest sheep might be expected to do the decent thing and stay away.'

Gareth stayed silent, his face impassive and his darkened eyes unreadable. For years unfounded suspicions had plagued his mind over Glyde's role in that ill-fated card game.

'Aren't you going to invite me to sit down, Mr Wendover?'

Glyde tormented. 'I'm presuming it *is* Mr Wendover? Why the false name, I wonder? A silly question no doubt. I imagine you would prefer to keep your identity hidden for all kinds of reasons. And staying in a place like this!' The smirk became more pronounced.

Gareth remained standing. His voice was cold and curt. 'State your business. Mine is none of yours,' he rapped out.

'Still hot-tempered, I see. Some things never change. Though you've aged—not quite as fresh faced as when I saw you last. Now, when was that? Ah, yes, the Great-Go. Quite a night, quite a sensation, I recall.'

'Cut to the chase, Glyde, what do you want?'

'Not you, for sure. Keeping company with the flotsam of society is not really my custom. But I am rather interested in the sister you appear to have acquired. If my memory serves me right—and, of course, I could be wrong, family genealogy was never my strong point—your father, another unfortunate I understand, had only one child and that child was you. So a sister?'

'It's none of your affair and I'll thank you to leave.'

'Now that's where we could disagree, I fear.'

'I've nothing further to say to you. Leave of your own free will or at the end of my boot, it's your choice.'

'Proud crowing from someone plainly unable to enforce their threat.' He gestured at Gareth's bandaged ankle. 'Tell me what I want to know and I'll leave as quickly as you could want. What about this sister?'

Gareth weighed up the odds of forcibly removing his antagonist from the room and decided it was probably not worth the pain he would inevitably suffer. He would give him the minimum of information and speed him on his way.

'She is merely an acquaintance who happens to be staying at the inn.'

'An acquaintance you call a sister. Come, Denville, that won't wash. Who is she?'

'She's a maidservant, no one you know and no one of any interest.'

'A maidservant? Pitching it rather low even for you, my dear Denville. A maidservant—and your doxy, I presume.'

Gareth's knuckles tightened until they were white. 'Get out!'

'Dear, dear, that temper again. Yes, I see, your doxy, and to pacify that dreadful harpy downstairs, you pass her off as your sister. You're right, of course, I have no interest in her. The woman I seek would not pass the time of day with you, and as for impersonating a maidservant and sharing this vile refuge, the idea is laughable.'

'Now you've had your laugh, you're at liberty to leave.'

'Indeed, and I shall do so very shortly. But first tell me how the cardsharping business prospers in Europe. Did you make a living?' Glyde glanced down at the elegant coat of superfine he was wearing and then at Gareth's outfit, daily looking more frayed.

'And I always thought such practised tricksters went on prosperously,' he murmured, 'but it would seem not.'

Ignoring the intense pain in his ankle, Gareth moved with unexpected swiftness towards his enemy and clasped him violently round the throat.

'If ever you call me a cheat again, you will not live,' he ground out.

The door had remained open throughout their acrimonious

exchange and with his hands still wrapped around Glyde's neck, Gareth thrust his adversary through the doorway and down the stairs.

At the moment Glyde had been dismounting from his carriage, Amelie had escaped through the back entrance of the inn. She ran wildly past the crumbling outbuildings and through the small wicket gate that led on to open pasture. Dismayed and frightened at the turn of events, she ran without thinking where she was going. Her mind was in chaos, refusing to accept that Sir Rufus had tracked her to this remote place. It was impossible. Nobody except Gareth Wendover knew her whereabouts and he was ignorant of her true identity.

Slowly through the confused toss and tumble of thoughts a chilling idea began to emerge. Was it possible that they were in alliance together, that Gareth knew who she was and had been Glyde's accomplice all this time? Was it coincidence that Rufus Glyde had appeared out of nowhere, just after she'd been abducted from the stagecoach? The fact that his carriage had mown Gareth down and thrown him into a ditch was probably an accident in their plan. Gareth had resolutely refused to tell her anything about himself. Was that in case she would unmask him too soon, before Glyde could catch up with them? And to think that she had so nearly put herself into his power, so nearly succumbed to his seductive charm.

By now breathless, she was forced to come to a stop. It was pointless running any farther across the fields. She had no idea where she was going and if she turned back again to regain the road, Glyde could overtake her in his curricle at any moment. A nearby clump of trees would provide shelter and from this vantage point she could observe the inn from a distance. She settled herself beneath a sturdy oak, her back against its grainy trunk. The gentle summer sun filtered through the leaves above and birdsong filled the air. It was hard to imagine there was anything wrong with the world. Gradually her breathing returned to normal and her disordered thoughts began to settle. It was madness to imagine that Gareth was in league with the man who was hunting her. How could he have arranged to be outside her house at the precise moment she'd climbed from the bedroom window? It was ridiculous. Even more ridiculous to think him an accomplice. She knew, as well as she knew herself, that he would loathe and despise a creature such as Glyde.

The time passed tantalisingly slowly. She told herself that her pursuer wouldn't be at the inn long. Even if he ran into Gareth, he would not know him and any description of Miss Wendover's appearance was unlikely to match that of the aristocratic woman Glyde sought. He would be eager to leave an inn as insalubrious as the George and make once more for the pleasures of London. And once he'd driven away, she could take shelter for one more night. Early tomorrow morning she would get her lift to Wroxall and be on the stagecoach to Bath and safety.

She waited for what seemed an age, although in reality only half an hour had passed since she'd fled the inn so precipitately. In that time she'd neither glimpsed any activity nor heard a sound from the distant building. Maybe, after all, her hiding place was too far away to hear the noise of any departure? She debated what to do. At this rate she could be sitting under the oak tree until nightfall. Gathering her courage, she decided to chance a return. With some stealth she began slowly to approach the inn and, meeting nobody, crept through the back entrance to the passage that ran the length of the building to the open front door.

Almost immediately she became aware of Glyde's carriage

being led back into the courtyard and turned to flee again. But at the same time raised voices sounded above and she was sure one of them was Gareth's. She strained to hear what was being said, but the voices were too indistinct. As she listened, there was a sudden noisy creak of bedroom floorboards overhead. In a trice she'd whisked herself into the shadows beneath the stairs. Just in time. Rufus Glyde clattered down the staircase, his face twisted in fury. He was so close that had she reached out her arm, she could have touched him. She remained frozen to the spot as he stormed past her and out into the sunlit yard, throwing himself onto the driving seat of the carriage and whipping up his horses in a frenzy.

She found she was shaking uncontrollably and her first thought was to seek the sanctuary of her bedchamber. But there were questions burning through her brain that needed answers. The angry scene she'd come upon in its dying moments made no sense. Her old suspicions began to return; she needed to know what connection existed between these two men.

Contempt was written large on Gareth's face. His ankle throbbed angrily, but it had been worth the pain to knock the sneering smile from the face of his foe. Glyde would be for ever associated with the scene of his disgrace and his heart rejoiced that he'd routed the man so completely. But if he were honest, it was the image of Glyde and Amelie together that had spurred him to extreme action. That image was seared on his mind's eye, even stronger for being intangible. He had no idea why Glyde had turned up at this remote inn or what connection he had to the girl, but speculation gnawed relentlessly at him. He doubted he would ever get the truth from her; he'd been a fool to believe that she was trustworthy.

He was still standing by the window, exactly where she'd left him. If she hadn't just heard that furious altercation, she might have imagined she'd been away for only a few minutes and that the intervening time was simply a bad dream. But Gareth's face told another story. She could see immediately that he was in a thunderous mood. He turned as he heard her footsteps, his eyes now blue flint and his mouth close-gripped. She started to speak, but was cut off abruptly.

'Why did you leave like that?' he flung at her. 'What is that man to you?'

She steadied her racing heart and replied in an even voice, 'He's nothing to me. I ran away because I feared being discovered.'

'Why should it matter that he saw you?'

'I told you, I feared being seen—by anyone.'

'Anyone? Do you take me for a fool? He came looking for a woman and I think that woman was you. You turned white when you saw his carriage in the yard. You fled. Can you really expect me to believe that it was because some stranger had suddenly arrived?'

'Believe what you wish, I don't know who he was seeking. I escaped from the inn because I didn't want to be found here. I'm an unmarried woman and have been living under the same roof as you for the last week.'

'You would have me accept that a girl who thinks nothing of throwing her lot in with a man she doesn't know is worried that others will see her with him?'

'I never threw my lot in with you. You forced me to accompany you.'

'It doesn't seem to have pained your sense of propriety too greatly.'

'You can mock all you wish. You may not have a reputation

to defend, but I do. I have a living to earn and I can't afford to attract any gossip.'

She hoped that this was an inspired invention, but instead Gareth immediately pounced on her words and shredded them to pieces.

'If you don't know this man, then how could it affect your reputation one way or another?'

'I didn't say I didn't know him,' she conceded.

'At last,' he muttered grimly, 'we're getting near the truth or as near as we're ever likely to with you.'

'What do you mean by that?' Her anger sliced through the airless room.

'Simply that you appear to have a rather slippery relationship with honesty.'

'If we are to call each other liars, then you hardly fare better. What about the lies you told my fellow passengers on the stagecoach? That was blatant.'

'And this isn't?'

'I was telling the truth when I said that I didn't want to be discovered. But I am acquainted with this man. He's an intimate of my young mistress's brother and visits the house regularly. Although I was only a servant there and beneath his notice, I was worried he might recognise me.'

Gareth was silent, seeming to turn this over in his mind. She was unsure he believed her and, to deflect him further, renewed her attack.

'I've told you how *I* know him, though I can't understand why it's any business of yours. Now perhaps you'll tell me how *you're* acquainted with him.'

He stared sightlessly through the window, once more in that overheated, overfurnished salon. The babble of rich men intent on their pleasure filled his ears, then the sudden silence, the incredulous stares, the shuffling of feet and finally the cool withdrawal of the well-bred from the social disaster in their midst.

Unrelenting, Amelie waited for his response, never taking her eyes from his face. Aware at last of her scrutiny, he raised his gaze to her, his expression bleak.

'My acquaintance with him is very slight.'

His discomfort was palpable and she decided to press home her advantage.

'You were quarrelling,' she insisted. 'You must know the man well enough to quarrel.'

'He angered me. He invaded my room without permission and then wouldn't leave.'

'And that was enough for you to throw him down the stairs?'

'A slight exaggeration? He's a particularly obnoxious man and I didn't care for his tone.'

'If all that annoyed you was his attitude, you seem to have argued for a long time. Why didn't you get rid of him earlier?'

'You may not have noticed,' he replied scathingly, 'but I've sustained an injury. You fled on the instant and I was left alone to deal with him. In the end I got tired of his importuning and decided to risk the ankle. It hurt like hell, but I'm glad I assisted him on his way.'

He seemed to have regained something of his poise and his face no longer bore the icy expression that she'd come to dread. She was almost encouraged to tell him her true situation—almost, but not quite. To do so might jeopardise her plans entirely. If Gareth were the man she believed him to be, he would be impelled to pursue Glyde when he knew the full extent of his infamy. That would cause a scandal she would never live down.

And if he were not that man, if he were untrustworthy, then she could be in real peril, in danger of kidnap or blackmail once he knew her true identity.

'Does he know that you have a sister staying here?' she ventured tentatively.

'He knows,' came the short reply.

'You didn't tell him my name?'

'No,' he said in a distant voice.

Her face wore such an expression of relief that his distrust once again blossomed.

'Your fears are unfounded, my dear, your identity is safe.' His tone was caustic. 'I doubt that a man of Glyde's position would consider it interesting or worthwhile to spread scandal about a maidservant, even if he knew her name.'

Euphoric at her escape, Amelie hardly noticed his tone and unwisely pushed onwards.

'Thank you for not giving me away.' And when he didn't reply, she said again, 'Thank you.'

'Spare me the gratitude,' he grated.

There was a pause as he looked her fully in the face, wondering how he'd allowed himself to be taken in by a girl so adept at lying. He'd begun to believe his judgement of womankind faulty, but it seemed that she shared generously in the attributes of her sisters—she was no different from any of the women who'd passed briefly through his life.

'He thinks you're my doxy,' he said deliberately, then added with undisguised bitterness, 'And who could blame him? You behaved like one—scuttling for cover instead of facing him honestly.'

The words came out of nowhere and fell like hammer blows on her ears. Scarlet with mortification, she ran from the room.

How could he throw such a vile insult at her? Even if she were the simple maidservant she purported to be, she would be justified in protecting her good name. Yet by his reckoning she'd committed an unforgivable offence in running away; she was no better than Haymarket ware.

Once in her bedroom, she grabbed the faithful cloak bag and hurriedly packed the few items she still possessed. Then she ran down the stairs and out into the backyard. Will was busy washing the cobbles.

'Will, come here,' she called urgently to him. 'Mr Wendover has taken a turn for the worst. He needs the medicine that the doctor prescribed in an emergency. I must get to Wroxhall immediately.'

Will rested from his labours, leaning on the broom with one hand and scratching his head with the other.

'Mr Wendover were fine this morning. Happen he'll come about again soon.'

'No, Will, he won't. He's been feeling poorly for hours, but didn't like to complain. Now his fever seems to have returned. We must get to Wroxall.'

'I'd like to help, Miss Wendover,' he said doubtfully, 'but I'll have to ask the missus. Mrs Skinner do like to know where I am. And she don't like it if the horse is taken out without her permission.'

'Mrs Skinner is out,' Amelie lied recklessly, 'and Mr Skinner, too. I saw them on their way to visit neighbours.'

Will shook his head slowly. The image of the Skinners visiting their neighbours was one he was having difficulty with.

'Please help me,' she pleaded urgently. 'You don't want Mr Wendover to become really ill again, do you?'

Will shook his head, but still looked unhappy.

'It could be a matter of life or death, Will. I wouldn't ask you otherwise.'

She felt guilty about deceiving him, but refused to think of his likely punishment for helping her. She had to get away. Unwillingly, Will put down his bucket and brush and went towards the trap, which stood backed into the corner of the rear yard. He carefully moved it into the centre and arranged the leather ties. The mare had then to be led from her stable and harnessed. For Amelie, desperate to leave the inn behind, every minute seemed an impossible age. One or the other of the Skinners could put in an appearance at any time and ruin her escape.

Will might be slow, but he was methodical. Finally the trap was ready and she jumped up on to the passenger seat.

'Please make haste,' she enjoined him as they turned out of the yard onto the highway.

Will, who had begun to enjoy his freedom from cobble washing and enter into the spirit of the adventure, whipped the placid bay into something approaching a trot. They were very soon out of sight of the inn and she sighed with relief. She never wanted to see Gareth Wendover again. His words flung at her so coldly and dismissively had finally cut whatever cord existed between them.

Chapter Six

She stood beneath the white portico of her grandmother's house. The rain had been falling in torrents ever since she'd alighted at the White Lion Inn and she was now soaked to the skin from the brief walk to Laura Place. The weeping skies seemed an echo of her present mood. After all the obstacles and alarms she had encountered since leaving London, the final leg of her journey to Bath had been deceptively simple. Once in Wroxall she'd given Will the slip, with only a few pangs of conscience. There had been less than an hour to pass before her coach had departed and she'd found it easy to hide herself away and board the stage without anyone recognising her. Now with her escape plan almost complete, she should be flushed with excitement. Instead, she felt a dawning fear. What if her grandmother were out of town? What if Brielle were so outraged by her granddaughter's conduct that she refused to receive her?

She stared at the ebony door with its brass lion head. In her disquiet it seemed to challenge her right to be there and she had to summon all her resolution to lift the knocker. The resulting clatter reverberated through the hall beyond. Tense minutes of silence followed. She was just lifting her hand to knock again when she heard footsteps coming towards the door and in a minute the butler's familiar person stood before her. Horrocks was looking at her strangely, seemingly trying to puzzle out just what or who had arrived on the front steps.

'You should go round to the back entrance,' he said reprovingly as he took in the bedraggled figure in front of him.

'Horrocks, it's me, Amelie,' she cried, pushing back the hood of her cloak to reveal her face fully.

'Miss Amelie?' Horrocks stared in disbelief. 'Whatever are you doing here? Her ladyship said nothing of your coming. And where is your escort? You surely cannot be alone.'

He peered up and down the empty street in a vain search. Then, recalled to his duties, he ushered her quickly into the house. She slipped gratefully past him into the warmth of the hall. The house looked little different from the last time she'd seen it as a child, perhaps a little smaller, a little less grand.

'Her ladyship is out this evening, Miss Amelie, but I can send a messenger to fetch her home immediately. She is only a few minutes away.'

'No, don't do that, Horrocks,' she said quickly. 'I'll wait until she gets back. I don't imagine that she keeps very late hours.'

The butler looked grateful. 'No, indeed. But you should get out of those wet clothes straight away. I'll send Miss Repton to you.'

She'd never heard of Miss Repton, evidently a new addition to the household whom she supposed must be her grandmother's dresser. Horrocks led the way upstairs to the small sitting room overlooking Laura Place. This was Brielle's favourite retreat, even though she had a far more elegant drawing room at the back of the house with views over a surprisingly large and immaculate garden.

Miss Repton turned out to be a disapproving middle-aged woman, manicured to within an inch of her life. She looked Amelie up and down with disbelief.

'You'll need dry clothes, miss.' She sniffed. 'Where is your valise?'

'My luggage was mislaid during my journey, Miss Repton. It will be coming on later.'

She hoped her lie would satisfy this haughty woman, but the dresser continued to gaze at her with barely concealed disdain.

'I'll try to find something of milady's to fit you, but it won't be easy.'

Amelie, unused to such disrespect from a servant, answered sharply, 'It really doesn't matter. If you will be so kind as to take my cloak, I will dry my dress by the fire.'

Miss Repton looked scandalised and even more so when the discarded cloak revealed Fanny's plain, and by now, severely dilapidated dress. Amelie looked her in the eyes, challenging her to make a comment. The woman remained mute and made for the door, carefully holding the sodden cloak at arm's length.

'I'll ask Horrocks to send up tea, miss,' she said tonelessly.

Relieved by the dresser's exit, she sank into a comfortable chair and closed her eyes. The fire burned brightly and warmed her chilled body. The peace of the room gradually soothed her and by the time Horrocks brought her tea and toast, she was in a fair way to thinking that all would be well once her grandmother returned. But as the minutes ticked by and there was no sign of Brielle, tormenting thoughts once more began to possess her. Her grandmother might have led an unconventional life, but she was a stickler for proper conduct. She would be greatly disturbed by her granddaughter's flight from home. Brielle must be won over, made to understand the nightmare that was in store for her if she were forced into marriage with Rufus Glyde. Perhaps that would not be too difficult. But how to explain where she'd been since leaving London, how to gloss over all that had happened this last week without provoking unwanted questions?

She suddenly felt very alone and a little scared. With a start she realised that all the time she'd been at the George, she'd never felt this vulnerable. Her mind drifted to Gareth and she wondered what he was doing. Was he thinking of her, too? What nonsense, of course he wasn't. He would never have spoken so shockingly if he'd had an ounce of feeling for her. From the start he'd made it clear that she was simply entertainment for him; when she'd refused that role, he'd pursued her out of pique. Any fleeting moments of tenderness they'd shared were just that, fleeting. He was a loner, happy to use any woman who crossed his path, but just as happy to dismiss them from his mind if they angered him or ceased to be of interest.

The noise of the front door opening and closing drifted up the stairs. She heard voices below and her stomach churned. Suddenly, her grandmother was there and she was swept up in a warm, perfumed embrace.

'Amelie, dear child, what is this that Horrocks is telling me? Let me look at you, you poor little thing.' Brielle held her granddaughter away from her, taking in the drab dress now dried in creases, the sadly bedraggled chestnut curls and the anxious pinched face before her.

'You're in a sad way, my dear, but I cannot tell you how relieved I am that you're safe. I've been out of my mind with worry. This evening was the first invitation I've accepted since I knew that you'd left your home. And this is the evening that you arrive on my doorstep! But thank God for that.'

And once more Amelie found herself pulled into the jasmine-scented embrace she remembered so well from childhood. Whether her grandmother approved or not of what she'd done, it didn't matter. Brielle loved her and would care for her. She bit back the treacherous tears.

'I'm so sorry to have worried you needlessly, but I can explain,' she pleaded.

Brielle took her granddaughter's hands in hers and squeezed them lovingly. 'I'm sure you can, but first we must make you comfortable. I really don't understand why you're wearing that dreadful dress, but you should have changed it immediately. I can't think what my woman is about. Why didn't she find you a dressing robe at the least and order your bedchamber to be made up?'

'It doesn't matter. I was comfortable here and Horrocks brought me tea.'

'Tea! What are my servants thinking of? What you need is a proper meal and to get out of those clothes. The next thing we'll know is that you'll be running a fever.'

She rang the bell energetically and her butler appeared rather too quickly. Like the rest of the household, he had been greatly intrigued by Miss Silverdale's dramatic and, unexpected arrival and hovering by the sitting-room door, had been hopeful of learning more.

'Horrocks, ask the housekeeper to make up Miss Amelie's bedchamber immediately, and get Cook to put together a tray of something nourishing, and I don't mean just soup.'

'Yes, milady, immediately,' the butler murmured, suitably abashed by his mistress's sharp tone.

Brielle was still fiery, Amelie observed, even though the years had begun to take their toll. Her grandmother, elegant in dove-grey Italian crepe, seemed smaller and frailer than when she'd last seen her.

'Horrocks is getting old,' Brielle said, excusing her butler's oversights. 'He doesn't think so clearly now.'

'He looked after me very well,' Amelie declared loyally, making ready to accompany the housekeeper upstairs.

She instantly recognised the room. Eau-de-nil hangings and bedcovers created a tranquil aura of pale green shadow: her mother's favourite colour. A portrait of Louise was displayed prominently above the dainty cherrywood writing desk. A deep tub was even now being filled with hot water by one of the house-maids. As soon as the servants had left, she quickly stripped off the despised dress and dropped it in a heap on the floor.

By the time her grandmother joined her once more, she was ensconced in one of the large easy chairs, wearing a robe of the finest chenille silk.

'This robe is far too beautiful for me to wear, Grandmama. Miss Repton must be in anguish.'

'Never mind about her. She has far too high an opinion of herself. Though she does have a way with my hair and makes her own complexion cream from crushed strawberries. Otherwise I would never keep the creature.'

Her grandmother put down the tray she was carrying. 'I've brought your food myself so we can be quiet together. Make sure you dine well. You look as though you've barely eaten all day.'

It was true. A sparse breakfast had not been followed by lunch. She'd been too busy hiding from Rufus Glyde to think of eating, and then Gareth's unexpected abuse had sent her flying from the inn to Wroxall and finally to Bath. She attacked the cold chicken with relish.

While she ate, Brielle kept her amused with anecdotes of Bath life. It was clear that she viewed English provincial society with some irony, but she had put down secure roots and now had many friends and acquaintances in the locality. The quintessential French woman had become almost English.

She let her granddaughter finish her meal in peace before saying, 'Now what's this nonsense I've been hearing?'

'Nonsense, Grandmama?' Amelie's stomach clenched. The inevitable moment had arrived.

'About a week ago I received a most unwelcome visitor. His name was Hyde or Glyde or some such. He told me some fara-diddle about your being pledged to him in marriage.'

'He was lying,' Amelie said quietly. 'I never agreed to marry him.'

'Then why did he think you had?'

'Papa decided I should marry him. I decided I would not.'

'But why should your father wish you to marry a man you so clearly dislike?'

'Sir Rufus Glyde is a very rich man, I believe. Papa thought to help the family by marrying me to him.'

'The family, perhaps, but not you, it would seem. Your father is a selfish man and I won't hide from you that I do not hold him in a great deal of affection. But I've always thought his love for you showed him at his best. Why would he try to enforce such a marriage, knowing how you felt?'

She had no idea how much her grandmother knew of the Silverdales' financial difficulties and did not want to alarm her unnecessarily, so she said as nonchalantly as she could, 'The family have a few money problems.'

Brielle looked at her straitly. 'Your father has always lived high, that's certain, but surely the income from the estates he holds must be sufficient to cover even his expenditure.'

'There are other problems,' Amelie began awkwardly. 'Robert...' And her voice trailed off.

'Ah, Robert, an unfortunate boy by all accounts. Even in this backwater we've heard tales of his legendary gambling.' Brielle fixed her granddaughter with a sharp eye. 'Exactly how bad is the situation, Amelie? Tell me the truth.'

'Sir Rufus holds the mortgage on the house in Grosvenor Square and that is all we have left.'

Brielle let out an audible gasp. 'I knew your father and brother to be foolishly extravagant, but I had no idea that things had come to this pass.'

'Grandmama, I cannot marry Rufus Glyde. Please help me.'

'My darling, you shall not marry a man you hate. Your father will have to think again. And until he does, you will stay with me here in Bath.'

Amelie's brown eyes sparkled through a mist of tears as she launched herself at her grandmother and hugged her so tightly that the older woman was almost crushed.

'Hush, child, you've squeezed the breath out of me. You're a loving and beautiful young woman. You deserve better. We may even find you a Bath beau to take the place of this Glyde person.'

Amelie's smile faltered a little. 'I'm not looking for any other man. I don't wish to marry. Just let me stay here with you. I can be useful, I'm sure, even more as you get older.'

'What nonsense is this? To waste your youth and beauty on running errands for an old woman. Certainly not! Why are you so opposed to the idea of matrimony? It is every woman's destiny, after all.'

'I don't think it mine,' she retorted. 'In my experience men are either frivolous and foolish or they feel compelled to dominate me. I've no wish to be either the master or the mastered.'

'You have been unlucky in those you've met. But that's not to say that a strong man with the confidence to allow you independence does not exist, or that you won't encounter him.'

'Even if I were to meet such a paragon, how could I ever be sure that he would remain so?' Amelie ventured. 'Mama...' And she allowed the rest of her sentence to fade into the air.

Her grandmother gazed unseeingly into the fire, and it was a while before she spoke. 'You must not allow your mother's difficult life to determine your own choices,' she said at last. 'A woman's duty is to marry. But we'll say no more for now. I shall introduce you to Bath society while you're with me and who knows, the right person might just appear on the threshold.'

Brielle's thoughts were already ranging across the eligible males she knew and had begun to centre on one name that she thought might just alter Amelie's mind. But for now she was content to change the subject.

'You haven't told me yet how you escaped from Grosvenor Square.'

Amelie recounted the tale of the sheets and the stagecoach, carefully omitting the entrance of Gareth Wendover into her life. Brielle enjoyed the story immensely, even more so because it was a rebuke to a son-in-law she did not trust and a suitor she had disliked on sight.

'Grandmama, can we send for Fanny, please? I promised her I would do so as soon as I could.'

'I'm not at all sure about that, my love. Fanny aided you in what was a foolish and dangerous escapade. I've been enjoying your tale, but that's because you're safe here with me. When I think what might have befallen you! And Fanny would have borne a grave responsibility for it.'

'That's unfair,' her granddaughter cried hotly. 'Fanny tried to persuade me not to escape, but I made her help me. And no doubt she's suffered already for her loyalty. I cannot make her suffer doubly.'

Brielle blinked with surprise at this passionate outburst. 'You're far too hot at hand, my dear. I'm not surprised you've emerged from your first Season unwed. A fiery temper is not perhaps the best asset a young woman can possess.'

'Forgive me, ma'am, I didn't mean to be discourteous, but I owe Fanny so much.'

'Including a dress by the look of it,' her grandmother remarked drily, looking askance at the miserable heap of cloth lying abandoned in the corner. 'I was about to send a message to your father to assure him of your safety—I will ask him to despatch Fanny to you. We must hope that he hasn't already discovered her perfidy and sent her packing.'

Amelie smiled her pleasure and then gently stifled a yawn. She hoped Brielle would take the hint and leave her to sleep. So far she'd managed to evade all mention of her stay at the George. But as she'd foreseen, her grandmother was not so easily satisfied. The stagecoach had left the White Horse Inn in London over a week ago—so where had Amelie been in the interval?

'The stage had an accident,' she lied, 'and we had to find accommodation at a local inn. One of the passengers was hurt and I stayed to look after them. As soon as they were better, I finished the journey to Bath.' How glib that sounded and how very far from the truth!

'And were you the only two passengers at this inn?' Brielle questioned shrewdly.

'There were only a few other people on the stage. And they lived a short distance away and were able to finish their journey on horseback.' More lies, she thought guiltily.

'Who was this passenger you were so devoted to? Wasn't there anyone else who could have offered their services?'

'I felt obliged. They'd been very kind to me.'

'But who was this person?'

This was the question Amelie had been dreading. 'An elderly gentleman.' Age is relative, she told herself. 'You wouldn't know his name. He was actually on his way to Bristol, so he's not local.'

'A gentleman? You were looking after a gentleman? Surely that cannot be right.'

'I had to help. There was no one else who could devote the time to nursing him. The doctor called a few times and the landlord assisted when he could.'

Her grandmother was silent for a moment. 'Just how old was this gentleman?'

'I'm not very good at ages,' she prevaricated. 'A good deal older than me.'

'And who else was at the inn with you?'

'The landlord and his wife, and some of their serving staff. I shared a bedchamber with the kitchen maid.'

Brielle looked relieved at this information and decided not to probe any further for the moment. Amelie was looking tired and distressed. She sensed her granddaughter was not being entirely truthful and was determined in the next few days to get to the bottom of whatever mystery there was.

'You must sleep now. Tomorrow we'll begin to make up the deficiencies in your wardrobe. I understand from Horrocks that you arrived with only a cloak bag.'

'I'm afraid so. It will be wonderful to wear a dress other than Fanny's.'

'I should think so indeed,' Brielle lightly scolded her. 'After breakfast, we'll start our campaign. In the meantime I'll make sure that Repton looks out a dress from my younger years—not too old fashioned, I trust—and alters it to fit you.'

'Thank you. You're too kind—I don't know how I can ever repay you.'

'I'm sure I shall think of something,' Brielle replied, her mind firmly fixed on the man she intended to present once the girl was looking her best.

Amelie stayed awake longer than she expected. Her body was exhausted, but her mind continued to plague her. How was she to avoid telling her grandmother the true nature of her stay at the inn, for she knew that Brielle would not be content to leave the matter to rest? She smiled at the description she'd given of Gareth—he was neither elderly nor a gentleman!—but somehow she must maintain this fiction. Her smile died as suddenly as it had come—she must not think of him ever again. It had been foolish of her to allow an early attraction to melt her usual reserve and flourish unchecked. She'd grown far, far too close to him. She had never before felt such longing, such desire, and was left now bruised and baffled.

The insults he'd flung at her should have crushed such troublesome emotions. But apparently that wasn't so. As she drifted half in and half out of sleep, his powerful frame invaded the room. It was as though he were there with her. If she reached out, she could trace the outline of his smile with her finger. If she reached out, she could know the raw strength of his embrace. Shaken by her need for him, she buried her head in the pillow and tried to sleep.

* * *

Gareth was also finding it difficult to sleep. His anger still burned brightly, but he knew that he'd offended Amelie beyond pardon. His fury over her wild escape and his deep suspicions of her relationship with Glyde were justified, he was sure. But to call her a doxy had been inexcusable. She was no such thing, as he knew to his cost. He smiled mirthlessly as he considered the countless women of his acquaintance who perfectly satisfied that description. No, she was not a doxy, but she was just as cunning and manipulative as any other of her sex. He'd learned his lesson well; a woman was worth only the pleasure she gave. Amelie had given him pleasure, it was true, but not as he'd expected: it had been something altogether deeper, more exciting and more disturbing—a dangerous delight. It was as well that she'd left when she had. There was no place in his life for loyalty, tenderness, love, even if he could be sure of her. And he couldn't.

He would leave her in peace to find a new situation and be on his way. Within the next day or so his ankle would be strong enough to begin travelling, but where he knew not. He was close to Bristol; a journey to the port would take half a day at most and once there he could book a passage to France. It would not be difficult to resume his old life at the tables of the slightly less respectable gaming houses or take whatever menial work was offered. That way he would never touch a penny of the inheritance so long denied him.

But why shouldn't he enjoy his legacy? Would it not be sweet revenge to plunder the fortune his grandfather had so carefully conserved? Perhaps he would travel back to London after all, deal with Mr Spence and his formalities, and ensure a constant flow of funds to his pocket over the coming years as he wandered Europe. That would certainly spare him the discomfort of living off his wits. But what an existence! The one thing that had sustained him in seven long years of exile was the excitement and intrigue of a life on the edge. Take that away and what was left? A tedious round of places you didn't know, people you would never see again, plans that held no interest.

One way or another, though, he would leave England and this time willingly and for good. There was nobody to mourn his departure—except perhaps Lucas Avery. He'd been his one true friend. He knew him to be living in Bath, a short distance away, with a wife and children that Gareth had never met. He wondered if he could risk a meeting or whether Lucas might have changed his mind about his old friend in the years since that fateful evening. The unknown wife, too, might not easily welcome a convicted card cheat. But he would have liked to have bid him a final goodbye.

And Amelie, he suspected, was also in Bath. If he chose to make the journey, he might even see her there. If he chose! In his heart he knew that the decision had already been made. Of course he would make the journey, of course he would see her. Be truthful with yourself, he thought savagely. She was dangerous to him; a threat to his plans and to his peace of mind, but somehow he couldn't keep away. He might try to justify the trip to Bath in a dozen ways, but he was going there for one reason alone. He'd willed himself to forget this girl, but he could not: she was a constant refrain singing in his mind. London or France would both have to wait.

Amelie woke to the swish of heavy silk curtains being drawn and felt the warmth of the mid-morning sun streaming onto her bed. She hadn't heard the entrance of the maid on the deep pile carpet, but turning her head she saw that a cup of steaming chocolate sat waiting and a large jug of hot water was already on the washstand. A refashioned dress of her grandmother's was draped across the armchair, hardly the height of fashion, but acceptable enough for this one day. Miss Repton had been busy. She supposed she must thank her.

She lay back on the pillows and stretched luxuriously. Eventually she'd slept long and deep, cocooned in the comfort of the four-poster, a far cry from the straw mattress of recent days. At last she was at her grandmother's. She'd succeeded in what she'd set out to do and the world felt good. Or at least a part of it did. Gareth's figure once more crept unbidden into the corners of her mind. He would soon be preparing to leave the George and then where would he go? Whatever his decision, she scolded herself, it concerned her no longer.

This morning she was intent on pleasure for she knew it would be fleeting. She had no false expectations that Brielle would agree with her wish to remain single. For a woman of her grandmother's generation, indeed for a woman of her own, marriage had to be the goal of life and anyone who rejected it was either unwanted or eccentric. How much better to live alone, she thought, than be chained to a man with whom she shared nothing but a roof. That was likely to remain a dream. There was one thing of which she *was* sure: her heart would stay her own. It would not be a difficult vow to keep; until now she'd felt nothing for any man she'd ever met. Until now. But Gareth Wendover was clearly ineligible and destined to travel through life alone. A misguided passion for him would ensure the very unhappiness she was trying to escape.

The bedroom door opened and her grandmother came into the room fully dressed and looking businesslike. 'Good, you're awake. Are you well rested?'

Amelie smiled her assent.

'That's as well—we've a lot to do today. I'll see you in the breakfast room in thirty minutes.'

Brielle's brisk commands were diverting. Her grandmother might be approaching old age, but she was as sprightly as ever and it was clear that she'd already been up some hours planning the day ahead. Amelie made haste to obey.

The carriage had been ordered to the door immediately after breakfast and very soon they were bowling along Bath's main thoroughfare. Brielle's destination was the small but elegant shop of a highly talented young modiste. She had heard on the grapevine that this new seamstress had the originality and skill of many a more expensive establishment. She had a very clear idea of what would suit her granddaughter, something in the French style, she thought, beautifully cut and simply adorned, to flatter the young woman's budding figure.

It seemed to Amelie that the next few hours were spent in a fantasy of fashion. There were outfits for every occasion: braided, embroidered, some adorned with knots of ribbon, others with spangled rosettes and silver fringes. Walking dresses, riding costumes, day *toilettes* and ball gowns floated past on a wave of elegance.

She tried hard to keep her feet on the ground, worrying about the mounting cost and how she could ever repay her grandmother even a fraction of the staggering bill for this dazzling wardrobe. Frantically she tried to catch sight of the price tags as the dresses were brought forwards for her inspection. An evening gown in sea-green tulle made her gasp as she gazed in wonder at her reflection in the mirror. She could hardly recognise the modish and graceful young woman looking back at her.

'How much did you say this gown was?' she asked the seamstress tentatively.

'That is one of our newest creations, *mademoiselle,* and made from the finest silk tulle. A very reasonable hundred guineas. It suits *mademoiselle* to perfection.'

Shocked by the price, Amelie began reluctantly to take off the charming creation when the modiste, catching a minatory look from Brielle, coughed apologetically and decided that she had made a mistake.

'Of course, for such a beautiful young lady we can come to an agreeable arrangement, I'm sure. You will wear the dress with a distinction that will bring honour to our small salon and build our reputation.'

After that Amelie gave up trying to keep count of the ever-increasing total. It was all way beyond anything she could ever have afforded from her allowance. The colours and fabrics flew past her eyes like a moving kaleidoscope. To the pile of dresses were added fur-trimmed pelisses, tiny pearl-stitched slippers, long white leather gloves and a Norwich silk shawl, all apparently necessities for a protracted stay in Bath. By the time they left the salon, the carriage was brimming with boxes and packages and had to be sent back to Laura Place while they made their way to Milsom Street to pay a call on Brielle's favourite milliner.

Amelie, who owned precisely two hats, was amazed by the information that she would need no fewer than six if she were to grace the Bath social scene successfully. One extraordinary confection followed another as Madame Charcot laid before them the finest of her wares. Amelie's London Season had been notable for its modesty. Lord Silverdale had neither the money nor the wish to expend large sums on his daughter's coming-out and expected her natural beauty to be sufficient to win a husband. An old acquaintance of his youth had acted as chaperone and since she also had a daughter to launch, she'd shown little interest in her new protégée or her clothes. Amelie had chosen almost single-handedly the restricted wardrobe her father had permitted for the three months of her London Season. Now Brielle, with her highly developed fashion sense, was intent on giving as much enjoyment as possible to her granddaughter.

Seated amidst a tower of hat boxes, waiting for the carriage to return, she revealed that she'd been busy first thing that morning putting together a guest list for a small evening party the following day.

'It will be more comfortable for you to meet a few people before going into society properly,' her grandmother explained.

Amelie made haste to reassure her, 'I won't be uncomfortable, Grandmama, not with you by my side.'

'That's as may be. I'm an old woman now. You need to meet younger people. It will be just a small, informal party. Nothing too overwhelming. But when we go the Pump Room or the Assembly Rooms, you'll already know a few faces.'

Amelie wasn't so sure. She'd expected to live quietly in Bath, but it was evident from the morning's shopping that this was not what Brielle had in mind. She was grateful for her grandmother's unstinting kindness and she would try her best to conform. She had little desire to socialise, but that was something best left unsaid.

Like her granddaughter, Brielle decided on silence. It had been difficult to conjure up interesting guests at such short notice, but she'd felt it essential to introduce Amelie as swiftly as possible to many of those she would see in the coming weeks. She was intent on establishing the notion that her granddaughter's stay had been planned for a considerable time and that Amelie would be paying a protracted visit. That way she would limit any damage that rumour might do.

This morning while her granddaughter slept, she'd cast her mind swiftly over the people she might invite who would not be offended by the very short notice. Celine Charpentier, of course, a fellow *émigrée* and friend since the time they'd both left France for exile. Celine would support her in whatever plan she was hatching, Brielle knew. Then Major Radcliffe was a genial soul, always ready to add his bonhomie to any party. Unfortunately she would have to invite Miss Scarsdale. Letitia Scarsdale was a permanent fixture at all her parties, a difficult neighbour who had constantly to be placated.

But one particular guest would more than earn his place. Brielle had high hopes of him. Sir Peregrine Latham was well known in Bath, a handsome man and delightful companion. Perry Latham was no country bumpkin, either. He preferred a quieter pace of life, dividing his time between the Bath mansion and his Somerset estate, but he visited London regularly and was not devoid of town bronze. He was well into his thirties now and, gossip had it, the victim of a sad history. The story went that he had lost his fiancée when he was a very young man and had never recovered from the blow. Nevertheless, Brielle reckoned he might be persuaded to think again by the sight of her enchanting granddaughter.

The following day brought with it another whirl of activity. The hairdresser called early to trim Amelie's chestnut locks into submission. Her shining curls were artlessly twisted into a knot on the top of her head and then allowed to cascade down the sides of her face in loose ringlets. Before she had time to properly admire this transformation, it was the turn of the dressmaker. Hours the previous evening had been spent thumbing through the latest editions of *La Belle Assemblée* to decide on suitable styles. Now for several uncomfortable hours she was draped with muslin and stuck with pins. The dressmaker, she was told, would make her gowns for wearing at home when no one of any importance was expected. She began to wonder when she would ever have time to don even half of the wardrobe she'd so suddenly acquired.

Shortly before their guests arrived that evening, Brielle appeared with a pearl necklace and earrings that had belonged to Amelie's mother. They were the perfect accompaniment to the simple pink crêpe-de-Chine gown she'd chosen for her first party.

'Wear them for Louise,' her grandmother said with a catch in her voice, the closest she would ever come to expressing the pain she still felt.

Now that the evening was here, Amelie determined to take pleasure in it, if only for Brielle's sake. It was true that the guests assembled in the elegant drawing room were something of a motley crowd, but they were evidently all well-wishers. All except Lady Lampeter, who had two very plain daughters of Amelie's age and who was furious to discover that her acceptance of such a late invitation had been pointless. Not even the fondest of mamas could expect the Lampeter girls to compete with Amelie's beauty.

'Claudia Lampeter will come at short notice,' Brielle had confidently predicted to Celine. 'She has a mountain to climb with those girls of hers. One has spots and the other a sad figure. She will take them anywhere in the hope of finding a marriageable man.'

Knowing nothing of her grandmother's wiles, Amelie remained serene and unruffled as she made her way slowly around the mingling guests. Moving from one chattering group to another, she attracted admiring looks from around the room and Brielle was happy to see that in company her granddaughter was both modest and assured.

'She does you credit,' Celine remarked. 'A beautiful and unaffected girl.'

The Major took a long pinch of snuff and gave his considered opinion. 'With those looks and that charm she will take Bath by storm.'

As the evening proceeded, Amelie began to appreciate the gentle rhythm of Bath social life. The great society gatherings of her London Season had been a strain, but here she felt soothed. Even the man she imagined had been invited to partner her was unexceptional.

'And how do you like Bath, Miss Silverdale?' Perry Latham began as an opening gambit.

He had been stunned by the beauty of this young woman and was eager to see whether her intelligence matched her looks.

'So far, Sir Peregrine, I've seen only the inside of dress shops, but I'm sure I shall enjoy it immensely.'

'And Bath will enjoy you, too,' he rejoined gallantly. 'Can we hope to see you at the Pump Room shortly?'

'Indeed, yes. I understand my grandmother is planning our first visit tomorrow.'

'Excellent. I'll make sure I attend. I'm afraid you may well find the town a little dull. You will see many of the same faces there as are here tonight.'

'I shan't mind that. I find familiarity comforting.'

'I'm not sure you'll continue to think so after you've met the same set of people a dozen times.'

Privately, Amelie thought that was more than likely, looking around at the less-than-stimulating collection of people gathered there. She couldn't stop herself smiling at the thought of what Gareth would make of the company. 'An assortment of gargoyles,' she could hear him say. One of the older women, the scrawny Miss Scarsdale, bore an uncanny resemblance to Mrs Skinner.

'You smile.' Perry Latham had been watching her closely. 'You see, Miss Silverdale, you're already beginning to have doubts about Bath society.'

'No, Sir Peregrine. I was smiling at how very pleasant it is to be among friends.'

Diplomatic as well as intelligent and beautiful, he thought, already half-smitten with this entrancing princess who had appeared so suddenly in his world.

'Please call me Perry. I hope you will count me as one of those friends.'

The last guest departed well before eleven. She wasn't sorry that Bath inhabitants seemed to keep early hours. The party had been convivial and undemanding, but it had still cost an effort to play the role expected of her.

'I saw you talking to Perry Latham,' her grandmother remarked casually. 'He's a good-looking fellow, don't you think?'

'Very presentable.'

'A thorough gentleman, too.'

'Indeed, yes.'

'And not without town bronze,' Brielle pursued.

Amelie smiled warmly back at her. 'He's a veritable pattern card of all the virtues,' she replied laughingly, while her thoughts roved dangerously elsewhere.

Chapter Seven

The next morning dawned fair, a perfect day Brielle declared for her granddaughter's first visit to the Pump Room. Amelie felt little enthusiasm, but knew that her grandmother had been delighted by the success of yesterday's small party and was now eager to introduce her to wider Bath society.

Brielle did not take the famous waters, which she privately considered disgusting, but many of her friends drank a daily glass for a variety of complaints, imagined or otherwise. And she made sure that she attended the Pump Room regularly as a way of keeping in touch with what was going on in Bath. It was said that a morning spent there would vouchsafe the visitor all the current gossip of the town.

The room they entered was spacious with a wall of tall windows giving on to carefully tended lawns. A richly moulded azure ceiling was hung with ornate chandeliers glittering with light even on this bright morning. Small golden chairs were positioned around the edges of the room or marshalled by visitors into friendship or family circles. The salon emanated wealth and leisure, capturing the essence of Bath as a town of affluence and pleasure.

Almost immediately they spotted Celine Charpentier, who had just procured a glass of water from the pumper and was busy wending her way through knots of people deep in conversation. Brielle began to follow in her wake, zigzagging to avoid the couples who slowly paraded around the room, arm in arm, intent on seeing and being seen. Amelie was acutely conscious of the many pairs of eyes staring at her, some curious, some measuring and some frankly admiring. She gave thanks for the familiar faces already gathered at the far end of the room. As her grandmother had predicted, it was comforting to recognise acquaintances among a sea of unknowns. Perry Latham's sunny smile beamed across at her.

But before they could greet Brielle's friends, they were intercepted by a very thin, very richly clad figure. Amelie caught her breath—the man bowing profusely before her grandmother was none other than Rufus Glyde! He had returned not to London, but to Bath. He must have suspected that she would eventually find her way here.

'Lady St Clair,' he purred, 'my most humble apologies for intruding, but allow me to say how delighted I am to see that your granddaughter has been safely restored to you.'

Brielle nodded briefly and went to move on, but Glyde was intent on detaining them.

'My lady, if I could beg you for a few minutes of your time... I wish to tender my heartfelt regrets for any misunderstanding that may have occurred when we last met.'

'I am not aware of any misunderstanding, *monsieur*,' Brielle said stiffly.

'I mean only that my motives for seeking your charming granddaughter were not clear and I fear I may have been misinterpreted.'

'Believe me, I understand perfectly your wish to pursue my granddaughter and since we are being frank, I will tell you now that your pursuit is unwelcome. Miss Silverdale stays with me for the foreseeable future. I am now responsible for her welfare.'

Amelie felt a glow of satisfaction. Surely that would get rid of him for good.

'Naturally I am more than pleased that Miss Silverdale has found sanctuary with a beloved relative. It is right and proper that she should do so.' Glyde's voice was smoothly persistent. 'My pursuit, as you term it, was a wish only to be of assistance to a young woman I had reason to believe was happy to become my wife.'

Unsure of precisely what Miles Silverdale had promised, Brielle was forced to concede the point.

Emboldened, he continued, 'Now that the position is clear to me, Miss Silverdale may rest assured that I will in no way incommode her in the future. Indeed, I would like to wish her very well whatever that future may be.'

Her grandmother had begun to look a little more gratified and answered neutrally, 'We thank you for your good wishes, sir, and for your reassurance.'

His thin lips arranged themselves into a tight smile, the sunken lines on either side of his mouth becoming more deeply etched. Amelie recoiled in distaste, but was forced to remain by her grandmother's side.

'In that case I hope that we may continue to enjoy a pleasant association. I had just begun a visit to friends here when I felt it necessary to interrupt my stay to search for Miss Silverdale. Now that the matter is happily concluded, I can look forward to enjoying the delights of Bath more thoroughly.'

'I hope the town will live up to your expectations,' Brielle murmured.

'If not, I have always the pleasures of my country estate, which lies nearby, but I can't imagine Bath will pall with two such charming ladies at the forefront of its society. I trust I am forgiven sufficiently to be included in your personal group of acquaintances.'

Brielle inclined her head slightly. 'Naturally, we are bound to encounter each other on occasions, Sir Rufus.'

'I look forward to meeting you and your granddaughter frequently. Bath is such a small society that I imagine that to be inevitable.'

Amelie had managed to put on a brave face during this interchange, but her heart plummeted at these words. She was sure they carried an implicit threat and, glancing up at his thin, white face, she saw the wolfish eyes staring out at her from behind the social mask. Her grandmother, though, seemed to sense nothing amiss and, with another bow in Glyde's direction, moved towards her group of friends.

Glyde turned swiftly on his heel and left the Pump Room. Now that he was gone, she found her limbs were trembling and she had to fight to calm her breathing. His trite commonplaces had cloaked his true intent, she was sure. He had not given up his intention to marry her, whatever platitudes he mouthed to her grandmother. And Brielle appeared to have been completely taken in. With a sickening jolt Amelie realised that the sanctuary she'd sought and found with so much difficulty might now prove as dangerous as her London home. She could see Glyde's strategy clearly. He would make sure that he was constantly in her grandmother's company, presenting himself as a loyal and dependable friend. Gradually he would chip away at her grandmother's suspicion until Brielle began to wonder why her granddaughter had taken such a dislike to him. There would be nowhere else for her to run and little by little she would be coerced into an appalling marriage.

Her grandmother was already deep in conversation with the Major, and she saw with dismay that Perry Latham had begun to walk towards her. Unable to face him immediately, she fled towards the entrance hall, intending to stand in the cool, fresh air until she regained her composure. Looking straight ahead, she moved swiftly towards her goal, barely noticing the figure standing in the shadow of the large palm trees that graced either side of the doorway.

In an instant Gareth Wendover stood before her. She had a fleeting glimpse of his muscular figure, clothed now in a perfectly fitting coat of blue superfine, his shapely legs encased in skin-tight pantaloons of the palest fawn. Hardly had she absorbed his new image, when he advanced menacingly towards her and grabbed her by the wrist.

'You've evidently managed to acquire a very liberal employer since we met last,' he snarled. 'Such elegance, Amelie, such a taking coiffeure, but hardly fitting for a maidservant.' He thundered out the last word, his lip curling with disdain.

'Or a doxy, I imagine.' Her retort was swift and equally angry.

His face shadowed and he let go of her arm. He should apologise, but he was damned if he would. She had utterly deceived him. The girl he saw before him, so beautiful he could devour her on the spot, was thoroughly false. She had lied and lied again to him.

'May I enquire exactly who or what you are?' His tone was scathing.

She replied with as much dignity as she could, 'My name is Amelie Silverdale. My father is Lord Silverdale.'

'Well, well, a poor little rich girl. Wasn't being Miss Silverdale exciting enough for you? Did you get some shabby thrill from dressing up as your maid?'

'There was no thrill. Disguising myself as a maid was the safest way to travel, or at least it would have been if I'd not been unlucky enough to meet you.'

'Not that unlucky, as I recall. You might still be dangling on the end of a rope if it were not for me. Or were you hoping your friend Glyde would happen by and execute a magnificent rescue? Was it a stunt to reel in a reluctant suitor?'

'How can you be so stupid! I was escaping from Rufus Glyde.'

'Another fantasy? I've just seen with my own eyes on what familiar terms you stand with the man.'

'Then your eyes tell you false. Sir Rufus has designs of his own. He wishes to ingratiate himself with my grandmother.'

'For what purpose?' he asked impatiently, pushing back the dark hair that had fallen across his brow.

'I don't see that it's any business of yours.'

'Really? You don't consider your constant lies give me any reason to demand the truth from you?'

She bowed her head slightly and said in a voice he could hardly hear, 'He wishes to marry me.'

'And…?'

'He hopes my grandmother will persuade me to agree.'

'How much persuasion will that take, I wonder?'

'I detest him,' she burst out. 'He's a vicious and depraved man. He's followed me here when I thought I was safe and is plotting against me still.'

'He's certainly vicious,' Gareth said measuringly, 'but why are you running from him? You've only to tell your father that he's plaguing you and you'll be free of his demands.'

'I wish that were true, but my father has decided that Sir Rufus is the suitor he wishes me to accept.'

'The last time I looked we were living in the nineteenth century. Forced marriages no longer happen. You must have given your consent or at least appeared to do so.'

'I did not. I tell you I hate the man, but my father is adamant. I cannot speak of my family's difficulties, but Glyde wields considerable power over us.'

Gareth considered this for a moment, his athletic figure reclining lazily against a carved pillar.

'So you were the mistress who was being forced to marry for money? And your maid's defiant independence a mere charade, I imagine.'

Amelie flushed, but said nothing.

'And why go to so much trouble to deceive me? Why couldn't you have told me the truth and asked for help? Didn't you trust me?'

She swallowed uncomfortably. 'I was worried you might react unthinkingly. You might have chased after him and caused an even greater scandal than there was already.'

'Chased after him? With an injured ankle? You can do better than that.' His tone hardened. 'Wasn't it rather that you thought I might use the situation to my own benefit?'

She blushed. That was precisely what she had thought, imagining if only in fancy that he might be capable of blackmail or kidnap.

He saw the telltale flush and concluded bitterly, 'You didn't trust me. Only now that I've exposed your deception are you willing to be honest.'

'You shouldn't judge me harshly. You can't know what it feels like to be so besieged, without a friend in the world.'

He smiled crookedly. 'Can't I?'

'It's different for men—you make your own rules. A woman is always subject to others. Even a strong woman,' she added.

'You must have known I would stand your friend, yet you disappeared from the inn without a word.'

'I had to—you treated me abominably.'

'I regret my intemperance,' he muttered unwillingly. 'It was unfair, but Glyde provoked me and I knew you were lying.'

'It was more than unfair. It was a vile insult—I wanted never to see you again.'

'Nor I you.'

They stood facing each other, their figures tense, the air between them scorched by anger. Then quite suddenly his expression relaxed and he said lightly, 'But here I am.'

'And why exactly are you here? I thought you were going to Bristol—or was it London? It seems to me, Mr Wendover, that you also have some explaining to do.'

'I have a particular friend in Bath. I wanted to say goodbye to him before I sail for France.'

She digested this news. 'You never mentioned this friend before. In fact, you were adamant you had no friends.'

'He slipped my mind.'

'Or maybe he's simply a figment of your imagination?'

'Like Amelie, the maidservant, you mean? No, he exists all right. His name is Lucas Avery and I'm staying in his house.'

'Even so, I'm not sure I believe you. Why suddenly do you

wish to say goodbye? You weren't intending to do so. You'd no plans to come to Bath.'

'I've determined to quit England for good and since our little adventure brought me close by, it seemed right to say a final farewell.'

'And that's the truth?'

'Not quite.' She looked up into the blue eyes and their disturbing gaze. 'I needed to see you again. I needed to say a proper goodbye to you.'

The warmth of his glance produced a feeling of breathless discomfort. She felt a flutter of panic—she must remember her doubts, she told herself, remember his insults, stay angry. She mustn't allow herself to falter.

'You've seen me now and said goodbye,' she said tightly. 'Let us end this chapter and wish each other good fortune.'

He did not reply, but took hold of her wrist again, this time with gentleness. Her heart turned a small somersault. Oblivious to the scandalised looks of people passing into the main room, he pulled her towards him and encircled her waist tightly. His mouth brushed her forehead and smoothed her hair. Crushed against his hard frame, she felt her body once more dissolve into the heat of his embrace. But it was over in a moment.

Breaking from her, Gareth took her hands and held them to his lips. 'We are deceivers both, Amelie. In another world we would belong together.'

Through a hot veil of desire, she became aware of the whispering voices around her and blushed deeply. Quickly, she disentangled her hands.

'I must go,' she managed in a constricted voice. 'My grandmother will be wondering where I am.'

And with that she turned and walked swiftly away.

* * *

Gareth made his way back to Lucas Avery's house, his mind a battleground of conflicting thoughts. He'd gone to the Pump Room that morning in the slender hope of finding Amelie in attendance on the new mistress she might have acquired. When he saw her across the room, he could hardly believe his eyes: not the beautiful but simple maidservant that he'd come to know, but an elegant and modish creature, moving effortlessly in the highest circles.

Transformed she might be, but she was still the same girl who had stirred his senses so fervidly and anger over her deception fought with desire to possess her. Then Glyde had appeared and all his questions over their relationship were answered. It seemed that Amelie Silverdale was indeed a true daughter of Eve. She had lied and deceived as expertly as any of the harpies from his past. His anger had exploded into blind fury. And it was Glyde who crystallised a ferocious desire for revenge; he could have run the man through if he'd had a sword. And in the back, he thought grimly. Glyde's ingratiating smiles announced clearly that Amelie was destined for him, a man he held in the deepest contempt. He'd been sickened by what he saw and was about to leave when Glyde had hurried from the room, unnoticing of Gareth standing silently in the shadows. When Amelie had followed suit, he'd been unable to stop himself confronting her.

But now it seemed he might have read the picture wrongly. According to Amelie she was escaping Rufus Glyde, not embracing him. Did he believe her? If she was in truth being pursued by the scoundrel, why hadn't she confessed her troubles at the inn and enlisted his aid? In his heart he knew why not. She mistrusted him, mistrusted all men, and she was right to. He'd told her as many lies as she'd told him. If not lies, then omissions, and even now she was still ignorant of his true situation.

Lucas was at home when he knocked for admittance. From the moment he'd arrived in Bath, he'd been welcomed with open arms. His fear that Lord Avery would no longer be the friend he remembered had vanished with the first emotional clasp of their hands.

'Did you enjoy an invigorating morning with the old tabbies?' his friend greeted him gaily.

'Not exactly. I didn't make it into the Pump Room.'

'Was it that daunting?'

'It was singular, shall we say.'

And Gareth, who had briefly sketched for his friend the details of his stay at the George, told him of that morning's meeting with Amelie and the very different circumstances he'd found her in.

'But that's wonderful,' Lucas enthused.

'How is that?'

'A maidservant was an impossibility, but Lord Silverdale's daughter will make the perfect partner for the Earl of Denville.'

'Hold on a minute,' said Gareth, only half-laughing. 'You go too fast. For one thing I've no intention of playing the Earl of Denville and for another I'm not in the market to become leg-shackled.'

'Tell me, why *did* you come to Bath? I'm quite sure it wasn't just to meet your new godson!'

His friend maintained a discouraging silence, but Lucas persisted.

'We may not have seen each other for the past seven years,

Gareth, but I know you as myself. In fact, I may know you even better.'

'I came to say a final goodbye, as you well know,' Gareth was goaded to respond. 'And if Amelie Silverdale has crossed my path, that's pure chance.'

'Doing it much too brown!' his friend said crudely. 'You've just returned from the Pump Room—the Pump Room, for Heaven's sake! Why ever else would you visit such a place?'

'All right, I admit that I had it in mind to seek her out. I thought I'd make peace with her before I left. But that was before I realised I'd nothing to apologise for. She's as much a jade as any other woman I've known.'

Lucas looked thoughtful and it was a while before he replied. 'Do you know that when you speak of her, your eyes say something quite different?'

'Do they say that she's been thoroughly dishonest with me?'

'I can understand your anger at being deceived, but you're equally to blame. Have you confided your troubles to her?' He looked searchingly at his companion. 'No, I thought not. Neither of you has been entirely honest with the other.'

There was a long silence until Lucas once more broke it. 'Face it, my friend,' he said, his voice amused but sympathetic, 'she's got under your skin. Whether you like it or not, love is in the air.'

'I know nothing of love,' Gareth countered lightly. 'Now dalliance, that's where I'm an expert!'

During the following days Amelie was caught up in a whirl of social activity, a round of dance classes, supper parties and recitals which left little time to think about her recent meeting with Gareth. Only at night, when she could escape to the solitude of her room, was her mind free to roam over their brief, angry encounter. She'd been astonished to see him at the Pump Room and looking every inch a gentleman. Where had this sudden wealth come from and who was his supposed friend in Bath? She wasn't at all sure that either existed.

His fury at her deception had been real enough, but he was surely as guilty—she knew no more about him now than at their first meeting. Yet he seemed compelled to seek her out; she knew without being told that she was the real reason for his presence in Bath. If she'd needed confirmation, his scandalous embrace in that shockingly public place had been proof enough. But what had he meant by saying that in another world they should be together?

She had little time to puzzle over his words; every day her grandmother chaperoned her to what seemed a dozen different engagements and every day she was forced to appear unconcerned and happy. The week sped past, a constant bustle of movement, culminating in her first ball at the Upper Assembly Rooms. Its Master of Ceremonies had visited the ladies early in Amelie's stay. Mr King was a man who took his duties seriously and he had been concerned to introduce Miss Silverdale to any and every suitable young man he could find. The advent of a splendid evening of dancing promised him even greater scope. Amelie's lessons in the waltz, a daring new dance for Bath, were to be put to the test.

Her interest in attending the ball was mild, but the minute she was ushered through the classical columns of the Assembly Room to its richly hung interior ablaze with light, she found herself responding to the colour and movement all around. Brightly clothed young women floated past on the arms of their black-suited escorts, while chaperones lined the walls of the ballroom, enjoying the opportunity for an agreeable exchange of news.

As she and Brielle entered the room, they were besieged. Within a very few minutes every slot on her dance card was filled; all the young men present, it seemed, wanted to dance with this beautiful new addition to Bath society. She couldn't help but give herself up to enjoyment. The sensation of being twirled around the highly polished floor in the arms of one admiring partner after another, and of knowing she was the toast of the evening, was gratifying. Perry Latham, revealing himself to be an excellent dancer, took to the floor with her twice, much to the delight of the Bath gossips.

It was certainly pleasurable to be the most sought-after girl in the room, but the froth and glamour of the night could not disguise the truth of her situation. This ball, like so many others, was part of an elaborate ritual that must lead eventually to the altar. It was a path she'd always been desperate not to tread, even as she'd realised her chances of escape were slim.

But recently it had become more imperative than ever that she stay true to herself. It was since meeting Gareth, of course. He was rude and overbearing, duplicitous, too, but he'd lit a flame within her that made it impossible to settle for the good enough. She'd believed herself to be cool, rational, even passionless. And yet within a few short weeks he'd destroyed that belief, but offered nothing in return. In the last moments of their meeting at the Pump Room, he'd shown her tenderness, but that altered nothing. He was getting ready to move on and his tenderness had simply been a prelude to his leaving.

Knowing nothing of what was passing in her granddaughter's mind, Brielle looked on complacently, secure in the knowledge that Amelie was the most beautiful girl in the room. Dressed in a gown of white sarsnet over a white satin petticoat with pearl fastenings and a circlet of pearls in her hair, she looked every inch a fairy-tale princess, Brielle thought with unaccustomed sentiment.

Halfway through the evening, when the gentlemen's starched shirt points had begun to wilt from the heat of the hundreds of wax candles burning in the wall-sconces, the orchestra took their break and everyone began to make their way towards the refreshments laid out in the adjoining room. Amelie had been dancing constantly and was grateful for the chance to sit down. As she went towards the door, Brielle following, Mr King caught up with them, clearly wishing to introduce an escort for the buffet which lay beyond. It was Rufus Glyde.

'Miss Silverdale, how very good to meet you again and in such pleasant surroundings. I hope you've enjoyed the dancing?'

The white mask of Glyde's face leaned towards her while his eyes ran lightly over her body. She felt herself squirming, but managed a brief curtsy without meeting his predatory gaze.

'Thank you, Sir Rufus, I have.'

'I wonder if you would be willing to add to *my* enjoyment by allowing me the pleasure of escorting you to tea?'

She looked desperately around for Brielle, who was now inconveniently deep in conversation with her neighbour. Following her glance, he said silkily, 'I have already asked your grandmother for permission and she is more than happy to entrust you to my care for half an hour.'

She was left with no other alternative than to agree. She felt the loathsome touch on her arm and stifled her repulsion, allowing Glyde to lead her through to the adjoining room. Here he found her a chair and went in search of food and drink. Escape was impossible.

In a very short while he was back and handing her a small gold-rimmed plate.

'I hope I've gauged your tastes correctly,' he murmured obsequiously, 'but tell me, please, if you would care for anything else.'

'This will do very well, thank you, Sir Rufus.'

'Please, Rufus. I feel we know each other sufficiently well to be on first-name terms. Do you not?'

'I would prefer our acquaintance to remain formal, Sir Rufus. I'm sure you will appreciate my reasons.'

'I'm not sure I do. I am a little disappointed that you lack faith in me. Your father evidently holds another view or he would not have wished me to make you an offer of marriage.'

'My father has nothing to say in the matter. And I beg you to refrain from mentioning your proposal.'

'As to that, I would think your father has everything to say, notwithstanding your temporary stay in Bath. And I do trust that it is temporary.'

'I'm unsure of how long I shall be here, but certainly for some considerable time.'

'We shall have to see.' His voice held a sinister edge. 'In any contest of wills, Miss Silverdale, I think I might back your father.'

'Sir, I find the tone of your conversation not to my taste and I beg you to cease harassing me in this way.'

'I see that I must mend my tone. I have no wish to upset you unnecessarily. Please be assured that in future I will not burden you by making any further requests for your hand. I am not, after all, in the habit of requesting—as you will come to know.'

'If you will excuse me, I must find my grandmother.'

Unable to stifle her disgust any longer, she hastily gathered up her reticule and fled back into the ballroom. Brielle was nowhere to be seen, but she knew that even if her grandmother were to materialise before her that instant, she would not tell her of Glyde's menaces. What could she say? He was far too clever to issue direct threats. There was nothing you could pin down. Nevertheless she was aware that she had just been issued with a warning. Glyde was planning his revenge and it would be coming soon.

Scared that he might follow her, she kept moving through the long French windows which stood open, scarcely a breath of wind stirring the curtains, which had been pulled back to welcome the warm night air. She made her way rapidly out onto the terrace that ran the length of the building and descended a shallow flight of steps to one of the many paths that intersected the surrounding gardens, making sure that she could not be seen from the lighted room behind her. The night was still, as if holding its breath. The crunch of her slippers on the gravel was the only sound to disturb the warm enclosing peace.

The smell of lilac newly in flower floated towards her. Ahead the trees were motionless, a black mass silhouetted against the pale night sky. Her eyes gradually adapted to the darkness and now she could see shades of grey emerging from the gloom and close by, a pinprick of glowing red. For an instant her eyes focused directly on the light and with a start she realised she was looking at the tip of a cigar. She turned to flee back into the ballroom where the musicians had once more begun to play. A sardonic voice sounded softly in her ear.

'Tired of dancing so soon, Miss Silverdale?'

She spun round and saw Gareth Wendover's derisive

smile. 'Surely as the belle of the ball, you cannot be leaving already?'

'I was merely taking the air. It's a beautiful evening.'

'Then perhaps we can take the air together,' he suggested in a voice that brooked no refusal.

They were now clearly visible from the ballroom and, not wishing to draw unwanted attention, she laid her hand lightly on the arm he proffered and retraced her steps along the pathway towards the knot of trees in the distance. The moon, which had been hovering behind clouds, swam free and the garden was suddenly bathed in silver. She saw her companion clearly for the first time. The white frilled shirt and black tailcoat and knee breeches deemed necessary for a formal occasion set off his tanned face and honed body to perfection. He looked magnificent. Her eyes felt bewitched, longing to linger on the seductive picture he presented, but she quickly averted her gaze. She had no wish to advertise the effect he was having on her.

'I see you've reacquainted yourself with your friend?'

'You've been spying on me,' she denounced hotly.

'Hardly.'

'Then why are you here?'

'I'm here because the Averys wished to attend the dance and I accompanied them.'

'I didn't see you dancing.'

'I prefer to watch. One notices all kinds of interesting things. Rufus Glyde, for example, your sworn enemy.'

'You don't believe that he is my enemy,' she said flatly.

'From where I was standing, it looked unlikely. That was a cosy little tête-à-tête—what did you enjoy most, tasting the sweetmeats or listening to sweet nothings?'

'I was forced into taking tea with him. They were threats he was uttering.'

'Forced? Threats?' Gareth looked quizzically at her.

'Hints, then, that I'd better do as he wishes and accept him as a suitor.'

'And do you intend to?'

'How can you ask me that?'

He gave a slight shrug of his shoulders. 'Your family is keen for you to make the match. Your life might be easier if you were to agree.'

'My life would be monstrous!'

Standing motionless in the cold, bright moonlight, her shoulders suddenly crumpled into defeat. She looked very young and very vulnerable and his heart was stirred.

'If you need help, you've only to ask,' he said, stopping beneath the broad leaves of a chestnut tree and turning to face her.

'Thank you, but I doubt you can aid me.'

'You could be wrong.' He reached out to trace the line of her cheek with one finger.

She took an involuntary step backwards; provokingly his brief touch had sent a shiver dancing up and down her spine.

'As you're leaving England very shortly, I'd be unwise to rely on your assistance,' she almost snapped.

His smile was lazy and assured. 'If you asked nicely, I might put my journey off.'

'Why would you do that? You believe me a trickster, a perfect deceiver.'

'You're certainly artful and scheming—like all your kind.'

'I bow to your limitless experience of women,' she said caustically.

'You should—it's been hard won and rewarding only for transitory pleasure.'

'If I'm no different from the countless women you scorn, why offer me help?'

'Maybe because you *are* perfect as well as a deceiver. And because you need help—it seems that the net is closing in.'

She shivered and he moved closer to her. Then, tipping up her chin, he gently kissed her on the lips. She knew that she should break away, ask him to escort her back to the ballroom. Already she had all the menace she could manage in her life without having to struggle against the temptation of this dangerous man. But the taste of his mouth was something she was desperate to know again and her lips opened unresistingly to receive his. He kissed her long and deep. She leaned back against the trunk of the tree, soft and pliant to his touch. He drew her towards him, the hard planes of his body pressing against her. His hands slowly and expertly caressed her bare skin until she was inundated by rolling waves of desire. The small pearl buttons of her dress were soon undone and the white flesh of her breasts exposed to his touch. His mouth found them and moulded them to his desire, his kisses becoming hotter and more urgent with every moment.

Somewhere an owl hooted and for an instant they were stilled, listening to the sounds of the night. Brusquely, he pulled away.

'You should go back and find your grandmother,' he said roughly.

Shocked, she began to put her dress to rights with shaking fingers. He watched her from a short distance, his expression impossible to read.

'You should be married, Amelie. And quickly. Surely there must be a suitor in the wings other than Rufus Glyde.'

She felt the anger exploding within her. How dare he use her like that and then suggest she marry another man? Was this just another version of the insult she'd already suffered from him? Did he indeed think of her as a doxy, permanently in a state of heat for any man who came her way?

She marched past him with her head high, but he caught her by the arm and pulled her back. 'I mean it, you know—if you're in trouble, send for me.'

She shook off his restraint and ran swiftly towards the ballroom. Thankfully, Brielle was seated near the window and alone.

'I'm afraid I cannot dance anymore, Grandmama, I have the most dreadful headache.'

Looking at her granddaughter's drawn face and hearing the agitation in her voice, Brielle hesitated only long enough to gather her belongings before summoning her carriage. Seated side by side in the town coach, her grandmother took her hands in a warm clasp and stroked them comfortingly. 'You're exhausted, my dear. We shall have a few quiet days and then you'll be more than ready to socialise again.'

If only she knew, Amelie thought, but she dared not mention the existence of Gareth or, even worse, her own impropriety. She needed to push the incident into the furthest recesses of her mind. She had behaved as unchastely as it was possible and with a man who cared nothing for her. It was obvious that he viewed her as an amusement, to be enjoyed when it suited. He'd made her frenzied with desire and then walked away. As she thought of their encounter, her face blazed scarlet with vexation and her whole body was suffused with shame. But she must not think of it, she must not!

'I admire your choice. A diamond of the first water!' Lucas grinned as Gareth entered the Avery family carriage. 'We caught a glimpse of her returning from your moonlight tryst.'

'She's a most beautiful girl,' his wife interjected. 'No wonder you're in love with her.'

Gareth glared at his friend. 'I won't ask who put that notion into your head, Katherine, but you have it wrong.'

She wrinkled her nose meditatively.

'I wonder,' she said gently.

'Admit it, you're in love, just as I said.' Lucas was jubilant. 'And what could be better? I was worried when I thought you'd fallen for a girl who was completely ineligible, but now the situation is different.'

'No, it isn't,' was the terse reply as the coach trundled a slow passage over the darkened cobbled streets.

Once at the house, Lucas took his friend by the arm and ushered him into his den. No one ever entered this room except by invitation. He poured two glasses of brandy and handed one to Gareth.

'I may be stupid,' he began, 'so explain to me exactly why you're determined to walk away from this stunning girl?'

'Amelie *is* a beautiful young woman and I'm as red-blooded as the next man. But there it stays.'

'But why?'

'Women are a complication I can do without.'

'Women, maybe, but forget all the others who've flitted through your life—this girl is different.'

'I don't see that.'

'You said yourself that you can't get her out of your mind.'

'I have to and I will.'

Then, seeing his friend's perturbed expression, he said grimly, 'I'm not looking for a bride, Lucas. I'm not even looking for love. That would involve trust and I don't have trust to give.'

Lucas's eyes were troubled. 'Trust can grow—if you give it a chance.'

'I did—once. But we both know the end of that story.'

'It's a story from the past,' his friend argued, 'It doesn't mean you can't start again.'

'There is no starting again. I chose my path years ago and I can't now unchoose it.'

'It wasn't a choice, it was forced on you. I'm reluctant to speak ill of your family and of someone who isn't here to defend himself, but your grandfather treated you shabbily.'

Gareth gave a small, mirthless laugh and his friend continued, 'I can see you're a changed man, but don't let that accursed scandal ruin the rest of your life. You're innocent of any wrongdoing.'

'I know that and, thank God, so do you. But to the rest of the world I'm a guilty man and always will be. I can never ask anyone to marry me—even if I wanted to. It's as well that I don't,' he concluded roughly.

His companion sighed with frustration. 'If we could discover what really happened that night… Have you any idea who might have cheated? If it wasn't you, and it wasn't me, then it was one of the other three people around that table. General Tilney is an impossibility and Petersham is so wealthy that it would be laughable to suggest his cheating. But Glyde? He's a man steeped in all kinds of murk.'

'Of course I've thought about who cheated that night. I've thought about nothing else for seven long years. It could only be Glyde. But what would he have to gain? The stakes weren't that high and in any case he's a rich man.'

'I'm not sure he's as well-breeched as he appears. There are tales that every so often he's forced to sell property and some of his horses. Then he has a lucky streak and all is well again. He replenishes his stables and says he merely fancied a change of cattle.'

'So where does that get us?'

'It means that Glyde might have had a motive after all—money. There's been a good deal of whispering lately about his keenness to play with very young men, those who have little experience, but are plump in the pocket.'

'I was certainly not one of those. Wet behind the ears, it's true. But I didn't have a fortune to lose. You know as well as I do how stringent my grandfather was. I received a very small allowance, hardly worth Glyde's effort if that was the plan.'

'It's true, I suppose, that he wouldn't have fleeced you of a great deal, but the man is spiteful and has a thoroughly malicious nature. He might just have wanted to destroy a young man with a golden future—good looks, charm, a title in waiting and a grandfather who loved and respected him.'

'It's not enough. It's never been enough. If there'd been a motive and concrete evidence of his wrongdoing, I'd have confronted him years ago, exiled and penniless though I was.'

'I think you may be underestimating our friend Glyde. He would destroy anyone—for a wager, perhaps, or even for fun, his kind of fun.'

Gareth was sunk in deep thought and when he spoke his voice was harsh. 'And now he's hanging around Amelie Silverdale. I thought at first that she was playing games with me, pretending to dislike his overtures while angling to become the next Lady Glyde. But she appears to detest him. Despite that, he's determined to pursue her. First in London, then at the George and now here.'

'Then if you have a care for the girl—I won't call it love,'

Lucas hastily interjected as he saw his friend's face, 'you must look out for her.'

'That won't be easy. She doesn't trust me and she's right not to.'

'Tell her the truth about yourself, then she will.'

'She's much more likely to turn away in disgust.'

'She needs to know the lengths to which Glyde will go, understand the peril she faces if she acts against him.'

Gareth stood up abruptly and began restlessly to pace the floor of the den. 'You're right,' he pronounced minutes later. 'France will have to wait. I need to warn her and defeating Glyde's plans will bring a certain savage pleasure.'

'Don't underestimate him, Gareth. He can be a dangerous man.'

'That I can believe, but *I* can be even more dangerous.'

Chapter Eight

It was the small hours before Amelie slept that night. Try as she might, she could not obliterate the stolen meeting with Gareth from her memory. Her mind replayed the scene constantly and every repetition made her feel worse. She knew that she'd behaved recklessly and immodestly. Yet what had she really been guilty of? Showing her feelings too obviously, allowing herself to trust? In return she'd been utterly humiliated. Witnessing her mother's distress all those years ago, she'd made a vow never to allow herself to get too close to any man. Now she'd broken that vow and was paying the price. Her only hope was that he would leave Bath instantly. She would never have to meet him again and see in his face the easy contempt he must feel.

A troubled sleep had left her tired and dispirited and it was with reluctance that she agreed to take a walk in the Sydney Gardens the next morning. Her grandmother had set time aside to wrestle with the household accounts and Fanny was deputed to accompany her mistress. Amelie had no wish to burden her maidservant with the emotional storm she was suffering, nor with her worries over Rufus Glyde. The girl had received a severe scolding for her part in her mistress's flight and the last thing Amelie wanted was to revive bad memories for her. It was best that Fanny thought her mistress perfectly happy.

The gardens were looking particularly inviting. An overnight shower had made the leaves gleam brightly and the flowers put on their most vivid colours. They strolled at a leisurely pace along meandering pathways that criss-crossed the well-kept lawns, making their way slowly around the grounds and back into Great Pulteney Street.

Fanny was eager to hear the details of last night's ball and her mistress was occupied trying to paint a reassuringly cheerful picture. Neither saw the clouds gather once more and the sky begin to darken until the rain started to pour in earnest. Snatching up their skirts, they ran for cover. A small wooden summer house at the end of the gardens offered what little shelter there was. They arrived there breathless and not a little wet.

'We should have brought our umbrellas, Miss Amelie, Bath weather is that changeable.'

The maid attempted to shake off the large drops of water that adorned her skirt and then turned to Amelie to help her do the same. But her mistress did not respond even when Fanny asked her with some puzzlement, 'Is everything all right, miss?'

Instead she stood, frozen and motionless, staring at the man who shared their shelter. Fate could not have been more unkind; Gareth Wendover was the last man in the world that she wanted to see. He bowed slightly to the two women, but remained silent. His blue eyes gazed into the distance without expression and a lock of wet hair shadowed his brow. The rain had moulded his coat of superfine to his form and the feelings she'd willed herself to suppress began to throb into life once more. Dumbly, she looked out at the teeming rain, unable to say a word.

At last, his voice broke the silence, the smooth tones seeming to travel from a vast distance.

'I trust I see you well this morning, Miss Silverdale.'

He'd turned towards her and his black brows were raised in enquiry.

Urgently, she gathered her wandering wits and somehow managed to reply in an even voice, 'I thank you, sir. I am well.'

'And fully recovered from the exertions of the last evening, I hope?'

She felt the anger seep through her; he was not content with mortifying her last night, but now must seek her out to taunt her with her shame.

'I'm not such a poor creature that dancing a few cotillions exhausts me, Mr Wendover,' she answered waspishly.

'Ah, *dancing*, naturally not,' he said with the slightest suggestion of a grin.

'You are unhandsome, sir.'

'How is that?'

'I may have been forced to take shelter here, but should not be forced to suffer your mocking.'

He looked genuinely surprised. 'That's far from my intention.'

'I find that difficult to believe, however. Since we first met you have treated me with contempt and last night you excelled yourself.'

Fanny, meanwhile, had gasped at the mention of Wendover. A distant memory had revived and she'd been gazing in astonishment, first at her mistress and then at the man who bore this disquieting name. Now, in an attempt to capture Amelie's attention, she shuffled her feet noisily on the bare wooden boards.

Reminded of her maid's presence for the first time, Amelie made haste to send her away.

'Go back to the house, Fanny, and find our umbrellas.'

'But, miss, the rain has almost stopped.'

'Don't argue. The weather looks like to remain inclement and I don't wish to get any wetter than I am already.'

Fanny looked doubtful, but her mistress wore such a severe look, that she scurried away with hardly a backwards glance.

They watched the maid out of sight before Gareth began to move towards her. She held up her hand abruptly, stopping him in his tracks.

'I don't know if you've happened here by accident or if you've followed me. It matters not,' she said bitterly. 'You've taunted me for the last time. I wish never to see you again, speak to you again, even hear of you again.'

A frown creased his brow. 'I've no idea why you should be so angry, but I'm sorry if I'm the cause.'

'No idea! When all you've ever done is play games with me. Save them for the women you meet and discard on your travels. I'm sure they'll be more appreciative. I'm not one of them.'

'As I know to my cost,' he murmured wryly. 'And I've never suggested you were.'

'No? Then how do you account for your despicable conduct last night?'

'I shouldn't have made love to you, I agree, but how is that despicable?'

'You were trifling with me.'

'Believe me, Amelie, I was far from trifling.' And he smiled in reminiscence.

She found herself remembering, recalling his smell, his touch, the feel of his body, and desperately sought to stoke her anger.

'You can't help yourself. You're so used to treating women as trophies that you think you can appropriate anyone.'

'It's true that plenty of women have passed through my life and I've let them go without regret.' His tone was sardonic. 'But they've hardly been trophies, merely ragged comfort along a stony path.'

'Very poetic, but it doesn't disguise the fact that you deliberately lured me into a compromising situation and then humiliated me.'

'You've a taste for the poetic, too, I see. I admit I should have resisted temptation, but you make that very difficult, you know.'

He smiled down at her in a way that made her body begin to crumple with desire. Alarmed by her own response, she sprang away from him, leaving as much distance between them as possible.

His expression turned wrathful. 'If you must cast blame, look to yourself. You're angry because last night you surrendered to your feelings. Be grateful that I saved you from betraying yourself further.'

'But of course, you're my knight errant, always rescuing me from disaster. I had forgot. How painful last night's episode must have been for you!'

'Inconvenient, shall we say. Such moments can benefit neither of us and you should have a care for your future.'

Her face wore a shocked expression, but he continued harshly, 'You don't want to hear it, but your best route out of the dangers that beset you is to find a good man to marry.'

'I shall never marry,' she said bleakly.

'Ah, the old refrain, but why ever not? There *are* decent men in the world, you know.'

'Few women find them or, if they do, manage to keep them. My mama did not,' she said in a subdued voice.

He looked at her for a long time and his expression softened slightly. 'Whatever your mother's experience you're not destined to repeat it.'

'Except that my own experience tells me otherwise. Did *you* play the decent man last night?'

'Do you really think that I wanted to lose control?' he grated. 'Of course I didn't. I've survived a brutal world by ensuring that I'm never at the mercy of my emotions.'

'Then why are you here, exposing yourself yet again to such peril?' she asked tartly. 'Or are you going to tell me that you accidentally just happened by?'

Even if his lovemaking had not been a deliberate ploy to humiliate her, it was at best an aberration, an inconvenience. And which was worse?

'No accident—I sought you out this morning. I saw you leave Laura Place and hoped to overtake you on your walk—it was fortunate that the rain brought us together.'

'*Fortunate* is not the word I would use. You deny spying on me, but spying is exactly what you're doing.'

'I sought you out,' he said deliberately, 'because I've something I must say. Don't fret, you'll be free of my presence very shortly.'

'I can't imagine why you're still in Bath,' she retorted childishly. 'How long does it take to bid your friend goodbye?'

He ignored her pointed rudeness and replied calmly, 'I've stayed because I have business to complete. When I go depends on you.'

'How very surprising—' the sharpness of her voice cut the air '—and there was I thinking you were a law unto yourself.'

'I need only a few minutes of your time, then you may be on your way. And I'll be on mine.'

His expression was impossible to read, but his tone was unusually serious.

'A few minutes then, Mr Wendover, although I cannot imagine that you've sought me out to exchange confidences. You seem to delight in posing as a figure of mystery.'

His face relaxed at this and he smiled. Once more the blue eyes were alight with warmth and, despite herself, she felt drawn into their orbit. He was standing very close to her again. She realised that just as his rain-soaked clothes had displayed his muscular form, hers were very revealing of her figure. The sheer sprig muslin she wore clung sensuously to her curves and he was looking his fill and clearly enjoying the sight.

'I'm glad you find it amusing,' she snapped, annoyed that her heart was once more in disorder.

'A figure of mystery sounds flatteringly enigmatic. My smile was simply for that.'

'And are you about to cease being a mystery? Do you intend to tell me your secrets?'

'Yes,' he said unexpectedly.

'Now?'

'Yes.'

'You're going to be honest with me at last?' she persisted.

'I'm going to be honest with you,' he replied solemnly. 'For your own sake, I need you to trust me. When you've heard what I have to say, you may choose to disown my acquaintance, but I still have to say it.'

The light had gone out of his eyes and his face was grave. She began to feel nervous. She'd always wanted to know his true history, but how troubling were the revelations he was about to make?

He remained standing close, their bodies almost touching, but not quite. He made no attempt to possess himself of her hands, no attempt to kiss her. She felt real fear now of what he was about to recount.

'Miss Silverdale, what on earth are you doing out in this dreadful weather?'

It was Perry Latham who had come bounding along the pathway with a large umbrella above his head. 'I met Fanny a while back and assured her that she could go home to dry and I would come to your rescue.'

'Thank you, Sir Peregrine,' she answered, flustered. 'That's most kind.'

'I am delighted to be of assistance. I am, in any case, a messenger from your grandmother.'

He caught sight of Gareth, standing still as a statue, and was somewhat disconcerted by the latter's scowling expression. 'Your servant, sir.' He bobbed his umbrella hastily as a token of respect.

'Yours, sir,' Gareth replied stiffly. Amelie hastily made the introductions, but Gareth was in no mood for social niceties.

'If you'll excuse me, I have a number of affairs to settle. Now that you have an escort, Miss Silverdale, you have no further need of my company.'

'But…' began Amelie.

'It was good to make your acquaintance,' Perry called after the rapidly disappearing figure, as Gareth strode towards the gates across one of the Chinese-style bridges that dotted the gardens.

'A pleasant fellow,' said Perry Latham, 'I think.'

'What message did you have from my grandmother, Sir Peregrine?'

'Perry, please.' He smiled happily. 'She wanted me to tell you that a splendid excursion is arranged for tomorrow. A picnic to Severn Abbey. Always providing the weather changes for the better, of course.'

'A picnic tomorrow? How can this be? We were not to have any social engagements for a few days. It seems strange that Lady St Clair has arranged this without first consulting me.'

'She didn't arrange it. No, far from it. Everything taken out of her hands, everything done for her.'

'You've arranged it?'

'No, not me. I could have, of course. I thought about it, but I was pipped at the post. Some chap called Hyde or something like that.'

'Glyde?' Amelie faltered.

'Yes, that's the fellow. Good natured of him, don't you think? He's gone to a lot of trouble apparently. Even booked musicians, I believe, and invited a big crowd.'

She had the presence of mind to pin on a smile of pleasure, but her heart was beating uncomfortably fast. This was to be the first strike in Glyde's renewed campaign. She had to go home and speak to her grandmother. Brielle must be made to understand Glyde's true purpose.

'Sir Peregrine—Perry, I was intending to visit the haberdashers after my walk, but I have just now realised that I've left behind the ribbon I wished to match. I'll have to return home after all.'

'Let me accompany you.'

'No, indeed, there's no need. The rain has stopped. Please don't let me keep you from your business. I will see you tomorrow, no doubt.'

And with that rapid dismissal, Perry Latham had nothing to do but bow politely and walk away in the opposite direction.

'Why are you so upset?' Brielle was clearly puzzled by her granddaughter's response to the invitation. 'It's simply a picnic, my dear. I shall be there and a good many other people that you know.'

'But so will Sir Rufus Glyde. The last thing I want is to be in that man's company. Why did you accept? Why didn't you ask me first when you know how I feel?'

'Dear child, strive for a little common sense. I accepted because to refuse would have been churlish. Sir Rufus has gone to considerable trouble organising this expedition—he made it clear to me that it was to compensate in some small way for the unpleasantness he unknowingly subjected you to. In those circumstances it was impossible to refuse.'

Amelie looked mulish. 'You could have said I was unwell and gone by yourself.'

'How could I have done that without appearing to lie? How many people have seen you today in the full bloom of health? You are refining too much on what has gone before. I do not believe that in the past Sir Rufus fully understood your feelings, but now that he does, he simply wishes to be a friend.'

'I love and respect you, Grandmama, but in this I believe you are judging wrongly.'

Brielle's expression was stern. 'You will allow me to know a little more about the world than you. I'll hear no more of this nonsense. The invitation is unexceptional, certainly nothing you need fear.'

'I do fear it. I loathe the man. I want nothing from him except his absence.'

'You are being unnecessarily alarmist, my dear. Whatever harm can come to you from going on a picnic?'

She had no answer and her grandmother continued smoothly, 'I'm sure that Sir Rufus means well. The trip to Severn Abbey is a kind thought on his part and will give you the chance of getting to know him better. It might even make you begin to change your mind.'

Horrified, she burst out, 'I will never change my mind as long as I live. The idea of marriage to such a man is abhorrent.'

'And yet you seem not at all interested in marriage to anyone else, despite having been introduced to some of the most eligible bachelors living in Bath. Perry Latham is clearly entranced and one small sign of encouragement from you would produce an offer of marriage, I feel sure.'

'When I said I never wanted to marry, I spoke the truth.'

'I also spoke the truth, Amelie, when I said that you will have to marry, unless you are content to beg shelter as a poor relation for the rest of your life.'

She knew only too well that her grandmother was right. Not unsympathetic to her plight, Brielle tried gently to coax her towards accepting the inevitable.

'If you have no preferences, why not go along with your father's wishes for the time being? You may even come to think he has chosen wisely for you.'

'Never, never, never!'

'No histrionics, Amelie. You must begin to think sensibly. I accept that Rufus Glyde may not be the partner for you, but you cannot dismiss marriage entirely. Take heed of the fact that once you are wed, you will no longer be under your father's control.

It will be your husband's duty to protect you from any interference from your family. If you choose a man like Perry, mature, independent and wealthy in his own right, he will have the power to do that. He will make you a good husband.'

'I don't want a good husband,' Amelie found herself saying while Brielle looked aghast.

In the silence that followed, her mind chased a maelstrom of thoughts, but always returned to a small insistent voice that would not be banished. What she wanted, she was learning, was a man who would possess her utterly, body and soul.

In the reaches of the night, she knew that man and he looked uncommonly like Gareth Wendover. But he was the last person who would feature as an eligible husband; marriage would never be for him. He desired her, that was obvious, and he would take her with a passion she could only begin to imagine. A streak of fire suffused her body as she thought of their lovemaking. But what then? She plummeted to earth. He would love her certainly, but just as certainly he would leave. He would cut loose with barely a backward glance.

Once again she lay awake for hours, a thousand different thoughts circling her agitated mind, Gareth always at their centre. His last words had disturbed her—what was it that he'd wanted to tell her with such urgency? She'd seen him angry, bitter, laughing and loving, but never before so serious as the moment when Perry Latham had interrupted their conversation. He'd deliberately sought her out that morning, but what was he about to confide and why now? Did it flow from that shared moment of passion in the moonlit garden? Did his feelings go more deeply than she suspected? Even if they did, he would not acknowledge them. He'd made it plain that emotion was a weakness he couldn't afford; the moment's pleasure was his only interest. And yet...

She longed to be able to seek him out on the morrow and know the answers. But convention decreed that a single woman must be sought rather than do the seeking. In any case the day was not even hers—it would be filled by an excursion she longed to forgo.

The heavy overnight rain had cleared by dawn and by ten o'clock the next morning the sky had mellowed to a clear blue, streaked with wisps of white cloud. It seemed there was to be no reprieve from the weather. She'd decided on the plainest of dresses, but her grandmother dismissed this plan immediately and insisted she put on one of the most fetching of the modiste's creations, a soft green lustring and matching cape. Miss Repton was sent to dress her hair. Her grandmother's maid had unbent slightly over time, Amelie's natural beauty providing her with the best opportunity she had ever enjoyed to display her professional skills. Her protégée acknowledged her efforts with courtesy, but with little interest. This was a day to be got through as quickly as possible.

From the outset it was clear that Sir Rufus had spared no effort or expense on the planning of his excursion. A cavalcade of carriages set off for Severn Abbey towards noon, the last two filled with servants, blankets, sunshades and hampers containing every conceivable kind of food and drink. The countryside was bathed in mellow sunshine and stretched before them fresh and green. As they swished through narrow lanes, the delicate scent of wild flowers wafted into the carriage from high banks on either side.

Amelie saw and felt none of it. This outing was simply a part of Glyde's plan to bend her to his will and she recognised miserably that her grandmother could no longer be counted as her ally in the battle against him. Sir Peregrine, dapper in dove-grey pantaloons and claret waistcoat, shared their carriage and ably maintained a flow of chatter. He tried and failed on several occasions to draw her into the conversation.

'Do you know the countryside around here, Miss Silverdale?'

'I regret that I don't. When I visited Bath as a child I never went beyond the town.'

'There are a great many places of interest, you know.'

'I'm sure, Sir Peregrine.'

'The Abbey we're visiting today, for instance? Do you know anything of its past?'

'No, I'm afraid not.'

He decided against regaling her with his potted history of Severn Abbey and said instead, 'You might be particularly interested in the legend that surrounds the building,' plunging into a somewhat confused account that interweaved a mad monk, a black crow and a murdered spouse who was forever dressed in white. She listened with an expression of interest on her face, but his words simply circled the air before disappearing without trace.

Once they had arrived at the Abbey, the carriages disgorged their occupants and the whole party began a walk around the ruins. Perry Latham, as an acknowledged expert on the Abbey's history, entertained a small crowd with anecdotes of its past. The most popular proved to be that of the ghost, although the story had grown even more confused in the retelling. Until called to order by their formidable mama, the Misses Lampeter giggled in nervous excitement at his description of the lady in white who floated through the ruins at full moon. Rufus Glyde pointedly ignored the storytelling, deciding instead to play the role of perfect host. He darted here and there, at one moment mingling with his guests and at the next snapping out commands to his servants. At his order the musical trio positioned a little way off struck up a cheerful air.

'This seems a little excessive for a simple picnic,' Amelie remarked to her grandmother.

'Don't be ungrateful,' Brielle chided. 'If the event is a little extravagant, I'm quite sure it is for your benefit alone.'

'I imagine it's rather to satisfy our host's love of ostentation.'

'You are unfair, Amelie, and unrealistic. It's clear to me that Sir Rufus cares for you a great deal and doubtless still wishes to marry you despite your stubbornness. You're not interested in Perry—I saw how you treated him in the carriage. If you won't take him, then you should seriously consider the very advantageous offer that's been made to you by your father's choice of suitor.'

Before she could respond, they were interrupted by Glyde himself, who appeared without warning at their side. Summoning up his most amiable smile, he turned to face Amelie.

'I hope you're enjoying our impromptu little affair, Miss Silverdale, and that all is to your satisfaction. Sir Peregrine's stories, I feel, have given the event an added *frisson*. Or perhaps, unlike the Misses Lampeter, you don't enjoy tales of ghostly visitations?'

'I've more interest in the present than the past, Sir Rufus.'

'How very sensible,' he murmured slyly, 'although one must never forget the future, either.'

'That is something I'm not like to forget, sir.'

'Exactly so. When one is young, the future is an exciting blank, is it not, just waiting to be filled.'

'And I shall fill it as I wish,' she retorted defiantly.

Glyde remained unruffled. 'He will be a lucky man who helps you.'

'I said nothing of any man. My future is mine alone.'

Brielle looked sharply at her granddaughter and decided to mediate. 'Sir Rufus is surely right to suggest that the most satisfying future is a shared one.'

'That's a matter of opinion,' Amelie replied, and looked pointedly away.

The excursion had started badly and continued so, even when the picnic lunch was served in the shade of the chapel ruins. As well as folding tables and chairs scattered across the close-cropped green, blankets had been spread for those who preferred the informality of eating close to nature. Servants circulated busily among the guests, offering platters spilling over with the finest food, followed by tray after tray of cool champagne in crystal glasses. Glyde hovered around their table, constantly offering Amelie a variety of delicacies, to which her reply was just as constant, 'Thank you, but, no.'

'In this heat I eat very little.'

'I really am not hungry.'

And as for champagne, 'I rarely drink wine and never during the daytime.'

Brielle became more and more incensed with her wayward granddaughter. Here was Sir Rufus making a concerted effort to give the girl an enjoyable day and Amelie appeared intent on treating him with an indifference bordering on rudeness. Over the past week Brielle had come to think that Glyde's proposal should not be dismissed out of hand. He appeared to be a man deep in the throes of love, but he'd shown a restraint and courtesy that she'd not expected of him. It was true that he was considerably older than Amelie, but that was no bad thing in Brielle's view. He was wealthy, a necessity now that the Silverdales' fortune was in such a parlous state. It was a little worrying to be sure that he'd acquired the mortgage over the house in Grosvenor Square, but Brielle thought that her granddaughter had perhaps misunderstood the nature of the transaction and that it had not been used as a threat, but as a way of helping a family with whom Glyde evidently wished to ally himself.

It was with relief that Amelie saw the servants begin to pile blankets and hampers back into the carriages and thought thankfully of the return to Bath. But the end of her misery was not yet in sight.

'Lady St Clair, I wonder if I might be permitted to drive your granddaughter?' Glyde had detached himself from the crowd of picnickers and was now bowing graciously to Brielle. 'I will undertake to deliver her safely at Laura Place.'

Brielle willingly gave her assent despite the pleading look on Amelie's face. It would be a chance for them to talk together without interruption. Perhaps they could sort through their differences, and if not, nothing had been lost.

'Grandmama, why don't you accompany Sir Rufus? I'm sure Perry will have room for me in his carriage,' Amelie appealed, hoping that Brielle would be content if she accompanied the second of her potential suitors.

'Perry has already offered me a seat, my dear—' her grandmother neatly cut the ground from beneath her feet '—and since Sir Rufus has been good enough to organise this wonderful excursion with you in mind, it would be fitting that you accompany him.'

This was the nearest Brielle had come to a public rebuke all day and it was one that Amelie could not ignore. Her face burning, she climbed into Glyde's carriage without another word. For the first few miles they drove in silence. She had no intention of playing the gracious guest and Rufus Glyde was biding his time. They were halfway back to Bath before he broke the ominous quiet.

'I'm so glad you felt able to accompany me, Miss Silverdale. I fear our acquaintance began badly and I have had no real chance to remedy this. You have given me now the opportunity to plead my true feelings for you.'

She remained mute and looked away at the blur of trees as they sped headlong through the country lanes. She was his quarry, hunted and cornered. She could escape ensnarement only by jumping from the curricle and that would mean injury for life, or worse.

Wholly undeterred by her silence, he began again, 'I would like to use this moment to tell you how much I hope you will consent to be my wife.'

'Did you not say, Sir Rufus, just one week ago, that you would not be renewing your proposal?'

'That is true, dear lady, but I think I was perhaps a little premature. I find that my feelings for you are stronger than ever and I am looking forward to making you Lady Glyde.'

'I thank you for your kind offer, sir, but I regret I must once more decline. I'm unable to return your affections.' She delivered her words as calmly as she was able.

'I hope in time you may be brought to change your mind.'

'I shall never change my mind.'

'Never is a very long time. You may think differently once you know me.'

'I know all I need to know, I assure you, and I will never wish to be your wife. I have no desire to hurt your feelings, but please accept this as my final word.'

'You don't hurt my feelings, Miss Silverdale. Very little does. But I've decided that you are the woman I shall wed. Your opposition merely adds spice to the quest.'

'If you persist in your delusion, there's nothing more I can say.'

'There is one word and that is yes.'

'I will never say yes.'

'I think you will. I have some powerful forces on my side. You see, I know you took at least a week to reach your grandmother's house from London and I ask myself just where you were during that time. Others might start to wonder, too, if they knew of your long absence from the protection of your relatives. I might even suggest to the inveterate gossips among us that you were up to no good. A possible love tryst? A scandal at all events. How would the *ton* react to that, I wonder? I imagine it might prove the end of all your hopes to shine in society, certainly all your hopes of a prestigious marriage.'

'I have no wish to shine in society. Nor have I any wish to make a marriage, prestigious or otherwise. Your threats leave me unmoved.'

They were now entering the outskirts of Bath and Amelie, her hands tightly clasped to prevent them shaking, could only hope that she would get to Laura Place with her head still held high. Her tormentor wore a marked sneer on his face and continued to drive at a spanking pace through the town's streets, seemingly undisturbed by her response.

They had begun to move into the more populated part of the town, when she gave an abrupt start. A familiar figure, his back turned, was walking purposefully along the pavement. It was Gareth. During the long day's ordeal she'd thought of him constantly—yearned for him, she admitted shamefacedly. And suddenly here he was, longing transformed into reality. Her start had not gone unnoticed by Glyde. He looked long and hard at the figure striding along the road, scarcely able to believe his eyes.

'And how do you know that fine gentleman?' he asked sharply.

'I doubt that is any concern of yours. But I believe I met him a few days ago at the Pump Room with my grandmother.' She was aware that this sounded less than convincing.

'Drinking the waters? Evidently, a new come-out for him.'

'Whatever do you mean?'

'I interest you at last! Strange, when the subject is a man you only *believe* you met.'

'He is of no interest to me—I simply did not understand you.'

'Then allow me to explain. The man we have just passed is a low scoundrel. A sharp, to be precise.'

'A sharp?'

'As a young lady of impeccable background, I doubt you will know the term. A sharp is a cheat who lives by his skill at manipulating the cards or dice. In effect, a thief.'

Her face paled, but she said in a voice that hardly wavered, 'I don't believe that he is any such thing.'

'Why? Is your knowledge of the gentleman so much greater than mine?'

'On what grounds do you accuse him of such base behaviour?'

'I saw him cheat with my own eyes. Pretty good grounds, wouldn't you agree, my dear?'

She sat rigid, in a state of shock. Glyde turned to her, a malicious smile on his face. 'The man is really not suitable company for any woman of quality.'

When she said nothing, he continued to taunt her. 'You seem a trifle upset at my revelation. Could it be that the gentleman is a little more to you than the casual acquaintance you claim?' And then slyly, delivering his crushing blow. 'So, we may have an answer to where you were for that missing week. With *that* man? And you refuse *me*!'

'I told you,' she said desperately, 'I hardly know him. And I doubt that you know him much better.'

She was far from feeling the certainty she expressed, haunted as she was by the remembrance of the quarrel she'd witnessed between the two men at the George.

'I hate to contradict a lady, but today I will make an exception. I know a good deal of him. He has recently returned from the Continent where I believe he has been pursuing his vocation with mixed success. He appears to have enjoyed better luck here. You are the first bird to be plucked, my dear, if not at cards.'

'How dare you! Kindly set me down. I'll not stay a minute longer in your company. I shall walk the rest of the way.'

'As you wish. But you are naive if you think you can flout society's rules and go unpunished. That is a grave error. If I know the truth, how long before others do, too? You will learn your mistake soon enough. Your biggest mistake by far is to tangle with me.'

Chapter Nine

She ran blindly towards her grandmother's house. Passers-by turned to stare at the young woman hastening past them, bonnet untied and hair flying free. Once in the house she rushed up the stairs to her bedroom and locked the door. She needed time and solitude to take in what she'd just heard. The threats by Glyde had hardly registered. She'd always known that he was a vicious man who would stop at nothing to gain what he wanted. But what he'd said about Gareth had turned her world upside down. It couldn't be true, it couldn't be true, echoed over and over again in her mind. Rufus Glyde would not hesitate to denigrate any man he thought might be a rival, but the confidence with which he'd delivered his damning judgement on Gareth had had its effect.

With all her heart she wanted to repudiate his words, but the fact that they accorded all too easily with what she already knew gave them a dreadful ring of truth. So many details fitted: Gareth's estrangement from his grandfather, his shabby clothes when she'd first met him and his air of having known better times, his wish to leave England and return to the Continent. The silence about his background would be readily explained if he were the disgraced man that Glyde had intimated. It would explain, too, the way he'd constantly deflected her questions and his anger when she'd continued to probe. And explain all too evidently why he'd looked so grave when she'd encountered him yesterday in the Sydney Gardens. He had something to tell her, he'd said, the truth about himself at last. Was that what he was about to confess when Perry Latham had interrupted them so inopportunely?

Perhaps after all not so inopportunely. If he didn't say the words, then maybe they wouldn't be true. She had no wish to hear such things from his lips, from the lips of the man she'd come to love. There it was…and she could no longer deny it. She'd fought so hard to preserve her heart, but in vain; she'd lost it to a man who cared for nothing and nobody, whose tenderness was a fleeting caress and who, it now transpired, was an outcast from society. She lay down on the silk bedspread and closed her eyes. She was too deeply upset to cry, but her head thudded painfully. Her mind darted here and there, going over and over all the conversations she'd had with Gareth, trying to find a chink of light, trying to find a different interpretation. The dreadful realisation dawned that there was no other.

How long she had lain there she had no idea but a discreet knock on the door brought her off the bed instantly. It was Fanny.

'Milady wants to speak to you, Miss Amelie,' she said softly.

'Tell her I'm indisposed, I have a headache.'

'I think you should see her now, miss, then I'll brew you something for the pain.'

'My grandmother will understand if you say I'm not well.'

'I don't think she will, Miss Amelie. She's in a rage and ringing a peal over everyone who dares come near. Best to go down.'

Why was Brielle in such a temper? She'd obeyed her grand-mother's wishes and suffered a hateful journey for her pains. What, then, could be wrong? Lady St Clair's inexplicable mood seemed the final straw for a day so wretched that she wished for ever to blot it from her memory. Reluctantly, she combed her hair, smoothed out her dress and made her way to the library.

'There you are at last,' Brielle greeted her impatiently. 'That woman of yours takes her time.'

Amelie bridled. 'Fanny came as quickly as she could. I was lying down, Grandmama. I have a monstrously bad headache.'

'Another one? This seems to be getting rather a habit with you. Though after what I've heard today, it hardly surprises me.'

She stared at her grandmother uncomprehendingly.

'Yes, you may stare. I have never been more mortified. To think I should hear of my granddaughter's appalling conduct from a man who, as yet, has no connection to the family!'

'I don't understand,' she murmured in a dazed voice, but her bewilderment did nothing to appease her grandmother's fury.

'I have just suffered one of the most uncomfortable interviews of my life. Sir Rufus Glyde made a point of calling on me after he'd set you down. He felt it his distasteful duty to relay the most shocking news. He wished to warn me of a thoroughly unsuitable friendship you have contracted with a man—Wendover was the name—a man who is an out-and-out villain.'

Amelie caught her breath. So this was Glyde's new plan. He intended to use her own grandmother to intimidate her and enforce his threats.

'I had to sit there,' Brielle continued bitterly, 'while he was kind enough to inform me that my granddaughter is acquainted with a man who is a proven thief, a man who has been shunned by his own family and is not accepted in decent society. This is a man apparently that you know well. Let's not be mealy-mouthed, a man you've stayed with alone in a solitary country inn. Sir Rufus was nothing but courteous, but can you imagine my feelings when he told me this? He expressed concern for your safety. He knows this man well and said he would be most anxious if it were his own sister involved. His feelings do him credit, which is more than I can say for yours, Amelie. You have let me down greatly—in fact, you have let the whole family down, by your scandalous behaviour.'

Her grandmother's harsh words struck a deep chill in her heart. There was no defence she could make without revealing her feelings for Gareth. And that could do nothing but make the situation a hundred times worse, if that were possible.

'I acquit you of any deliberate wrongdoing,' her grandmother was saying, 'but your naivety and lack of prudence are likely to make you the talk of this town and beyond. If that happens, you will be lucky ever to live it down.'

Questions nagged in Amelie's mind and forced her to speak, though she knew it would infuriate her grandmother further.

'How could Rufus Glyde know I'd spent time at the inn with this man? And what right has he to accuse him of such wrongdoing?'

'He *is* a wrongdoer. Sir Rufus would not voice such a serious charge if it were not true. And as for him knowing of your indecent stay with this man, he has been most discreet, never hinted that he imagines there is any more than a casual acquaintance between you. He didn't have to say more—I worked that out for myself. The patient you looked after so devotedly? An older man whom no one else could care for? How could you have deceived me so badly? Haven't I deserved better?'

Amelie turned a stormy countenance towards her grand-mother.

'You are unfair, ma'am. You know that I would never hurt you. Please believe that I've done nothing wrong. I was at the inn by accident, that is the truth, and I only withheld the full story from you because I didn't want you to worry unnecessarily, not because I wanted to deceive.'

'It's certainly necessary for me to worry now. How are we to avoid this becoming common knowledge?'

'I left the inn as soon as I could and no one knows I was there, except you.'

'And Sir Rufus, if only by supposition. However, he appears to be an honourable man and I'm sure will not spread rumours. In the circumstances he is hardly likely to. We must trust that the scandal will not leak out.'

Her grandmother looked at her sharply. 'You're extremely fortunate that, after this dreadful misdemeanour, a man like Sir Rufus is still willing to marry you.'

She turned sheet-white as her grandmother's words sank in. Of course Glyde was willing to marry her. He would get his desire and she would no longer be able to say a word against it. She had lost any moral advantage. Brielle was right: her family would consider it very lucky that anyone wished now to marry her, least of all a notable member of the *ton*.

Looking at her granddaughter's woebegone face, Brielle's heart softened. Amelie was so like her mother. She remembered seeing too often that same expression on Louise's face when things between her and Miles Silverdale had begun to go awry. She took her granddaughter's hands in hers.

'You've made a bad mistake, but you can recover from this. I have every faith in your good sense. Whatever may have happened in the past, you must immediately cut any links you have to this unsuitable man.'

Amelie said nothing and her grandmother tried to rouse her with a brisk smile. 'Put this behind you, my dear, you're still very young and you have your whole future in front of you. You should give thought to what that future is to be. Sir Rufus is not the only man who admires you. It's possible...' she pursed her lips thoughtfully '...that an early wedding will prove the best way out of this predicament.'

She felt too distressed to ask her grandmother what she meant and excused herself as soon as she could. Crushed by the shower of troubles that had descended, she could hardly drag herself up the stairs. The faithful Fanny was waiting in her bedroom with camomile tea and a handkerchief soaked in lavender water. At her insistence, her mistress lay down on the bed and almost immediately fell into an exhausted sleep.

It was daybreak before she stirred. As her mind swam out of slumber, a tide of wretchedness swept through her and drowned her in its misery. But she knew that she had to rise and dress and pretend all was well.

At breakfast her grandmother looked approvingly across the table as she sat pale-faced but composed. Whatever ailed the girl, Brielle thought, she had spirit and would recover.

'I thought we might make a short visit to the Pump Room this morning,' her grandmother suggested over tea and toast.

'If it's possible, I would prefer to spend the day quietly, Grandmama.' The thought of the crowded room and the noisy chatter filled her with something near despair.

'Very well—' Brielle smiled agreement '—but you must not withdraw from society for too long. That way rumours start.'

She knew her grandmother spoke the truth. She would have to appear in public again very soon and could only hope that when she did, she would be able to wear an indifferent face. After breakfast she picked up one of the marble-backed novels recently arrived from the Circulating Library, thinking to divert herself, but it turned out that she had no interest in fantasy worlds. All the time her mind was tussling with the dreadful news that she'd learned and she could give thought to nothing else. Whatever occupation she chose was the same. It was a wearisome business and she was glad when at last the long day dragged to its close.

Two equally long days later Brielle rose unusually early and made her preparations. By the time Amelie came down to breakfast, she found her day already arranged and to her grandmother's liking.

'Perry Latham is calling this morning. We haven't seen him since the picnic and I thought it a friendly gesture to discover how he goes on.'

Amelie smiled absently and took a sip of tea. Whether he called or not was unimportant. Her grandmother, though, continued to pursue the subject.

'I know he has business at Duffields and I thought you might wish to accompany him and choose some new reading for yourself.'

She didn't bother to disagree. Her grandmother obviously wanted her to take a walk with Sir Peregrine and, since she felt guilty at upsetting Brielle so badly, she was more than willing to go. She was even persuaded to wear the bronze-and-green walking dress that became her so well and to allow Miss Repton to dress her hair. She was determined to make it up to her grandmother in whatever way she could, short of consorting with Rufus Glyde.

When she returned to the drawing room, Sir Peregrine was already there, discussing with her grandmother the weather prospects for the next few days.

'Lady Blandford holds her open-air ridotto the day after tomorrow, but the omens are not good. It's said that the Blandfords have spent huge sums on the party. No doubt an attempt to launch the youngest girl in some style—a nice enough girl, but rather too plain to take, I fear.'

'It will need more than a ridotto to launch Georgiana Blandford successfully,' her grandmother was saying caustically as she entered the room.

'Miss Silverdale—' Perry Latham leapt to his feet '—allow me,' and he drew out a chair for her, smiling deferentially as she took the seat. 'Lady St Clair tells me that you have been slightly unwell. I hope you are now fully recovered.'

'I am well, Sir Peregrine, but thank you for your concern,' she answered tranquilly.

'You've been missed, let me tell you. You have been constantly looked for. Your army of admirers will be delighted to see you return to our midst.'

'You were talking of a ridotto, I believe,' she said to deflect the conversation away from herself. 'That sounds exotic.'

'Not so exotic, I fear, if we do indeed suffer the thunderstorms that are threatened. But I don't wish to put you off—I hope you will come.'

Her grandmother looked meaningfully at her. 'We have received our invitations.'

'Of course we shall come,' Amelie said quickly 'but perhaps take our umbrellas.'

Brielle relaxed and Sir Peregrine smiled with pleasure. 'We shouldn't need them this morning in any event. I hope you will feel able to accompany me to Duffields Library, Miss Silverdale?'

'That would be most enjoyable—it's time I explored the shop,' she lied glibly. 'I understand that you've already selected your volumes.'

'I'm most excited about them. I've ordered them especially from London—they are serious histories of this part of the country and one in particular is lavishly illustrated. If you are interested, I would be most happy to loan the books.'

'That is kind of you.'

'Perhaps you had better start for the library or they will be closed for luncheon,' Brielle reminded him. He looked a little concerned and rose quickly from his chair before he remembered his manners.

'When it is convenient with Miss Silverdale, of course.'

'I'm ready to leave now. I'll fetch my bonnet and gloves.'

Walking through the Sydney Gardens brought back some uncomfortable memories. Had it only been a few days ago that she'd met Gareth here and he'd said those fateful words about needing her to trust him, about wanting to tell her something that might change her feelings towards him? In the event, he had not told her anything—someone else had, and what she'd discovered had shaken the foundations of her world.

They threaded their way through the park and Sir Peregrine continued gallantly to make conversation. She felt sorry for him, trying so hard to entertain a companion whose thoughts were far away. When she looked up, she saw that he'd led them to the small summerhouse in which she and Fanny had taken shelter, the place she'd had her last meeting with Gareth.

Her instinct was to flee from the spot, but instead she asked with only a slight tremor, 'Sir Peregrine, why are we here? I thought we were making haste to Duffields.'

'You must forgive my little deception, Miss Silverdale. We will, of course, go to the library but I was hoping to have a few words with you in private and I thought this would be a perfect setting. I know how much you like it.'

She wondered fleetingly how he could have got things so wrong, but it was his desire for a private interview that gave her greatest pause. Before she had time to question, he had begun on what was obviously a well-honed speech.

'Miss Silverdale…Amelie, I would like you to know how much I honour and respect you. These last few weeks your company has given me so much pleasure. It is not too much to say that you have transformed my life. Meeting you has given me a second chance of happiness.'

She looked alarmed and held up her hand as if to stop him, but he was now well and truly embarked on his address and he was going to finish come what may.

'I said I respected you, Miss Silverdale, but my feelings run far deeper than this. I truly love you, Amelie, and I ask you to do me the honour of becoming my wife.'

She was stunned into silence and he went on quickly, 'In case you think that your grandmother would not approve of my having spoken, I have confided my feelings to her, and she has given me permission to address you.'

So this was the reason for Brielle's cryptic comment that an early marriage would be the most satisfactory outcome: she'd decided that it was time for Perry to declare himself. He was looking at her beseechingly. She felt sorry for him and angry with her grandmother for her interference.

'Sir Peregrine,' she managed, 'I am greatly honoured that you wish to marry me. I esteem your good opinion very highly. You are a true and dear friend, but I fear that is all. I regret that I cannot accept your kind offer.'

He looked crestfallen. 'Perhaps I have been too precipitate,' he suggested. 'You may want time to think it over and I am more than happy to wait.'

'No, Sir Peregrine, it's only fair to tell you that I'm quite sure of my decision. I need no further time. I esteem you as a friend, but I'm not in search of a husband.'

'I see. I was led to believe that perhaps you would not be averse to marriage.'

'Then I regret that you've been misled.' She saw his face fall further. 'I hope that we can still continue to be friends. I wouldn't wish this uncomfortable situation to make that impossible.'

She held out her gloved hand to him and he took it rather limply.

'Of course, Miss Silverdale, I shall always be your friend,' he murmured chivalrously, looking abjectly into the distance.

'Shall we continue to Duffields,' she suggested gently, 'or would you prefer to abandon our visit?'

'No, no, naturally we will continue.'

'I'm sure you're eagerly awaited. The shop must be looking forward to showing you the volumes they've managed to obtain.'

For the first time in the interview his face relaxed a little. 'By Jove, yes,' he exclaimed. 'I'd almost forgotten them.'

She took his arm and they once more moved off, this time towards the delicate wrought-iron gates that led them out of the gardens. His step had a slight spring in it now and by dint of talking to him about the publications he'd ordered and getting him to describe them in every particular, they managed to arrive at the library with Sir Peregrine in unusually good spirits for a man whose marriage proposal had just been rejected. In her desire to comfort him, she had for the moment forgotten her own plight.

Once in the shop he made haste to the counter and was soon lost in the new treasure awaiting him. She left him to his reading and began to wander around the shelves, listlessly picking up and putting down books without any real interest or intention of borrowing them. She drifted towards the back of the library where the shelves were even higher and the tomes even more dusty. A large volume bound in dark brown calf took her eye. The gold lettering seemed to leap out of the battered cover as though the title were intent on seeking attention. She lifted the book from the shelf better to decipher the words on its spine and found herself looking through the empty space at a face she knew well. In a second, Gareth Wendover had walked quickly around the end of the bookcase and was at her side.

'I've visited every shop in Bath these last few days, trying to find you,' he began abruptly. 'Where have you been hiding?'

'I've been indisposed.' The bald statement hid an avalanche of pain.

'And are you fully recovered?'

It was unlikely she thought that she would ever recover, but she answered in a toneless voice, 'Thank you, Mr Wendover, I am well.'

'I wanted to find you,' he repeated urgently. 'I never finished what I had to say.'

'There really is no need.'

'I think there is. Let me speak. I'll be brief.'

'There's no need, I tell you,' she said with anguish. 'I already know what you're about to say.'

'How can that be?'

'Others have told me.'

'Others? What others?'

She didn't answer.

His brow furrowed. 'Glyde? Was it Glyde?'

She nodded silently, a miserable expression on her face. The furrow deepened. 'How did he know I was in Bath?'

'He saw you as we were driving back into town a few days ago and was kind enough to apprise me of your history.'

'What exactly did he say?'

'Do you really want to hear?'

'Yes, I imagine his account differs markedly from mine,' he said curtly.

'He said you were a card thief—a card sharp, I think he called it—who preyed on naive people and made your living by taking their money. He said that you worked on the Continent usually, but hadn't been successful lately, so you've returned to England to try your luck here.' Her voice was dead and her eyes opaque. She could hardly bear to hear what she was saying.

He reached out and took her hands. They felt ice cold through her light gloves. 'Let me tell you the truth,' he urged.

'Truth? You once told me that my relationship with the truth was slippery. Yours, I think, does not exist. Spare me any more lies!'

With a sharp jerk she snatched back her hands just as Perry Latham came into view. He had been lost in the dream of his new acquisitions, but suddenly remembered that he was escorting a lady and one he had just asked to marry. He came bustling up to them, raising his hat to Gareth whom he vaguely remembered.

'Your servant, sir. Miss Silverdale, I am so sorry I abandoned you. Call it the excitement of an enthusiast. I can't wait to show you the books that have arrived. They are truly magnificent. I know you will be as entranced as I am.' He fairly danced with pleasure.

'Books!' Gareth growled.

'On the history of this area. Priceless volumes. Don't tell me that you are an amateur historian, too?'

Gareth's face was a mixture of astonishment and rage. He wheeled around to face Amelie. 'I can't talk to you here. Come with me.'

And without a further word he grabbed her arm and pulled her through the shop, leaving Sir Peregrine to gape helplessly after them. Once outside, he hailed a passing hansom and bundled them both inside. It was all too reminiscent of a previous journey she'd taken with him.

'How dare you kidnap me in this way!' she protested.

'I need to be alone with you.' With that he pulled down the blinds on the cab windows and commanded the jarvey to drive on.

'Where to, mister?'

'Anywhere, drive in circles if you wish, just leave us to be private,' he said abruptly.

'I geddit.' The jarvey gave a low whistle.

Incensed, Amelie made to open the cab door, but before she could jump to freedom, they'd jolted forwards and were bowling along the cobbles at some speed. He steadied her with one hand and turned to face her.

'You must listen to me, Amelie. Whatever Glyde told you has to be a distorted version of what happened. Give me the chance to tell you my story.'

'It would seem I have no option,' she returned, and stared rigidly ahead.

She'd spent fruitless hours trying to hate him, remembering

every slight she'd suffered, every insult, every mockery. She'd told herself again and again that for all his charm he was as untrustworthy as any man and worse, guilty of a low crime for which he'd been justly punished. Pure chance had brought him into her life and now the dice had rolled once more and chance was setting her free. But try as she might, she could not forget him, let alone hate him. He was always there, always with her wherever she went, catching at her heart at each and every unexpected moment.

Undaunted by her silence, he began to relate the events of that long-ago evening. She listened to him, at first smarting and angry at being kept against her will, but then with growing concern as a very different account emerged from the shadows. Imperceptibly, her heart began to lighten; she wanted so badly to believe him.

'Why would Glyde have marked the cards?' she asked guardedly. 'What was in it for him?'

He shook his head. 'I've no idea. He must have known that I had little money and Lucas not much more. Petersham is a very wealthy man, of course, and as for the General, I imagine he's reasonably well-breeched. But to risk a thing like that makes no sense.'

'And to accuse you? That makes no sense either.' Maybe, she mused, it didn't have to make sense. Glyde was simply a vicious man.

As if to echo her thoughts, Gareth said, 'Lucas insists he did it out of malice, that he resented me for having what he didn't—a loving family and a promising future.'

'And do you agree?'

He shook his head again. 'I can't think a man like Glyde would care a jot about family and as for a golden future, his own was secure enough. It was an excessive thing to do out of spite. He didn't even know me well.'

'If it was spite, he was successful.' She reached out for his hand and gripped it very hard.

Gareth's expression was bleak. 'My grandfather disowned me on the spot and we remained unreconciled. Whatever Glyde's motives, he ensured that I lost everything.'

Her lovely face was alight with warm solicitude. 'And you've never tried to clear your name?' she prompted.

'A small matter of how,' he said grimly, 'without money, friends or influence. Glyde, on the other hand, was rich and well respected, if not greatly liked. I had not a shred of evidence against him.'

'Is that still the case?'

'Evidence? No, none.'

'But you have friends—Lord Avery for instance. And you appear now to be in better circumstances.'

He looked at her sharply, but then relaxed. She could have no inkling of his changed position.

'Let's say that I've come to a point in my life where it's immaterial to me whether society believes my story or not.'

'So why tell me?' she asked gently.

'I need *you* to believe, to trust me sufficiently that you'll heed my warning. Glyde will not easily give up his pursuit. He's a ruthless man and so steeped in vanity that he'll go to any lengths to achieve his goal.'

Amelie snuggled closer, a happy curve to her lips. Her heart was singing. Gareth had faced scorn, faced shame, in order to warn her and keep her safe—he must truly love her!

'I will be doubly on my guard,' she said at last, 'but I've always known that beneath his mask Sir Rufus was a vile creature.'

'It seems that others do not—unfortunately those who should protect and care for you.'

'I'm lucky, then, that they don't include you. If indeed you do care for me,' she ventured, catching her breath a little and blushing at her boldness.

He did not answer immediately and when he did it was to say obliquely, 'You could wreak havoc on my life, Amelie, and I on yours. But I'll not let that happen.'

His reply left her hot with embarrassment at having once more exposed herself so baldly. How stupid she was! Of course he didn't care for her, at least not enough. She was more to him perhaps than the women who'd previously skimmed the surface of his life, but she was not the anchor that would bring him home for ever. Well, she had her pride; she would take his warning and expect nothing else. He need not fear she would hang on his shoulder.

Silence descended. He sat unseeing and grim faced, a lock of hair shadowing his set expression. She sensed he was waiting for her to speak, but she felt too mortified to utter a word, and the silence between them gradually built in intensity. So intense it could shatter the carriage walls, she thought. But then he was turning to her, slowly, almost unwillingly, a storm-tossed question on his lips. 'You do believe me?'

The urgency in his voice made her look up and she found her eyes caught and held by his gaze. The unexpected longing that she saw there shocked her.

Stunned by the well of emotion she'd glimpsed, she tried for a light reply. 'Would you prefer I believe Rufus Glyde?'

But lightness was not what he was seeking. He pulled her roughly towards him. 'Don't ever say that name again in my hearing!'

Held tightly against his chest, she felt the magical warmth of his body begin to weave its spell once more; her doubts were stifled, her hurts submerged. Shyly she put up her face to his, aching for his touch. It was not long in coming. In a moment more she was in his arms and he was smothering her face with kisses, his breath warming her skin. Then his mouth was on hers, hard and demanding.

Even as she opened her lips to him, he knew that he should stop. He'd told her what he'd needed to say and she'd believed him. That was all that mattered. There could never be anything more between them. He did not belong in her world, nor she in his; they were always destined to journey apart.

Her mouth was soft and inviting beneath his and he could not bring himself to break away. His lips sought hers more and more urgently. He needed to taste her, all of her. He slid the loose sleeves of her dress down, exposing her shoulders to his kiss, his mouth working its way towards the soft swell of her breasts. His lips lit a fire in her. She was breathing quickly and he had an unbearable urge to make her his if only for this time. He must fight it, but she was matching him kiss for kiss; she was stroking his body until it was burning out of his control. He laid her down on the seat and she moaned with pleasure as he began to move against her. He would allow himself this one moment; he would take the memory with him and cherish it.

Suddenly the carriage came to a juddering halt and their entwined bodies were forcibly parted. There was loud shouting coming from close by. Dazed, they scrambled to their feet and Gareth carefully inched the blind upwards. A scene of carnage greeted him.

'There's been some kind of accident,' he said, still breathing hard. 'There's a large crowd milling about and people shouting at each other.'

She swiftly put her dress to rights and joined him at the small pane of exposed glass. They were at a crossroads and an over-turned cart blocked the road opposite. Scattered sacks of potatoes bore witness to a collision and loud accusations of blame rent the air. She was alarmed at the number of people standing so close to the cab. At any time someone might notice them at the window or might even choose to open the door. She could not afford to be recognised.

'I must go,' she gasped. 'If someone sees me and tells my grandmother…'

'Your grandmother knows of me?'

'Glyde has told her and she's warned me that I must never see you again. If I disobey, she'll send me back to my father.'

'Then you must go. We should say our goodbyes now, Amelie.'

Still drifting on a hazy cloud of love, she was shaken from her dream by this splinter of ice.

'But why, why must we say goodbye?'

'I'll be gone from Bath very soon and we're unlikely to meet again,' he replied tautly.

'But—'

'Don't make it more difficult,' he ground out. 'This has to be. You know my story now—convince your grandmother of its truth and she'll send Glyde packing. Then you can look forward to a peaceful future. I have no part in that.'

His face was an expressionless blank and she felt like hitting him very hard. How could he be so obtuse? Whatever he was, whatever life he led, she was now a part of it. Glyde's shocking intelligence had forced her to confront her deepest and truest emotions. Even when she'd thought Gareth a cheat and a liar, she'd loved him, longed for him.

An idea flashed into her head. It was daring and dangerous, but it was what she wanted most in the world.

'Come to me tomorrow,' she said and her voice was clear and joyful. 'Meet me behind the Abbey after the lunchtime service. I'll be on my own—Grandmama attends the Catholic Church early in the morning.'

He shook his head. 'We cannot continue to meet, Amelie.'

'Come to me,' she pleaded again urgently.

He knew he must remain adamant. He must say goodbye for ever, right here, right now. He looked at her glowing loveliness and felt a wild confusion of tenderness and desire wash over him.

'I should not. We should not.'

'Come!' she beseeched.

At last he said, 'I'll be there,' and his voice was thick with emotion.

He held her fingers to his lips for an instant and then she was slipping swiftly out of the carriage door, facing away from the mayhem. They had stopped near Pulteney Bridge, a walk of only a few minutes to Laura Place, and she hurriedly began to make for home. Before Perry had a chance to speak to her grandmother, she needed to concoct an explanation for her sudden disappearance. Stopping for a moment, she glanced back at the crossroads where an angry crowd of people were still spilling across the road.

'Such a shame you had your carriage ride curtailed,' a cold, reedy voice sounded behind her.

She wheeled around. Rufus Glyde blocked the pavement, a contemptuous sneer on his face. But where had he come from?

He must have taken to tracking her through the town! She shivered inwardly at the thought of this base creature dogging her footsteps.

'I cannot think why you should choose to travel in such a disreputable conveyance,' he continued, gesturing in disgust at the distant hansom. 'And with the blinds closed!'

'I don't understand you, Sir Rufus.' She felt her stomach clench.

'Do you not? I believe I spoke in English. You alighted just now from a hansom cab, eccentric behaviour in itself, but with the blinds down? My dear!'

She flushed involuntarily, but her gaze did not waver even as he taunted, 'You are surely not bored already with the delights of Bath? Or was the view inside your carriage particularly enthralling?'

'Your remarks are offensive, sir. Allow me to pass, if you please.'

'Not so fast. I have, after all, a vested interest in your conduct.'

'On the contrary, my conduct has nothing whatsoever to do with you.'

'There we must disagree, yet again.' He sighed softly, but his face was alight with malice. 'I consider myself your affianced husband, you know, barring the formal announcement, and as such I have every right to concern myself with your activities.'

'You will never, ever be my husband,' she rejoined wearily. 'Please accept my decision and let me alone.'

'You are very wrong, my dear. I shall be your husband and soon.'

She shook her head with impatience and he said sourly, 'Let

us have no more of this nonsense. You will do as I require. If you think to make a fool of me, you had better think again.'

'Only you can make a fool of yourself, sir. Now let me pass.'

'You will show me respect whether you like it or not. I have only to tell your grandmother that you are still consorting with a known criminal, and she will shower me with blessings if I still agree to marry you.'

'You may tell her what you wish. I have no fear of you or your threats.'

'I think you will find you will be very afraid. I shall do more than tell your grandmother of this incident. I will make sure that I publish your loose conduct far and wide. Your disgrace will soon be circulating way beyond Bath—it will make you the talk of London society.'

'I have little interest in what society says of me. Publish all you wish,' she threw at him belligerently.

'You may find that your interest quickens however, my dear Miss Silverdale, when your grandmother ejects you from her house and the rest of your family shuns you in disgust. Where will you go? Who will you find shelter with? Not a pretty future, is it?'

'I think I can endure it,' she said lightly and slipped past his outstretched hand to continue her journey home.

Glyde looked after her and snarled. He could not understand why she despised his threats. What could be lending her the strength to flout him? But that could not continue. If he was unable to intimidate her by menace or blackmail, he would do so by force.

Unaware of the cauldron of anger that she'd stoked, she walked away with a smile on her face. Glyde was a repugnant creature and it had cost her dear to maintain her equanimity in the face of his threats. But throughout the ordeal she'd held tight to the magnificent idea that had come to her as she left Gareth. A hansom cab ride had changed everything. It had begun with her believing that she'd given her heart away to a man incapable of caring deeply, but ended with a revelation: that profound flash of feeling that she'd surprised. She'd known then that she was loved and that was sufficient.

She believed Gareth innocent of any wrongdoing and willed the world to believe it, too. Yet it was clear that he no longer cared for society's judgement. His mind was made up and she would not seek to persuade him differently. He was determined to leave England and she was equally determined to leave with him. She would be ruined in the eyes of the world, but no more so than if Glyde made good his threats.

From childhood she'd set her face against marrying, her mother's fate hovering always before her. But she'd known that in reality she would be forced eventually to conform; the best she could hope was to be tied to a dull, well-meaning suitor such as Sir Peregrine. Yet her whole being cried out to live life large, to live for passion. How splendid, then, to follow her destiny with the man she desired and to do so on equal terms. She would go with Gareth to the Continent and share the rigours of his life, travel where he travelled, sleep where he slept. She had no illusions. His way of life was transient and insecure and their future together might prove the same. Poverty imposed its own tunes and desire could become blunted. But whatever dangers she faced, she would be fully alive at last. Tomorrow when they met, she would tell him her plans.

Chapter Ten

She awoke to a joyous morning—in just one day her life had been transformed. Though her head had acknowledged the likely truth of Glyde's accusations, her heart had always told a different tale. Now head and heart were one. Tomorrow she and Gareth would be together, friends, companions, lovers, for as long as he wanted her; she'd discovered the freedom she'd been seeking ever since her escape from Grosvenor Square.

Brielle did not appear at the breakfast table that Sunday morning. She was still suffering from a chill contracted a few days previously and sent a message to say that she would keep to her bed for most of the day. She would take tea with Amelie after her granddaughter had returned from church. Amelie was relieved. There was no possibility now of an accidental meeting with her grandmother while she was hurrying to the tryst she'd arranged.

Fanny was to accompany her to the Abbey and would have to be told of the appointment with Gareth, but she was sure that she could persuade her loyal maid to keep silent. It would be unfair to involve her any further. Whatever plans she and Gareth made that morning would be known only to the two of them. 'The two of them'—the phrase had a magnificent ring to it. He would be bound to oppose her wish to go with him to France and would paint in vivid colours the evils of permanent exclusion from polite society. But in the end he would capitulate. She would persuade him that a life lived with him was all she desired—and she knew just how to persuade him. He wouldn't hold out for long.

Her stomach churned with excitement and she ate little of the lavish breakfast that Horrocks served. Impatient to be gone, she slipped out of the front door as soon as the clock struck twelve and was soon walking briskly to the Abbey with Fanny in tow. She would wait until after the service before she revealed the meeting she'd planned. It was pointless to worry her maid before it was necessary. The weather had changed dramatically today and the sun now hid itself behind dark scudding clouds, but she was in no way downcast by the lowering skies. She bubbled with an inner joy.

As they approached the pathway leading to the Abbey's impressive front entrance, she paused for a moment at the lych gate. A few paces away a carriage was drawn up at the side of the road. It had a strange, solitary air about it. No one was in sight and horses and carriage seemed to have been abandoned. It struck her as odd. Normally residents walked to the Abbey for Sunday services or, if they were driven, their carriage was ordered to return for them at the appointed hour. She remarked on the waiting coach to her companion.

'It must belong to old Mrs Warrinder,' Fanny suggested. 'She hates to be kept waiting and never allows her carriage to return home.'

Amelie nodded and promptly lost interest, walking quickly along the paved way and in through the Abbey's main door. The church was full, as it was on most Sundays. Visitors and residents alike enjoyed the sensation of attending a service in such ancient precincts. The opportunity to show off one's finery and the chance to glimpse new arrivals in town was an added pleasure. She glanced briefly around the congregation and at first recognised no one. But when she looked again, she saw Perry Latham sitting in the shadow beneath the pulpit and carefully avoided him, making her way to a pew at the back of the church. He'd not visited Laura Place since she'd left him at Duffields and she had still to offer him an explanation for her abrupt departure. But this morning she couldn't afford to be delayed by conversation with anyone. Once the service had finished, she would have to make good her escape before he could catch up with her.

The well-remembered hymns and prayers proceeded at a leisurely pace. She heard hardly a word, making the responses automatically with her mind elsewhere. Surreptitiously, she looked at her pocket watch. In just over half an hour she would be seeing the man she loved, and for the first time they would be meeting as equals, all deception past. Then the rector was giving the final blessing and the congregation knelt for a last prayer. As soon as she felt she could, she got to her feet and made swiftly for the door. Fanny had to scramble up unceremoniously and move at a trot in order to keep up with her mistress. They both shook hands briefly with the rector, who was waiting at the door to greet his parishioners, but they did not dally. A quick smile and a nod and they were through the church porch.

'Why such a rush, Miss Amelie? You mustn't worry about milady, you know. I'm sure she'll be better soon.'

'I'm sure she will, too. Forgive me for hurrying you so, Fanny. It's not my grandmother I'm thinking of. I have an appointment to get to and I don't want to be late.'

'An appointment? Where? Who with, miss?'

'An appointment with Mr Wendover.'

Fanny drew her breath in and said with decision, 'I don't think you should go, miss. That man is trouble if ever I saw it.'

'Nonsense. This is a business arrangement only. I shan't keep you long. I need to see Mr Wendover for just a few minutes and then we'll be on our way home. You may walk round the churchyard while we talk.'

'Would your grandmother like you to be meeting him?' Fanny asked feebly. She had a lively apprehension of what Brielle's reaction would be and who would most likely be held responsible for Amelie's rashness.

'My grandmother need never know. If you don't wish to be involved, I'll understand. I'm going to meet Mr Wendover—you can come with me or not, as you please.'

'Miss Amelie, you know I would follow you anywhere, it's just…'

Suddenly her words died in the air. Two burly men had leapt from the coach they'd noticed earlier, and blocked their path. The women looked startled, but before either could make any move to escape, the men had scooped Amelie up and thrown her through the open door of the carriage. Fanny dashed after her, trying to hold on to her arm, but one of the men turned back and cuffed the maid soundly around the head. She fell to the ground, momentarily senseless. In a second, the horses had been whipped up and the coach was disappearing along the street.

'Fanny? It is Fanny, isn't it?' A kind voice sounded in the maid's ear. 'Are you all right? You look terrible.'

It was Sir Peregrine Latham. He bent solicitously over the girl and tried unsuccessfully to drag her to her feet.

'My mistress,' Fanny whispered urgently, 'Miss Amelie…'

'What about Miss Amelie?' Perry demanded. 'Where is she?

I was trying to catch her up to have a word, but you both left the Abbey so quickly that I lost sight of you.'

The maid sat up groggily. She was shaking now, hardly able to speak. 'My mistress,' she moaned, 'those men have kidnapped her.'

'What men? Are you sure, Fanny? You're probably suffering from concussion—you must have hurt your head when you fell.'

She looked blankly up at Perry, who was still bending anxiously over her. 'They hit me around the head and then I fell.'

'Hit you around the head? In Bath, in broad daylight and on a Sunday? Surely not!'

She nodded in a bewildered fashion while Sir Peregrine struggled to understand what had happened. 'Who are these men? Who could be guilty of such barbarism?'

At this a jumble of disjointed words gushed forth from the tearful Fanny. 'I don't know, I don't know. They were waiting… My mistress and I were passing a carriage and they sprang out and grabbed her and I tried to hold on to her, but the one with the crooked teeth turned round and hit me round the head and I wasn't able to hang on any more, and now they've taken her.'

She collapsed back on the pavement, sobbing violently. Sir Peregrine began to feel extremely agitated. He was not sure whether this poor maidservant was deluded or telling him some monstrous truth. And he had no idea how to cope with a woman deluged in tears. He was very worried that she would succumb to hysterics any moment now. It was obviously time to be decisive.

'We must return to Laura Place, Fanny, and tell Lady St Clair what has happened.'

'But my mistress…' Fanny moaned.

'Yes, yes,' Perry said soothingly. 'Her ladyship will know what to do, I'm sure.' His voice carried a certainty that he was far from feeling.

It was a matter of moments before they arrived back at Brielle's house. With encouragement from Sir Peregrine, Fanny haltingly told her tale. Brielle looked first astonished and then infuriated.

'What nonsense is this that you're telling me, girl?'

The maid looked crestfallen and ready to burst into tears again. Perry Latham thought it prudent to intervene.

'My lady, the girl is speaking the truth when she says she was attacked. I found her lying on the pavement, clearly having been injured in the head.'

'And why should that mean she has been attacked? She could have tripped. This girl has a history of not telling the truth. I have never found her to be wholly dependable.' She bent a basilisk stare on the unfortunate maidservant.

'But, Lady St Clair, your granddaughter is missing,' Perry pleaded. 'She has vanished into thin air.'

The stare became more pronounced, 'And where, Fanny, is my granddaughter precisely?'

'I don't know, milady,' she sniffled. 'Miss Amelie was took. I couldn't stop them.'

'Are you expecting me to believe that my granddaughter was abducted in broad daylight?'

'Yes, ma'am,' Fanny asserted, her voice trembling a little.

'As she came out of church?'

'Yes, ma'am.'

'Ridiculous,' Brielle pronounced. 'And who do you suggest is responsible for this outrage?' Her dawning fear was making her more imperious than ever.

'I think I recognised one of the men,' Fanny managed. 'He had crooked teeth.'

'Yes...' Brielle prompted crossly.

'He was at the picnic Miss Amelie went to.'

'What picnic?'

'The one at Severn Abbey. The one organised by Sir Rufus Glyde, ma'am. He was one of Sir Rufus's men, I'm sure.'

'Are you suggesting, you stupid girl, that Sir Rufus Glyde, a respected peer of the realm, has abducted my granddaughter? How dare you! If it were not so laughable, it would be a shocking accusation.'

Fanny hung her head. 'Miss Amelie was very afraid of him,' she muttered defiantly. 'She was scared he would force her to marry him.'

Sir Peregrine had listened to this interchange in growing bewilderment. The idea that Amelie might be forced to marry a man she feared, and that this man had been responsible for her disappearance, seemed to him something out of one of the local legends he so eagerly devoured rather than anything approaching real life.

'Sir Peregrine, will you put a stop to this nonsense once and for all. Please call at Sir Rufus Glyde's lodgings and ascertain his whereabouts. I'm sure we will find that he is as ignorant as we are of Amelie's plight. In the meantime I will send Horrocks and the footman to make other enquiries. I'm sure there must be a rational explanation for my granddaughter's disappearance and—' she favoured the maid with a contemptuous glare '—for this girl's sudden malady.' Inwardly, though, she had begun to feel very uneasy.

* * *

Sir Peregrine was not long in returning. His face was grave as he entered the room.

'I regret to tell you, Lady St Clair, that Sir Rufus left his lodgings this morning. Apparently, he quitted his rooms quite suddenly. The landlord was given no notice of his departure and…' Perry coughed delicately '…I understand there is a considerable amount of rent owing.'

'I cannot believe that of a gentleman such as Sir Rufus.' Brielle looked ashen. 'I'm sure if we can discover where he's gone, he will be able to tell us something of Amelie or at least reassure us that he has had no part in her disappearance.'

'As to that, the landlord naturally has no idea where Sir Rufus might be.'

'And you?' Brielle looked painfully at her young friend.

'I regret, my lady, that my acquaintance with him is of the slightest.'

A soft tap sounded at the door. The butler had returned from his mission and came quickly to the point. Neither he nor Thomas had been able to find any trace of the young mistress. The rector remembered a girl who matched her description leaving the Abbey at the end of the service, but after that the trail had gone cold.

When Horrocks had bowed himself out, Brielle rose with unaccustomed difficulty from her chair and began slowly to pace the room.

'Who on earth can we turn to in this predicament? Who is likely to know where Sir Rufus would go? Who can we trust?'

There was no answer from her small audience. Suddenly she turned on Fanny.

'Sir Peregrine said that you were lying on the pavement beyond the Abbey. You must therefore have been walking away from the church. Why was your mistress heading in the opposite direction to her home?'

The maid swallowed hard, but did not reply.

'Come, girl, the truth, if you care anything for her.'

Fanny's voice was barely a whisper. 'She said that she had a business meeting, milady.'

'What do you mean, a business meeting? What has business to do with Amelie? Who was this person she was meeting and why?'

Fanny saw no escape from the question. 'I don't know why she was meeting him, milady,' she stuttered. 'Miss Amelie didn't tell me, but it was a man called Gareth Wendover.'

The name galvanised Brielle and she rushed over to the girl, and shook her violently.

'You allowed your mistress to meet that man? A man she was expressly forbidden to see?'

Sir Peregrine intervened in his quiet voice. 'I don't think we can blame Fanny, my lady. I know she would only have gone with her mistress to protect her.'

Fanny nodded gratefully while Sir Peregrine continued thoughtfully, 'I'm sure she knows as little as I do about this man. I have met him on a few occasions. A somewhat fierce person, I thought, but nevertheless decidedly a gentleman.'

He turned to the maid. 'Where was this meeting to take place, Fanny?' he asked her gently.

'Behind the Abbey, Sir Peregrine, I believe. I was to walk around the churchyard. Miss Amelie said she would only be a few minutes.'

'Then we must go there and find this man immediately. He may know more than we,' Brielle declared, invigorated now that she could take some action. 'Sir Peregrine, would you be so good as to assist in this?'

With an inward sigh, Perry Latham agreed and once more hurried from the house. It was beginning to be a somewhat energetic day.

Gareth arrived early at their meeting place, knowing he shouldn't have agreed to the stolen encounter. He had needed to tell Amelie the truth of his past, needed to be sure that she understood the full evil that was Glyde. But once she'd heard his story, he'd vowed that he would bid her a final goodbye. Why had he been unable to keep that vow?

Ever since he'd met her, he'd been acting irrationally. How could a slip of a girl do that to him? He'd never felt love for a woman, but that had been no hardship. Exiled from home and country, he'd been swift to put on the armour of indifference. An unsettled existence roaming Europe demanded nothing emotionally. But then Amelie had erupted into his life. He'd felt an immediate attraction, seeing her pirouetting uncertainly above him on that ridiculous rope, the chestnut locks framing her beautiful heart-shaped face. He'd been drunk, but not so drunk that he hadn't realised the pearl he'd stumbled on.

Since then he'd fought a constant battle with himself. Over and over again he'd argued the stupidity of a serious involvement with any woman, least of all with this green girl, and by dint of concentrating on her deceptions, her lies, he'd thought he'd managed to keep her from invading his heart. But it seemed that the heart wasn't interested in this tired ploy; it had its own ways to follow.

Sitting close in that musty cab, watching her beautiful face alight with happiness, and feeling her soft hair against his cheek, he'd been overwhelmed not only with desire, but something more, something deeper. He'd been unable to resist the urge to hold her, to caress and be caressed, to give himself to her body and soul. To take with him that one moment of love—yes, love. He'd been crazy; it should not have happened.

And here he was foolishly meeting her again, but this time there must be no repeat of yesterday's lovemaking. He could never offer her the marriage she deserved; even as the rightful earl, the taint of scandal would follow him wherever he walked and he could not bear to expose her to the venom of a spiteful society. She would say she cared nothing for her peers' judgement, but in time she would come to. They were destined always to travel different paths. His bags lay half-packed at Lucas's house: that was his future. Hers was the sensible marriage and no doubt Sir Peregrine Latham was being groomed at this moment for the role of husband. As for Rufus Glyde, he would cease to be a threat once Amelie's engagement to another was announced.

He made himself as inconspicuous as possible while he waited for the end of the service. The patch of grass where he loitered was shaded by overhanging trees from the churchyard and he was able to watch people coming and going without himself being seen. For some time there was little activity, but then the Abbey bells rang out and churchgoers began to saunter past in twos and threes. He felt a rising impatience to see her. He tried to remind himself that they had only a few hours left to them, but all he could think of was forbidden delights: to touch her, smell her, taste her again.

Time moved on and still Amelie did not come. He began to wonder if she were unwell or perhaps had been forcibly stopped from keeping the appointment. Perhaps her grandmother had discovered their intended meeting and kept her at home. The minutes ticked by. Surely, though, she would have sent an emissary to tell him if she'd been prevented from coming. That maid of hers, Fanny, was a devoted servant. She would have found a way of slipping out of the house and letting him know what had happened.

He stopped his pacing for a moment. She might have decided not to come. She might have thought better of it. In the fervour of their encounter yesterday she'd appeared to believe his account of that night at Watier's. But recalling their conversation word for word, he realised that she'd never actually committed herself. She'd pushed his direct question to one side. What if she'd had second thoughts once she was back in the quiet of her own room? Perhaps she was uncertain that this was finally the truth. After all, he'd consistently lied to her or at least avoided being honest. She might imagine that this story was yet another deception. She would think that the heat of the moment had deceived her and, now in the coldness of a new day, she would doubt. And doubting, she would not come.

Or perhaps this had always been her plan. The monstrous thought struck him off balance, apprehension turning to anger. She'd never had any intention of meeting him today; she'd meant him to wait fruitlessly. She'd enjoyed the physical pleasure he offered, but she didn't trust him. She didn't love him. He was the deceiver and always would be. This was her final riposte: she'd decided that she would be the one to practise the last deception.

That was the explanation, he was sure now. Why had he ever imagined otherwise? Amelie Silverdale was no different from any other woman he'd ever met. They'd shared a fleeting passion and that was all. He turned to go, disgusted with himself that even for a short time he'd thought he could know love. As he walked towards the corner of the street, a now familiar figure came into view. Of course, Peregrine Latham, her chosen go-between, he thought bitterly.

Perry Latham raised his hat and looked uncertainly at the glowering man in front of him.

'Mr Wendover, do excuse me for accosting you in this way,' he began with a worried look on his face, 'but would you be so good as to accompany me to the house of Lady St Clair?'

'Why on earth should I?' Gareth asked belligerently.

'Her ladyship is most anxious to speak with you,' Perry said in his most placating manner.

'But I'm not anxious to speak to her ladyship. I've nothing to say to her,' Gareth growled. Not only was he to be made a fool of by his false love, but he was to receive a raking-down from her grandmother.

Perry tried again. 'Lady St Clair is most worried about her granddaughter and feels that you may be able to help. I hope you will reconsider your decision.'

'Worried—why is she worried?' Gareth was seized with sudden foreboding.

Sir Peregrine answered repressively, 'That is something I cannot discuss in the street. If you will be so good as to accompany me, we can speak of the matter in private.'

'Has something happened to Amelie?'

'If you would come with me, Mr Wendover?'

'What's happened to Amelie?' Gareth rasped out, grabbing the other man by the coat lapels and nearly lifting him off his feet.

'I beg you, sir,' Perry gasped, 'let me go. All will be explained.'

Gareth reluctantly released his hold. All thoughts of Amelie's supposed treachery fled from his mind. She was in trouble and he must get to her.

Brielle looked long at the man who was ushered into her drawing room. He was lean and tanned and his dark hair fell carelessly over eyes that were as blue as a summer sky. At the moment they were blazing with a mixture of anger and alarm. As a woman Brielle could appreciate why her granddaughter had proved so wayward, but as a grandmother she recognised danger when she saw it. This man had no time for social niceties, she could tell—he was a soldier of fortune, a vagabond.

She wore her most haughty expression, but Gareth met her with an equal disdain. Neither cared for the other, but both were united in their desperate concern for Amelie.

'What do you know of Rufus Glyde?' she began.

'He's a villain,' Gareth replied shortly.

'You are entitled to your opinion,' Brielle conceded, even now finding it difficult to accept that she had been so badly mistaken in the man. 'But I meant—what do you know of his habits? Where might he go if he left Bath suddenly?'

'What is this about?' Gareth asked bluntly. 'I'm here because something has happened to Amelie, not to discuss a blackguard such as Glyde. What trouble is she in? I need to know.'

Once more it was Perry Latham who intervened at a difficult moment.

'We very much fear that Miss Silverdale has been abducted, and possibly by this man Glyde.'

'What!' Gareth's voice exploded in their ears. 'And you're sitting here doing nothing!'

Sir Peregrine glanced at Brielle, but she remained bolt upright in her chair, her lips firmly compressed. 'Her ladyship hoped that you might know where this man could have taken her,' he explained tentatively.

Gareth regained something of his calm. Now was not the time for outrage. He needed to be in control of himself, to think rationally and to think fast.

'Glyde has a country estate some thirty miles from Bath,' he said curtly. 'That would seem a likely destination. Do you know what he was driving?'

'Fanny described a coach and pair.'

'Hardly designed for a lengthy journey, so I doubt he has decided to go out of the county.'

Brielle turned to Gareth and her voice shook very slightly. 'Do you have any idea of why he should do such a dreadful thing?'

'His threats against Amelie haven't worked,' he said roughly. 'Your granddaughter is a spirited woman. That would be intolerable to a man like Glyde. My guess would be that his abduction is a way of punishing her and making sure he wins in any contest of wills.'

Brielle wrung her hands and suddenly looked a very old lady; he felt a slight stirring of compassion.

'I will find her,' he promised and his voice held absolute conviction. 'I'll travel on horseback—that way I can ride cross-country and get there quicker. Time will be of the essence,' he ended grimly.

Brielle nodded, her face a study of wretchedness, understanding his meaning only too well. She came forwards and shook his hand.

'Mr Wendover, if you can rescue this dear child I will be for ever in your debt.'

'I have no need of gratitude, my lady. I do this as much for me as for you.'

He walked swiftly to the door and was gone. Sir Peregrine, who had been hovering by the window, felt it an opportune moment to escape. He preferred his dramas to be safely confined within the covers of a book.

Left alone, Brielle sank into her chair, exhausted and sick with fear. She had believed Gareth Wendover when he'd pledged himself to find Amelie. Despite what she knew of his reputation, she had instinctively trusted him. But he did not know the local country well and he was just one man. It was clear that Glyde had hired a team of thugs to do his bidding. What if Gareth never found her or, having found her, was overpowered, which seemed more than likely? She could not bear to contemplate what might happen to her beloved girl. And she, Brielle, would be responsible. She had promoted the pretensions of a man who had turned out to be a scoundrel. How could she have fallen into such gross error? She had always felt pride in her judgement, but now she would never trust herself again. And Amelie, all the time in this very house, fearful and alone, not daring to tell her grandmother of the threats against her. The tears began to trickle down Brielle's cheeks and she put her head in her hands and sobbed.

She was not allowed to indulge her grief for long. A diplomatic tap on the door by Horrocks heralded another visitor, and one who could not have been less welcome.

'Lord Miles Silverdale, milady,' the butler announced.

'How good to see you, Brielle.' Lord Silverdale's hearty voice sundered what little peace was left. He seemed to fill her dainty drawing room with his presence and she was forced to her feet, offering him a feeble smile as he came towards her.

'Miles, what a surprise! Whatever brings you to Bath?' she asked somewhat inanely.

He looked nonplussed for a moment. 'Amelie, of course. My daughter? I need to see her. She is here, I take it?'

Brielle made a brave attempt to mask her discomfort. 'I hope to see her soon,' she extemporised.

'When exactly?' he sounded agitated. 'I've urgent business with her. I've been travelling since dawn to get here.'

For the first time Brielle regarded her son-in-law closely and saw that he was looking tired and travel-stained.

'I'm so sorry, Miles, you must be fatigued,' she prevaricated. 'Where are my brains wandering? I must order refreshments to be brought and have a room made up immediately.'

'Yes, yes,' he said testily, 'but Amelie—when will she be back?'

'Why is it so urgent to see her?' Brielle parried.

It was his turn now to look uncomfortable. He shifted uneasily on his feet and fixed his gaze on the far wall. 'You might as well know, Brielle, I've been a damned fool. The man I was intent on her marrying has turned out to be a complete blackguard.'

'Sir Rufus Glyde?'

'Yes, Rufus Glyde. The man is a very devil. He has deliberately set out to ruin this family!'

He began pacing jerkily up and down the room, evidently labouring under a great upswell of emotion. Hoping to calm the situation, Brielle gestured to him to sit down beside her.

'He started with Robert, you know,' he blurted out, then trying to compose his voice, 'gradually drew him into gambling well beyond his means—truth to tell, the boy needed little encourage-ment—but until he met Glyde the sums he wagered were within reason. Since then he has become more and more reckless. I've had to sell just about every piece of property we've ever owned to cover the boy's debts. The last straw was the mortgage on Grosvenor Square.'

Brielle said nothing, but took his hand. He looked tired and defeated. 'I believed in Glyde,' he continued. 'I thought that if he married Amelie, the family would be saved. And she would have a secure future.'

'And now?'

'Robert came to me late last night. For once he wasn't drunk and he hadn't been gambling. He told me a dreadful tale. A young friend of his had blown his brains out. Just twenty-two. Such a tragic waste. He owed money to Glyde and Glyde was threatening to foreclose on his parents' property.'

Brielle could not speak. This was the monster who had taken Amelie. She hoped desperately that the story was false or at least exaggerated.

'Could there have been any mistake?'

'No mistake, I'm afraid. Robert said that as soon as the suicide became known, half a dozen other young men came forwards with similar stories. They'd gambled with Glyde, lost heavily and been encouraged to pledge more and more until they were ruined. Glyde would make sure they paid up—his threats were taken seriously.'

'And nobody realised what was happening?'

'Not until now. The young men—boys, really—were reluctant to publish their troubles.'

'How dreadful,' Brielle said faintly.

'Dreadful indeed. It was the shock of losing his friend that gave Robert the courage to tell me last night just how badly things have gone with him. It is worse even than I knew. There's nothing I can do about the money or the estate—the Silverdales are ruined. But I can prevent another of my children becoming Glyde's victim.'

Miles opened his arms as if to plead for absolution. 'I've been so stupid. I knew that Glyde had followed Amelie to Bath and I hoped she would get to know him better here and be more willing to contemplate marriage to him. That's why I left her with you.'

'It didn't make her any more willing. She hated Glyde and has continued to hate him despite every effort he's made to attract her.'

'Thank God for that.'

'Don't be too thankful,' Brielle said with difficulty. 'I fear that Sir Rufus Glyde has lived up to his reputation.'

'What do you mean?'

'I hardly know how to tell you. Glyde has abducted Amelie.'

'Abducted!' Miles Silverdale's voice reverberated around the room, making the crystal decanters on the sideboard tremble.

'If you please, Miles, we must be as calm as we can.'

'Calm! How can I stay calm when you tell me my own daughter has been abducted and by this villain? When did this dreadful thing happen?'

'This morning. Amelie attended the lunchtime service at the Abbey and Glyde's men swooped on her as she walked away from the church.'

'And what has been done to get her back? Have Bow Street been alerted?' His face had turned a bright red as he once more began furiously to pace the carpet.

'You really must seek to compose yourself, Miles, or you will become ill. I am trying to find Glyde privately. Calling in the Runners would lead to a scandal that neither of us would want.'

'But how are you trying to find them?' Miles Silverdale was almost pulling at his usually sleek silver hair. 'Can you trust the servants you've sent?'

'I haven't sent servants. A man called Gareth Wendover has gone. He knows where Glyde's country estate is situated. He is a friend of Amelie's.' She passed over this quickly, hoping he would not enquire too deeply.

'I've never heard of him. What do you know of this man?'

'Little except that Amelie trusts him and he is intent on finding Glyde and bringing her safely home.'

'And meanwhile we are to sit here and wait like clunches.'

'What else do you suggest we do?' his mother-in-law asked, an irascible edge to her voice. Her nerves were overwrought and the constant effort of appearing self-possessed was beginning to take its toll.

Miles pulled himself together. 'You're right of course. It wouldn't be sensible to career around the countryside looking for this wretch. We can only pray that this Wendover fellow runs him to ground. If he rescues my girl, he will have deserved the highest reward—though God knows I have nothing left to give him.'

Brielle thought otherwise, but decided to keep her counsel.

Chapter Eleven

It seemed as though she were emerging from a pitch-black tunnel. The echo of far-off sounds filled her ears, but she could see nothing. A suffocating darkness enclosed her. Her breath came in short, sharp gasps.

Now the tunnel was expanding and the darkness was not so opaque. There seemed to be a slight chink of light in the distance. She opened her eyes a fraction and pain arrowed through her head. In response, her eyelids quickly shut and she drifted back into a black haze.

When she tried to look again, she was sure that she could see sunlight. Her head was heavy and throbbing and seemed detached from the rest of her limbs. Minutes ticked by and gradually her body began to come back to life. She stretched out her hands and realised that she was lying on a bed. A shaft of light lay brightly across the faded counterpane. Cautiously she turned her head and saw the sun streaming through dusty, mullioned windows. She turned her head in the other direction and this time the shape of a door swam into her vision. She felt wretchedly sick.

There was a bitter taste filling her mouth, which she couldn't understand. Her throat felt raw. She puzzled over this for some time and gradually her mind began to recall incidents, voices, actions. She'd been in a coach, she remembered, and her arm was hurting badly. She tried desperately to focus her wandering mind, to piece together the fragments of memory. She'd been in a coach, against her will—yes, that was it, someone had thrown her into the coach and she'd hurt her arm. A large, rough hand was covering her mouth. She'd struggled, she'd bitten that hand and freed herself. But not for long. Her head was being jerked back. What then? A hot, evil-tasting liquid was forced between her lips—she'd been drugged! Two men there'd been, nasty and brutish. She'd recognised one of them from somewhere. And Fanny had cried out. Fanny, where was Fanny?

And where was she? Gingerly she tried to raise herself into a sitting position, but instantly fell back onto the bed. The walls were moving in disturbing circles. After a while she tried again and saw that she was in a large room, wainscoted with dark oak panelling. Heavy Jacobean furniture filled the chamber, sombre and intricately carved. The bed she lay on was massive, the bedstead as black as jet. Leaded windows filled the entire side of a wall, diamond-shaped panes giving on to tall trees that swayed in the wind. Their branches scratched against the glass. She was in an old house and in the countryside, but whose house and where remained a mystery.

She lay back on the pillow and tried to concentrate her mind, but it wasn't easy. Waves of nausea constantly engulfed her. She'd been with Fanny, she remembered, they'd been walking along the pavement, just past the Abbey. They'd been to Sunday service and were going to…meet Gareth, she finished in a rush. She'd been going to meet Gareth when two men had jumped down from the coach she'd seen earlier, scooped her up and thrown her into the carriage and driven off at high speed. She'd struggled, but it was hopeless. She'd been forced to swallow the drugged liquid and she'd known no more. Until now.

She sat up groggily, then very slowly swung her feet to the ground. So far, so good. She tried to stand, holding on to the bed for support, but was forced to sit down again as the floor spiralled up to meet her. Allowing herself a short rest, she once again tried to stand. She had to get out of this house, wherever it was. She had to get back to Bath and find Gareth.

He would think she'd failed their appointment, that she was no truer than any other women he'd met. He would not wait long before deciding that he was wasting his time. His eyes had spoken a depth of feeling that had taken her breath away. But she knew him well enough to realise that if he thought himself rejected, he would cloak his emotions in ice. He would cut his losses there and then and start immediately on his journey. She had to get to him before he left Bath.

Dragging herself up to a standing position, she shuffled very slowly to the door. She tugged at the handle, a huge, plaited-iron circle, but the door did not budge. Slowly she inched her way in the other direction towards the windows. Looking through the dusty panes, she saw that she'd been right: she was in the country. Rolling hills were the backdrop for what appeared to be a neglected park. The grass almost reached the window sill and ragged bushes ranged far into the distance. The room had an air of neglect and the grounds of the house were no better.

If she could just open one of the windows, she might be able to climb over the sill. She fumbled with the latch, but it was stiff with rust and appeared to be jammed. As she struggled with it, the door of the room opened. She turned quickly, too quickly. Head spinning, she clung to the window seat to prevent herself from falling. She looked at the man framed in the doorway. She had always known who it would be, of course. Rufus Glyde. It could be no other.

'I'm delighted to see you on your feet, my dear. You have a strong constitution, which is most gratifying.' In the gloom of the doorway, his thin mouth was like a knife slash across the white face.

She tried to speak with authority, but her mouth was dry and her voice came out in a hoarse whisper. 'You are a villain, sir, to serve me thus.'

'A villain? Quite possibly, although I have been called worse.'

'You have drugged me, kidnapped me and now I am imprisoned.'

'Yes, all those things. But it will get better, I promise.' His thin face broke into a mirthless smile.

'Let me go immediately!' she demanded in as strong a voice as she could manage.

'I don't think so, not immediately. What would be the point of all the hard work in bringing you here? There is some business outstanding between us and we must first attend to that.'

'What possible purpose can you have in locking me up here?'

'I warned you, did I not, that you would bend to my will?' His cold voice slid icily through her consciousness. 'My purpose is to ensure that you do just that. Really quite simple.'

'And what is your will, pray?'

'I think you know very well, Miss Silverdale. By the way, do tell me when you think I may call you Amelie. Miss Silverdale is a trifle formal, I feel, for what lies ahead of us.'

'If you're referring to marriage, you must surely know that I will never agree.'

'Indeed I do.' He sighed with tedium. 'However, I regret that I must disappoint you a little. I find I am no longer desirous of marrying, or at least not just yet, so perhaps we should not be too previous.'

'Then why am I here?'

'So that we can become more closely acquainted. What else? And what better place to get to know each other intimately? No one lives within ten miles of this house and there is no staff to speak of. Only your two gallant companions of the coach and they, of course, do my bidding like the faithful dogs they are. We shall be completely alone. Won't that be pleasant? Just the two of us, getting to know each other.' His voice jeered, and a wave of revulsion broke over her.

He looked at her face, which had grown even paler as he spoke. 'But you must not despair, Miss Silverdale. Not entirely. I may still discuss marriage at a later date. We shall just have to see how you please me.'

She said nothing and he continued, his voice now harsh and peremptory, 'And you *will* please me, you know. You are completely at my disposal.'

She sank back on to the window seat. Her body was weak, but her mind was racing. Let him but go and she would try the window once more. Ten miles was a long way, but if she could once reach the road, she might garner help from a passing traveller.

He seemed to know exactly what she was thinking. 'I do hope you won't try to escape.' His voice was languid but its arctic menace was clear. 'It would be so tiresome. As you've already discovered, the windows are bolted and the door securely fastened. You will remain locked in this room and whenever you leave it, for whatever purpose, you will be accompanied. I shall leave you now. You will find hot water by the dressing table and fresh apparel in the wardrobe. I wish you to wear the dress I have selected for you.'

Despite her weakness, Amelie felt her temper rising. 'My own clothes are sufficient, I thank you,' she exclaimed.

'Perhaps I did not make myself clear. You will do as I command. Your own clothes are no longer fit to be seen.' And he gestured with distaste at her dusty skirt and torn bodice.

'And who is responsible for that?' she demanded angrily. 'The men you employ are thugs.'

'Regrettably so, but very efficient, would you not say? I'm sure you will find the clothes I have provided more than ample recompense. You will put them on and wait to be fetched for dinner.'

Her heart lurched. Might this provide her with an opportunity for escape? The relentless voice told her otherwise.

'So far you have been treated with restraint, but if you should attempt to escape or resist in any way, you will be bound closely. Do I make myself clear?'

She made no sign that she had heard his words as he went out of the door, locking it noisily behind him. Once he had gone, she sat for a long time looking into nothingness. She would not weep. Somehow she must find a way to escape this evil man. She dared not think of the threats he had made. Instead, she must concentrate on getting away, but her spirits faltered as she looked at the locked door and the bolted windows. The sun had disappeared over the horizon and a cold darkness had stealthily encroached on the room, finding a cheerless echo in her heart.

Once he'd left Brielle's house, Gareth moved rapidly. He went first to the livery stables and ordered them to saddle their fastest mare as quickly as possible. His urgent tone sent the usually sleepy ostlers scurrying to do his behest. From the livery stables he hurriedly retraced his steps along the main thoroughfare towards the Averys' house. The family was visiting friends and he was relieved to find only the servants at home. No time would be lost trying to explain the situation. He dashed off a brief note to his friend and left it with the footman to give Lucas immediately when he returned. Then up to the bedroom two stairs at a time and a rapid change into riding breeches and topboots, headlong down the staircase once more and quickly back to the stables.

The head lad was fastening the last buckles on the harness as Gareth walked through the gate. Minerva stood waiting, her legs twitching with anticipation and her head jerking up and down as if to shake off the bridle and be gone. He was in the saddle and away within minutes.

The location of Guestling Manor, Glyde's country estate, was already known to him. Just last night Lucas had related the latest *on dit* from town, now going the rounds of Bath. It was said that Sir Rufus Glyde's affairs were not flourishing and he would very soon be putting his country estate up for sale. It was generally held that he'd be lucky to find a purchaser. The mansion was old and dilapidated and its surrounding park untamed. It would require a mountain of money to make any improvement and was, in any case, not large enough for the needs of a gentleman and his family. It was large enough to conceal a prisoner though, Gareth thought grimly.

He was soon out of the environs of Bath, making for the country roads beyond. Almost immediately Minerva fell into an easy stride that seemed to devour the miles effortlessly. But Gareth did not relax for they had far to travel and the time was short. The image of Amelie, bewildered and frightened and in Glyde's power, tormented him and he was tempted to spur the horse forwards in a headlong gallop. But he knew he had to save her strength for the cross-country riding, which would soon be upon them. He felt the mare trembling with excitement, eager to speed like the wind, but reined her in and forced her to maintain a slower pace. The hedgerows were ablaze with pale gold honey-suckle and the scarlet of poppies newly opened, but he saw none of it.

Amelie was the picture that filled his mind. He knew she would fight with every breath in her body, but how could she successfully defend herself, a vulnerable girl held prisoner in a hostile place? He could only guess what Glyde intended towards her and none of it was good. Back there in Brielle's genteel salon, that scoundrel's name had sent his mind blazing, hot enough to set the room on fire. He'd been overwhelmed with the need to choke the life out of a man who sowed wickedness wherever he went. Such bloodthirsty ferocity was new to him. As a young man, wandering Europe friendless and penniless, he would have given his soul to wreak revenge on the man he suspected had authored his downfall. But he'd lacked the power to do so; all his energy and ingenuity had been employed in simply keeping alive.

His situation today was very different and he might have avenged his injuries any time since he returned to England. Yet he hadn't done so. He hadn't wanted to soil his sword on such a contemptible creature, but in truth he no longer cared enough. He believed Glyde responsible for sending him into exile, but it was exile from a society he despised; responsible for severing the ties to his family, but his grandfather had proved cold and unforgiving. Was avenging such wrongs worth more scandal and possible death? He'd considered not. But now it was no longer just about him; it was about a girl who'd lodged herself deep within his heart. His face hardened into an expressionless mask as he considered the revenge he would exact.

And he would exact revenge. He'd insisted to Lucas that he knew nothing of love, unwilling to acknowledge the powerful feelings Amelie had stirred in him from the very beginning. It had been easier to concentrate on her shortcomings. He'd taken refuge in anger at her deception. He'd pretended that they shared only a physical passion, which would burn itself out as quickly as it had ignited. But in the end he'd failed to subdue the emotions shaking him to the core. If he'd ever doubted that he knew the meaning of love, it had been put to flight the instant he'd realised she was in such desperate peril.

He would rescue her or die in the attempt. He would bring her safely back to Bath and to those who should have the greatest care of her. She would, must, find happiness in a match deemed suitable by her family; for all his title and wealth, that could never be him. It was ironic that after all the years of uncaring liaisons with women of the *demi-monde*, he should have finally fallen in love with a virtuous daughter of *ton* society.

He'd had a taste of that society as he'd stood in the doorway of Watier's salon. He would not be ignored—his inheritance would make sure of that—but he would attract the worst kind of attention. For himself, it mattered not a fig, but for Amelie… Confronted by the whispers, the nudges, the nuanced glances, she would die a thousand deaths. She would trust him to defend her and he would be unable. He loved her too much to put her through that. No, she was destined to be another man's bride and when he found her it would be to say a last farewell.

His mind thus occupied, he rode onwards, hardly conscious of time passing. The going was easy at this stage, the country lane soft underfoot. For the first hour, he made excellent time but just outside the village of Marksbury he received a check. Precious minutes were wasted at the toll where the keeper had absented himself. Gareth was forced to bribe a small boy to go and find him. After what seemed a lifetime, the guardian of the tollgate returned, very much the worse for drink, and was only persuaded to allow Gareth through by another hefty bribe. It was fortunate that only that morning he'd withdrawn a large sum of money in anticipation of his journey to France.

The experience of Marksbury decided him to avoid the toll roads and begin to travel cross-country where possible. The young boy had described a short cut through Witham Woods, which lay ahead and to one side, its eastern border running parallel to the toll road. The sky had gradually been clearing and the afternoon become hot, but the woods were blissfully cool. Strong branches reached skywards, interlocking overhead to form a shadowy vault, hardly pierced by the sun. The mare showed her appreciation of this welcome change of temperature by a willingness to pick up speed once more, but again Gareth reined her in. The forest floor was uneven; dead branches were strewn here and there and tree roots erupted haphazardly through the soil. The path, pleasant though it was, meant potential danger. Whatever happened he had to keep the horse in good shape.

From Witham Woods he took the path that skirted the southern end of a lake. Once past this large expanse of water, the countryside opened up and he could at last allow the horse an unrestrained gallop. Pounding over the soft turf, he was able to make up the minutes forfeited earlier at the tollgate. And even when the open country was left behind, he continued to make good time, speeding through leafy lanes and along rough tracks.

Candlelight began to appear in the few lonely cottages he passed, but still he travelled on, never slackening his pace.

The last rays of the sun had created shaded folds in the patchwork of surrounding hills. It was a beautiful evening, breezy but warm, and the pink tinged clouds that streaked across the wide sky promised another fine day on the morrow. But he was too anxious to care much for nature. A dilapidated signpost warned him that the manor house was still some five miles distant. He had to get there before nightfall. A moon gently climbing into the sky offered little help, its light diffused and pallid behind the scudding clouds. The thought of Amelie in Glyde's power as night came close was unbearable. Once more he spurred Minerva onwards, whispering in her ear to make one last effort. She whinnied softly in response, and though her breath was beginning to come short and fast, she redoubled her pace. They were back now in open country and leaning low over her neck, he urged her to a last gallop. The miles once again flashed by. The mare was almost spent when the rusting iron gates of Guestling Manor at last came into view. They were locked and barred, but an overgrown screen of dark ilex surrounded the property. Gareth sidled the horse along the hedge and very soon found a small gap. He pushed the horse swiftly through and prayed he was not too late.

Reluctantly, Amelie took the gown from the wardrobe. It was an elaborately embroidered silk gauze and the diaphanous folds billowed over her arms. A very expensive dress, she thought, its amber sheen lustrous and its beadwork intricate. But when she slipped it over her head and viewed herself in the tarnished mirror, she hated what she saw. The sheer material and the low-cut neckline made her feel horribly exposed and she looked in vain for a handkerchief to cover her breasts as they surged above the plunging bodice. Eventually she tugged a faded cloth from the small table, which stood nearby, and fastened it around her shoulders. It made her feel considerably braver. The shoes she was forced to wear were as flimsy as the dress, and would surely make any chance of escape impossible. She saw with satisfaction that her face was chalk-white and made even paler by the deep gold of the gown. Her hair was left tumbled and unkempt. She aimed to be the least attractive of dinner companions.

She had only just finished dressing when the ancient lock once more ground into action and one of her erstwhile captors stood on the threshold.

'Come with me,' he ordered abruptly and seized her by the arm, dragging her out of the room and along a maze of flagged passages. Small, cell-like doors dotted the stone walls, but appeared to lead nowhere. There was no other sign of human life. They seemed to walk for ever, the man striding ahead and dragging her roughly behind him. It took all of her strength to remain on her feet. She had completely lost her bearings by the time he arrived at a door that was more imposing and less dilapidated than the rest.

The man's knock was discreet, a surprise given his general brutishness. But she imagined that Glyde was an unpleasant master to serve and his hired hand would want to be as inconspicuous as possible.

'Come!' The thin tone rose clear in the air and she shivered. She could never hear Glyde's voice without feeling an upsurge of disgust.

She was pushed unceremoniously into the room and the door locked behind her. The furnishings here were slightly more comfortable, but the room still bore all the signs of prolonged neglect.

The brocade curtains, once a deep sapphire, now hung greyly at spotted windows, their fraying material incubating layers of dust. The *chaise-longue* beside the window had lost most of its gold embellishment and the two wing chairs that guarded either side of the fireplace had sunken seats and stained coverlets. Someone had attempted to polish the large rectangular table that dominated the middle of the room. Its surface reflected the light of a wrought-iron chandelier hanging above, also newly cleaned, it seemed. The table was set for two.

Glyde was lolling at his ease in one of the massive carved chairs drawn up to the table, but as she stood wavering in the doorway, he rose in a leisurely fashion and moved towards her. With a twitch of his hand he tore the material from around her shoulders and cast it on the floor.

'Allow me to see just what my very considerable efforts have purchased,' he sneered.

For what seemed minutes on end, he stared lustfully at her, his sulphurous eyes undressing her inch by inch. She could do nothing but stand and endure his gaze. Then reluctantly he stepped back, waving a negligent hand at her as he returned to his seat.

'Come to the table, Miss Silverdale. You must be hungry after the exertions of the day.'

She'd never felt less like eating, but she feared that he would return to her side if she did not obey. She could not bear him anywhere near. She moved slowly towards the end of the table and sat down. Glyde had evidently been drinking while he waited. His face was already slightly mottled and drops of red wine stained the frilled white shirt that he wore beneath a suit of rich ruby velvet. He saw the direction of her glance.

'Don't worry, my dear. I've merely been filling in time until you got here. No more wine this evening—at least not for me.

I need no Dutch courage.' He smirked unpleasantly. 'But allow me to pour *you* some. You will undoubtedly find it beneficial. Such an excellent relaxant.'

'I thank you, no.'

'You will drink some wine. It is my wish.'

He said it with a finality that brooked no argument. Before she had time to realise what was happening, he was at her shoulder and filling her glass to the brim.

'Now drink,' he ordered.

She did as she was told, but tried to sip as small an amount as possible. Satisfied that he was being obeyed, he resumed his chair and reached for the tattered bell pull. Its noisy clang echoed through the passageways beyond. Almost immediately, the man who had brought her to the room appeared in the doorway. He carried large bowls of soup and was followed by a companion bearing the remaining entrées, the man with the crooked teeth.

'This is most pleasant,' Glyde murmured expansively as he sipped from the bowl in front of him. 'The moment has been so very long in coming. But triumph is even sweeter when it is hard won.'

She didn't answer, but played with her spoon, pretending to consume the soup while in reality watchful and alert, hoping for a chance to escape. She'd noted that this time the door behind her had not been locked. It was possible that Glyde's two henchmen were lurking just beyond, but she reasoned they would have to return to the distant kitchen after each course to collect the next serving. For a few minutes at least the door would be unguarded. If only she'd not been forced to wear these stupid shoes! Perhaps she could slip them off under the table without being noticed. She hoped Glyde might forget his vow and begin drinking again. She needed him torpid and lacking in vigilance.

When the next course arrived, though, it was brought by just one man. Where was his companion? She could not be sure and if she made a dash for the door and he was on the other side, she would have lost any chance of escape. Her fate would almost certainly be another drugging, only this time when she awoke she would find herself securely bound.

Serving followed serving and there was never more than one man in the room at any time. She felt bitterly disappointed.

Glyde read her mind with uncanny ease. 'Escape is impossible. You might as well sit back, my dear, and enjoy the evening. For my part I can assure you of many hours of future pleasure.' He leered hungrily across the table, but almost immediately recovered himself and continued smoothly, 'The food, for instance, is in a class of its own. Naturally not cooked by the clods who have served it, but produced by the very finest chef that my money can buy.'

She wondered, but only for a moment, whether the chef was still on the premises and, if so, whether she would be able to appeal to him for help.

'Of course he isn't here now,' Glyde said, reading her mind once more. 'As I told you, there is just Amer and Figgis—yes, they do have names—and myself. A cosy little foursome, don't you think? Though naturally Amer and Figgis will be absenting themselves very shortly.'

She tried to eat slowly and delay each round of food as it came to the table. He saw through the ploy immediately.

'I have all the time in the world, Miss Silverdale. Do please savour your food. I like that in a woman. It suggests appetite.'

She continued to eat at the same pace, trying to maintain an air of indifference. His face, scored by the gash of his thin mouth, broke into the familiar icy smile.

'The longer the meal, the greater the anticipation and the more satisfying the finale. Do you not agree?'

All too soon the fruit was removed and coffee served. She was allowed to decline the liqueur, which Glyde tossed off in one gulp. He nodded sharply at his two henchmen, who were clearing the last vestiges of the meal, and they disappeared promptly. The occasional noises emanating from the passage gradually ceased.

Glyde strolled to the door and turned the heavy rusting key. He returned to his chair and leaned back with a cruel smile on his face. She cast around for ways of deflecting him, anything that would win her freedom.

'Sir Rufus,' she ventured, 'my grandmother is a wealthy woman. She would come to an accommodation with you—you have only to say the word.'

His face wore an expression of incredulity. 'You foolish chit, I do not desire money. Money is mine whenever I wish,' he boasted. 'What I require is a far rarer prize, as you well know. Spare me the play-acting. After all, you are hardly an innocent.'

'You have been misinformed. I am a virtuous woman.'

He scanned her cynically. 'As you wish, my dear. Your recent conduct would suggest otherwise. The man in question is fortunate to be many miles away, else I would have ordered his disposal. Chastity is not a requirement of mine—virginal pleasures in my experience are much overrated—but when I make a woman mine, that is how she will stay.'

He gestured to her. 'Come here to me, Amelie.'

She made no move.

'Now,' he barked, 'unless you wish me to come and drag you here.'

She got up and walked with as much dignity as she could

summon to stand in front of him. He pulled her down roughly onto his lap, his eyes devouring her greedily.

'You are very beautiful, Amelie, and you are now mine—mine as and when I desire. You will stay with me here until I have finished with you. If you entertain me well, I may consider renewing my proposal of marriage.'

One hand fitted itself around her waist while the other stroked her hair. She was overcome with nausea and fervently hoped that she might be sick over him.

'However, if you do not please me, you will be sent back to your family,' he continued impassively. 'They may do as they wish with you though their options will be severely limited. Damaged goods are so difficult to sell. And the family home will be no more. I will be forced to foreclose on the mortgage. Dear, dear, let us hope that it will not come to that.'

She remained immobile, dazed by his depravity, while he held her tightly against his chest. Her body was rigid, withdrawn into itself in a desperate attempt to avoid contamination. He began stroking the inside of her arm and crooning to himself. It was too much. She leapt to her feet and ran across the room to the window.

'Of course,' he jeered, 'I must not forget how young you are. Naturally you want to make it a little more exciting. I'm only too willing to oblige.'

And he was there beside her, grabbing her round the waist again, only this time managing to encircle her whole body with his arms and pulling her tight against him. His shirt smelt of wine and his breath on her bare skin was noxious. She tried to escape his grasp, but this only caused him to tighten it still further.

His right arm imprisoned her, holding her so that her face was buried in his chest and she could hardly breathe. With the other hand he began caressing the soft cream of her shoulders. She cried out in disgust, but this seemed only to excite him further. He pulled at her dress, trying to untie the ribbons single-handed. Taking advantage of his preoccupation, she managed to tear herself away. But not for long. He came after her immediately.

This time she had fled to the corner of the room nearest the door in a vain attempt to effect an escape. But there was no help from that quarter—the door was impenetrable. She was fighting for breath and knew she would not be able to hold off her abductor for much longer. A vision of Gareth, sparkling blue eyes and mocking smile, sprang improbably to her mind. She clung to it as though it would somehow save her. But how could that be? It was a figment, a phantom only. By now he would be well on his way to France, unknowing and perhaps uncaring of her fate.

Glyde was advancing on her once more, incensed now by her recalcitrance, and tore at her dress, exposing her breasts to view. For a moment he stood back, examining her with a salacious intensity as she cowered partly naked against the wall. Then he threw himself at her, hoisting her skirt upwards while he fumbled urgently with his breeches. She knew that he would have no compunction. He would rape her, here in this dreadful room. She closed her eyes, trying to abstract her mind from the frightful deed that was to be perpetrated on her.

A loud crash sounded from across the room. Then suddenly all was changed. There was a whirl of movement, a muttered curse from Glyde, and she was left alone, her hands trembling and scrabbling to cover her nakedness. An intruder had smashed his way through one of the leaded windows and stood brandishing two swords. One he retained in his right hand while the other he threw to Glyde, who caught it awkwardly. The man waited for his adversary to regain his balance. Glyde, deliberately ignoring the courtesy of touching swords, lunged without warning at the stranger, attempting to catch him off guard as the man's eyes adjusted to the lighted room. In response the intruder cut the chandelier cord and brought it tumbling down on to the table, the small crystals tinkling eerily as they shattered. The only light was that of the moon, now floating free of its cloudy coverlet, and streaming through the open casement. The two men faced each other.

Chapter Twelve

Glittering moonlight flooded through the window pane, lighting the centre of the room like a stage complete with its actors. The two figures circled each other cautiously for some minutes, their swords disengaged. Then Glyde, impatient to free himself of this unwanted visitor, delivered a lightning strike. In return he was parried gracefully. He lunged again and was once more deftly countered. Over and over again he pressed forwards, often seeming to be on the point of breaking through the other man's guard, but miraculously his opponent always regained his position, meeting Glyde's blade with steel.

In one of the pools of darkness that filled the corners of the room Amelie stood, hardly daring to breathe. She had snatched a cloth from a side table and wrapped it around herself to conceal her torn dress. Her lips were parted and her eyes wide. She had recognised Gareth instantly, a phantom miraculously made flesh. He had found her! How he'd done so, she had no inkling. It was enough that he had found her. He was here and fighting for her life, and for his: a darting force, lithe and nimble, biding his time, waiting to make a kill. She saw his eyes aglow with the primitive joy of revenge.

The fight went on, their blades clashing harshly in the silence of the room. Glyde continued to attack fiercely, but his opponent was able to parry the blows with ease. Gradually the younger man began to gain ground, his thrusting sword pushing Glyde back farther and farther. It seemed he would pin his adversary to the wall. Then, in a sudden violent movement, Glyde gathered all his strength into the riposte and with his whole body weight lunged straight at his opponent's chest. Gareth stepped back as quickly as he could, but the blade caught him on the arm and ripped the sleeve of his shirt. A trickle of blood seeped through the white cambric and began to drip on to the floor.

Amelie's eyes closed in horror, but when she looked again she saw that Gareth had managed to steady himself. Tight-lipped and with a deep furrow scarring his brow, he had recovered his ground. He began to fight more defensively, hoping that an opportunity would occur that would enable him to snake below his enemy's guard. Sensing his advantage, Glyde continued to assail his opponent savagely, strike after strike. At any moment Amelie expected to hear the dull thud of her lover's body falling to the floor. A dozen times he might have been run through, but he always managed to block the attack, disengage his blade and return to the fray. He was tiring, though. The loss of blood was taking its toll and he was no longer as nimble on his feet nor was his swordplay as sharp as it had been. Every fresh charge from Glyde tired him further. His face had turned ashen and his breathing was laboured.

Glyde's face wore a devilish expression. Once more he drove forwards ferociously, intent on making an end of it. But with an almost superhuman effort, Gareth blocked the blow and with a supple flick of his wrist twisted his sword in a rapid half-circle and slid smoothly under his opponent's guard. Glyde's sword hand wavered and he staggered back. With a mighty slash, Gareth struck the weapon from his hand and directed the point of his own blade to the other man's throat.

'Villain, I have you.' He was breathing raggedly, but his voice rippled with triumph.

In a moment he had staunched his bleeding with a tightly bound strip from his shirt sleeve. The fallen man, his face whiter than ever, snarled defiance. With the point of his sword Gareth pricked the skin of his enemy's neck and brought a pinhead of blood to the surface.

'If you wish to live, you will do as you are told.' He looked down commandingly on the prostrate figure.

'And what might that be?' Glyde spat out, infuriated by the ignominy of his position.

'You will grovel to Miss Silverdale for the torment you've inflicted and then tell her exactly what happened on the night you say I cheated at cards.'

Glyde, his head awkwardly angled away from the sword point, looked contemptuous. 'I will not grovel. Naturally as a *gentleman*, I apologise to Miss Silverdale for any misunderstanding.'

Gareth's expression remained one of iron control, but his sword hand gripped the weapon ever more tightly.

'You are a cur and I would whip you if *I* were not a gentleman!'

Unperturbed by Gareth's disdain, the fallen man sneered. 'A somewhat besmirched gentleman, however. You will never free yourself of that particular stain, I fancy.'

The sword quivered and the gash on Glyde's neck grew redder. 'You mistake—you are about to free me from the lies I've lived with for so long.'

'How very dramatic. But hardly likely.' Glyde's smirk became more pronounced even as the wound in his neck began to bleed freely.

Gareth ignored him and continued in a voice that was icily indifferent. 'You will recount the circumstances of that evening and you will do it truly. If not, I can assure you that you will feel more than the tip of my sword.'

His implacability seemed to affect his enemy more than any show of anger. The man glared at him, his face sullen and set.

'I must first ask you to remove your weapon from my throat. It is hardly conducive to talking.'

Gareth reluctantly withdrew the point of his sword a little, but still held its position fast.

'You have it. Now talk.'

'What am I to say? It was an evening like any other. I was engaged to dine with Petersham and we wandered into the Great-Go to make up a table with the General and whoever else was in the mind for a little light gambling.'

'Hardly light, as I recall.'

'Not for a Johnny Raw, that's true. It was unfortunate for me that you and your friend Avery, such an innocent, should happen to arrive at that moment. I would have preferred a plumper bird for the plucking.'

'That was your purpose for the evening?'

'I had some debts that were becoming a little pressing.'

'And you decided to pay them by cheating those you played with.'

'Not entirely, but the cards fell badly for me that night. I really had no choice.'

'So you marked the cards?'

'A very little, just sufficiently for me to recognise the ones I needed.'

'And when it was discovered?'

'I was amazed. Tilney spotted it. His eyesight must be a good deal sharper than his brain. Nobody else at the table had a clue. Petersham is so indolent that he hardly looks at the cards. And so disgustingly rich, that the result of a game matters nothing to him.'

'When General Tilney alerted the table to the cheating, you didn't own up.'

'Are you mad?' Glyde's voice was waspish with irritation. 'Of course I did not "own up." One would think I was some cadet on probation.'

'But you had no compunction in implicating me.' Gareth's hand quivered on his sword, but, controlling his fury, he kept the point just short of Glyde's throat. He was finding that after all such gross treachery roused an incendiary rage.

'None whatsoever. Striplings who think they are old enough to play with the grown-ups get all they deserve.'

'You must have known that I had little money of my own.'

'That's what made it so perfect. I saw in a moment that you were the one who would shoulder the blame. The General was out of the question, Petersham's too rich and as for Lucas Avery, everyone knew that his trustees were liberal to the point of insanity and would pay his debts instantly. But it was also common knowledge that your esteemed grandfather kept you on a tight allowance. So who more likely to cheat than you?'

'And that was your sole reason to tarnish the name of a man you hardly knew?'

'There was an additional pleasure, I must admit. I had a score to settle with your grandfather. You settled it nicely.'

'And now? Are you still settling debts in the same way?'

'Naturally one must live and, contrary to society's opinion,

I am not a wealthy man. Fortunately, there's an inexhaustible supply of callow youth. The money I've won off that fool Robert Silverdale has kept me afloat for many a month.'

Amelie's eyes had been wide with dismay, but now she looked stricken. It was bad enough that her brother had gambled so stupidly, but to know that his downfall had been deliberately plotted by this depraved man was horrifying. She could not stop herself crying out, 'You are the worst of men.'

'Indeed, and it is a great pleasure to know that I exceed in this,' he gloated.

'And Miss Silverdale, was she to be part of the debt?' Gareth asked savagely, thrusting the sword once more against Glyde's throat.

'We are all fools for something, are we not? She has been my one failure. I should have known she would be more trouble than she was worth. But as soon as I saw her, I meant to have her. The mortgage on the Grosvenor Square mansion was a master stroke. I had thought to make her my wife and then sell the house to provide some much-needed funds. But damaged goods...'

His vanquisher's weapon cut into Glyde's flesh. 'You will pay for every moment of suffering you've caused her.'

'How touching,' the injured man croaked, his voice faint with pain.

Gareth ignored him and for the first time looked directly at the frightened girl standing transfixed in the corner of the room. He gave her an encouraging smile.

'Unlock the door, Amelie, and ring the bell for those ruffians to come.'

'Are you sure we should? They may overpower us,' she said uncertainly, emerging from the shadowy darkness.

'Have no fear. They're as cowardly as their paymaster. I need a light and paper and ink. This black-hearted monster is about to make a full written confession, a little keepsake from our encounter this evening.'

The prostrate man recovered sufficient strength to snarl angrily, 'I'll not be signing anything. My men will finish you in a second.'

But when Amer and Figgis appeared over the threshold and saw Glyde's situation, they seemed in no hurry to come to his aid. Gareth snapped out his orders, warning them to follow his commands or he would execute summary justice on both them and their master.

They scurried from the room and he looked down at his antagonist.

'Somehow I can't see them staying for too long. My guess would be that they'll be gone from the house as soon as they can make their escape.'

In a few minutes the men returned, bringing the items he'd demanded. He moved towards the door to take the lighted candlestick and momentarily released his sword grip. In that instant Glyde staggered to his feet, his hand crept into his pocket and he withdrew a small duelling pistol. Standing behind him, Amelie saw in an instant what he meant to do and shouted a warning.

Gareth spun round as his adversary lifted the gun to eye level and made ready to fire. He waited for what seemed an endless moment, knowing there was no way he could escape, but then Glyde's body was crumpling to the floor, the gun harmlessly firing into the ceiling. Amelie, her breathing coming fast, stood clutching a branch of the broken chandelier.

Gareth smiled with relief. 'You certainly know how to fell a man,' he murmured wryly.

'Have I killed him?'

He felt for a pulse. 'Fortunately not. We don't want him dead yet.'

Amer and Figgis turned tail at this new course of events and made off towards the nether regions of the building. Gareth, meanwhile, had bound Glyde's legs with curtain ties and was busy throwing a jug of water from the table over his face. He came round, groaning and looking decidedly green.

Gareth dragged him roughly across the floor and into a chair, propping him up against the solid oak table. He dipped the quill in the ink and placed it in Glyde's hand.

'Now write to my dictation.'

For long minutes, the pen scratched across the paper, the writer looking ever more sickly. Inwardly, Amelie fretted that he would faint or worse before he could finish, but she remained silent while Gareth's inexorable voice spelt out the long confession. When the last word had been written, and Glyde's signature appended, he carefully rolled the document and stored it safely in his shirt front.

'That is the price for my not killing you,' he said, binding his adversary's hands behind him. 'The price of my silence, however, is a little more exacting. You will leave England within the next five days. And leave for good. You will never show your face in society again.'

Glyde started angrily, but his legs were still bound and he was unable to move.

'You would do well to heed my words,' Gareth warned. He patted his chest. 'I have here the means to expose you to your peers for what you are.'

'And if I choose exposure?'

'Somehow I don't think you will. A life wandering the world isn't the most fulfilling, as I can testify, but better far than being blacklisted by your fellows. Think, too, of all those opportunities to exercise your talents. Johnny Raws are everywhere!'

He opened the door and ushered Amelie through. Glyde was already struggling with the ties that bound him as Gareth turned to leave.

'Remember,' he warned, 'five days and you will have left these shores.'

His voice was implacable and with a last hard look at his enemy, he followed Amelie into the passageway and walked her slowly through the hall and out of the front door.

Once outside she turned to him and said wonderingly, 'You came.'

'How could you doubt that I would?'

She smiled slowly in response and held her hands out to him, but he took them only briefly. For a moment she wondered at his reticence, but a more important matter needed an answer.

'Why did you let him go?' she asked, perplexed.

'What else could I do? If I called in the Runners, your abduction and my pursuit would be the talk of the town for months. There's already been more than enough scandal and I don't want any more to taint your life. This way, Glyde has his liberty, but only to spend it miserably—and you're free of him for good.'

'But if he disappears, you may not properly clear your name. People may continue to think ill of you.'

'I have his signed confession, but, in any case, I've no interest in what people think. You know the truth and that's sufficient for me.'

He smiled gently down at her and she looked once more for the warm embrace she'd been expecting ever since they left Glyde to his fate. Instead he tossed her up into the saddle of the waiting Minerva, and said, 'I'm afraid that this time you *will* have to share a horse with me!'

The mare, still tired from her earlier exertions, ambled placidly along the same lanes that she had flown down just a few hours ago. Although night had fallen and the surrounding countryside was in inky darkness, a shaft of moonlight revealed clearly the thread of packed earth that was the pathway leading back to the main Bath road.

Amelie leant back into her rescuer's arms, weary but overwhelmingly happy. Above, the clear night sky was silvered with a cascade of stars and only a breath of wind sighed through the trees as they passed on their way.

It was she who broke the calm. 'How did you know where to find me?'

'I didn't. I knew it was Glyde who'd abducted you, thanks to Fanny, but I had no means of knowing for certain which direction he'd taken. It was a hunch. I'd been told that his country estate lay nearby and I guessed that he would instinctively go to ground there once he'd got his prey.'

She shuddered. 'You talk of him as though he were a wild animal.'

'What else is he, beneath the paint and the polish?' he asked grimly.

'How clever of Fanny to recognise Glyde's men.'

'She got precious little thanks for it.' Gareth smiled reminiscently. 'Your grandmother has the devil of a temper. Do you know that?'

Amelie didn't reply.

'Like grandmother, like granddaughter, I guess.'

'Why do you say that? Is that what you thought when I failed to arrive at the Abbey? That I was angry for some reason and wanted to punish you?'

'I thought you might have regretted making the appointment.'

'But we made a promise to meet. You didn't trust me to come.'

'Of course I did,' he blustered.

'No, you didn't. You didn't trust me!' She paused. 'But then I haven't trusted you, either.'

There was a long silence between them until she said quietly, 'Neither of us is blameless, Gareth, we've both been guilty of deceit.'

His lips brushed lightly against her soft curls. 'We've done a lot of silly things,' he murmured, 'but they're in the past. Now we can both face our futures honestly.'

She hardly noticed the odd expression as she once more nestled against his strong frame, Minerva slowly and surely carrying them towards Bath. They had been passing along a stretch of the road where the trees overhung, pressing tightly together and almost barricading the moonlight from view. Then quite abruptly the trees fell away from either side and they found themselves in clear country, with the lake before them, the moon shimmering across its surface like a lustrous ribbon. Carefully, the mare began to pick her way around the shoreline. The warm night air wrapped them in its velvet touch. All was tranquil.

But dozing in Gareth's encircling arms, Amelie suddenly became aware of a warmth dripping on to her hand. She raised her fingers slowly in the moonlight and gasped when she saw them blood-red.

'Gareth, your arm!'

In the semi-conscious state into which he'd sunk, he hardly heard her.

'Gareth, wake up. You're bleeding and badly. We must stop. We must bind up your arm immediately.'

She tugged urgently on the reins and the horse came to a halt. Slipping from the saddle, she pulled him down, trying to support his weight as he slid to the ground. His face in the moonlight was chalk-white, but he was alert now and tried to reassure her.

'I'm pretty sure it's just a surface wound.'

'Surface wound or not, you seem to be doing a good job of bleeding to death.'

'One of your faults, Amelie, is that you're prone to exaggeration.'

'One of your faults, Gareth, is that you're prone to stubbornness.'

And with that she pulled down her silk petticoat and ripped off a large strip of soft white material. She led the way down to the lakeside and gently took off his shirt. The wound looked livid. She only hoped it hadn't already become infected. She bathed the angry weal with care and swiftly bound it up again, this time more tightly and thoroughly than Gareth had managed in the heat of conflict. With some difficulty he shrugged on the remains of his shirt.

The horse had followed them down to the lake and was now thirstily drinking the water. After a few moments they took hold of her bridle and led her back to the trees where she began placidly to crop the grass.

'She should have a rest,' Amelie said, 'and so should you. Here…' and she quickly pushed a mound of leaves together to form a bed '…lie down for a while and try to sleep.'

He protested, but only feebly. He knew that if he were to return her safely to her family, he needed to be in stronger case. A short rest could only do them both good. In a moment he was asleep while she watched over him. At length when he showed no sign of waking, she curled up beside him and slept herself, her head on his chest, the glinting curls fanned out across his body.

It was one of those curls tickling his chin, as the breeze ruffled her hair, that finally woke him. He ran his fingers through the soft tresses and kissed her gently awake. Her eyes opened and for a moment fear engulfed her as she recalled the locked and darkened room of her imprisonment. But the rustle of the leaves and the breeze on her warm cheeks steadied her racing heart.

Gareth was looking down at her tenderly. 'I have no idea how long we've been sleeping, dear child, but your grandmother must be going out of her mind with worry. It's time we were gone.'

He looked over at Minerva. 'The mare is well and truly rested. She should carry us swiftly back to town.'

Amelie stretched lazily. Her ordeal was over and the man she loved was by her side. 'I've never thanked you properly for rescuing me.'

'Thanked me? What nonsense is this?'

'You risked your life.'

'But think of the prize,' he said lightly.

'You came for me because I'm yours and always will be.' Her voice grew husky and her eyes glistened with unshed tears.

'You'll always be the one girl I've truly loved, Amelie,' he said carefully.

She felt a shiver of apprehension and sat up swiftly. 'Why does that sound like a farewell?'

'Because, my dear, it is. As soon as we reach Bath and you're reunited with your grandmother, I must be on my way. Lucas will be wondering what on earth has happened. I've my valise half-packed and ready to go.'

'You can't still mean to leave England,' she burst out.

'I must, Amelie.'

'I don't understand you,' she cried passionately. 'Why must you go? You have a confession from Glyde. Everything is changed.'

'Nothing is changed, my love. I'm still the same man with the same history—and it's not an edifying one. I'm not a proper suitor for you.'

'But you've proved Glyde a villain, you can clear your name.'

'No matter how much I may wave his confession, scandal is like to follow me wherever I go. You deserve better.'

'This is nonsense.' The alarm in her voice hurt, but he must keep to his vow for her sake.

'It's the way the world wags,' he said as calmly as he could. 'And your grandmother will know that better than anyone. She will advise you.'

'You mean in the same way she advised me about Glyde.' Amelie's tone was acid.

'She's learned a painful lesson, I think you'll find. She'll be anxious to discover a man who is good and kind and not at all like Glyde. And not like me, either—someone whose skeletons from a misspent life will not always be threatening to reappear.'

'I don't care how many skeletons are hidden deep in your past, Gareth,' she said in a taut voice. 'They may all make an appearance if they will. I want no other man, and I intend to have no other.'

'Fighting talk,' he said, with a sad attempt at a joke.

'And why not?' she demanded. 'You've just fought for my

life, but now you seem intent on denying it to me. So, yes, it is fighting talk.'

In the silver light that threaded the landscape her face was ardent with feeling and her eyes, no longer velvet soft, sparkled with indignation.

'Why am I not to be allowed to choose my own destiny?' she went on. 'Why should everyone feel they have the right to make my decisions for me? First my father, then my grandmother and now, unbelievably, you!'

In her vexation she'd moved a little away and sat facing him, her back ramrod straight and the chestnut tendrils of her hair blowing in the breeze. The torn dress had been hastily patched together, but now the cloth she'd wrapped around herself slipped from her shoulders, revealing an expanse of luminous skin, gleaming pearl-like in the moonlight. Gareth had to force himself from feasting on this radiant vision, for both his heart and his body were urging him to forget his steadfast resolve to walk away and never return.

He cast around in his mind for an argument that would convince them both, but she was in no mood to listen.

'*I* have made my own decision,' she was saying proudly, 'and I'll allow no one to gainsay it, not even you, Gareth. When I asked you to meet me at the Abbey it was to tell you that I wanted to go away with you, that I wanted to live with you for as long as you desired me.'

Astonishment ranged across his face. Did she love him so much that she was willing to relinquish all vestige of virtue, in order to be with him?

'And I still want to,' she announced defiantly.

'But…' A vagrant part of him began to leap hungrily to life. He found his resistance crumbling, the power of her love destroying his last defence.

'No buts, I'm sick of buts,' she commanded. 'Sick of other people trying to arrange my life. You followed me to my prison and from now on I intend to follow you—wherever you go!'

'What a spitfire!' He was gathering his scattered wits. 'I see you do have your grandmother's temper.'

'I may pull caps with you from time to time,' she admitted, 'but only when you deserve it. Will you still be able to love me?'

In response he pulled her roughly into his arms, the misconceived vow consigned at a stroke to oblivion. 'Now it's your turn to hear *my* decision, my fiery one,' he whispered into her ear. 'You *will* go with me wherever I go, but with a wedding ring on your finger.'

His expression shadowed for a moment. 'If we stay in England, it won't be easy—there'll be gossip, innuendo, even direct snubs. You'll have to learn to bear it all with an indifferent face. Do you think you can? Brave the world with me?'

'I can and I will, but I'll need kisses, endless kisses.' She sighed slyly. 'You've been particularly mean with them of late.'

He pulled her down onto their bed of leaves and searched her face lovingly.

'You're sure of this, my darling?'

'I couldn't be more sure,' she breathed and stroked the hard planes of his face as he bent over her.

His eyes were the deepest blue, dark and mysterious, and his gaze penetrated to her very heart. He gave her a long, lingering kiss and the heat of his mouth made her hungry for him. She closed her eyes, drinking in his musky scent and melting, melting into his body like warm honey as he hardened against her. Her fingers buried themselves in his dark hair and pulled him closer as his kisses became ever more urgent, covering her face, her arms, her neck, with a fierceness that left her breathless. Then, more gently, he pushed aside the tattered remnants of her bodice. Cupping the soft swell of her breasts, he brought them to his eager lips. A deep, aching pleasure shot through her body.

'I see your arm is a good deal better,' she managed to murmur.

'Don't be pert, miss, or…'

'Or?'

'Or this', and with one deft movement he rolled her beneath him, fitting his form to hers. Slowly and thoroughly his hands began to move over her body, undressing her as he went, his mouth following where his hands led. The warm night air caressed her bare skin as it took fire beneath the heat of his lips. Gradually she began to move as he did, responding to his forceful rhythm until every fibre sang with hot pleasure. Her body ablaze, the world around her vanished into nothingness—the soft grass, the hushed lake, the clear night sky. Her world was contained only in this moment and she gave herself up to it.

Neither Brielle nor Miles Silverdale could bring themselves to eat. They sat at either end of the mahogany table, maintaining the pretence of dining while their faces, mirrored in the sheen of the wood, reflected back at them an overwhelming anxiety.

Horrocks carefully served the modest meal: soup and entrées followed by salmon, then a braised ham and a haunch of venison, and finally an assortment of pastries, jellies and creams. They sat in silence as the butler expertly brought and removed courses. But every dish was returned to the kitchen barely touched.

The dismal meal at an end, they removed to the drawing room and settled themselves in seats flanking the fireside. It was early

June, but Horrocks had thought it wise to kindle a small blaze and provide a little cheer. Both had given up trying to make polite conversation and instead gazed intently into the flames, sunk in their own thoughts. Forbidding images danced in front of them, pictures of Amelie terrified and alone, at the mercy of a villain they had both championed. Older heads had not been wiser and it was their lovely girl who was paying the price.

At around ten o'clock Horrocks brought in the tea tray. They sat still silent and cradling their two cups, their eyes now forever drawn to the hands of the clock slowly turning. An hour later the door bell pealed. Miles, slumped in the brown leather chester-field, jumped from his seat in one movement. Brielle held up her hand for silence and strained her ears. Two voices sounded from below, but she was certain one of them was Horrocks. Could it be that Gareth Wendover had returned empty-handed? She sat perched on the edge of her chair while Miles paced up and down, unable to rest.

Horrocks opened the drawing-room door and in a voice muted by disappointment announced, 'Lord Lucas Avery.' The servants, too, were keeping their own vigil below stairs.

Brielle pulled herself together sufficiently to make the neces-sary introductions. Their visitor looked uncomfortable, but also extremely worried.

'Please accept my apologies for this intrusion at so late an hour. Only very real anxiety for my friend's welfare could prompt me to impose on you in this way.'

'Your friend?' Brielle queried.

Lucas turned to her and in his overwrought state, the words poured out unchecked. 'I had a note from Gareth… He's staying with me, and I couldn't really make head or tail of it. Something about his having to leave Bath at short notice, but that he'd be back to collect his baggage. He was due to leave for France tomorrow.'

He paused for breath and then continued more slowly but with some awkwardness, 'He mentioned in the note that Miss Silverdale was in danger. Naturally, I've no wish to intrude on a private family matter, but he hasn't returned, and it's now many hours since he left.'

'Don't apologise, Lord Avery. As you see, we are in similar case, waiting helplessly for news.' Brielle sank down in her chair. She looked very tired and very old. 'You're most welcome to sit and wait with us.'

'But where has he gone, ma'am?'

'To find Rufus Glyde. It appears that the man we trusted—' and she included Lord Silverdale in her gesture '—is an out-and-out villain.'

'That I have always suspicioned, but your granddaughter?'

'Abducted,' she said abruptly, but her voice faltered. The young man looked horrified.

'This is the most shocking news. What can I say? But don't despair, Lady St Clair. Gareth is a resourceful man and a tough one. He's had many years shifting for himself in difficult circumstances. If anyone can help her, it will be him. Depend on it, he will bring her safely home.'

'So I hoped when I agreed to his going, but that was many hours ago. Will he even find Glyde?'

'I'm sure he will. Glyde will not travel far with an unwilling woman in tow. His country estate is not too distant from Bath and Gareth knows its general direction.'

She refused to be comforted. 'Glyde is not alone. Amelie's maid has told us that two ruffians in his employ swooped on her mistress. Your friend is just one man. How will he fare against the brutality of such low creatures?'

'*And* Sir Rufus is a notable swordsman,' put in Lord Silverdale, still pacing the room and in despair for his daughter's safety.

'Gareth is a first-class fencer. He will be more than a match for Glyde,' Lucas said staunchly, but his heart felt leaden. He had a very good idea of the odds his friend would face. If only he'd waited. But Gareth would have refused his help, he knew. Lucas had a wife and children and the mission was dangerous, if not suicidal.

Frustrated, he suggested riding out towards Glyde's estate. 'I could try to discover news of them. At least I would be doing something useful.'

Brielle shook her head. 'I appreciate your offer, Lord Avery, but I doubt that you would learn much. You might, however, give rise to speculation. One of the reasons that persuaded me to let your friend go alone was the need to keep this whole shocking business from becoming an open scandal.'

Lord Silverdale interjected with a sombre shake of his head, 'We shall know soon enough what has happened to them, I fear.'

His words effectively silenced the trio and they sat mutely, each encased in private thought. The hours wore on. Horrocks appeared regularly to make up the fire and offer unwanted re-freshments. As the minutes ticked by, Gareth's mission looked increasingly hopeless and by the time the small hours arrived what little spirit had earlier been present had vanished entirely.

The breaking dawn, chill and grey, found the three of them dozing fitfully by the embers, unwilling to give up their watch, but knowing in their hearts that whatever news came, it could only be bad. Then a bell pealed below. A sudden noise, a flurry of voices, footsteps springing up the marble staircase, and the door flew open.

Gareth and Amelie stood framed in the doorway, tired and travel weary but with hands held fast and faces lit with gladness. Brielle started forwards and flung her arms around her granddaughter, tears streaming down her face.

'It's all right, Grandmama. I'm all right,' Amelie calmed her.

She smoothed Brielle's hair and kissed her on both cheeks and then, putting her grandmother gently aside, moved towards her father where he stood alone and forlorn. His emotions choked him and for a moment he could only cling to his daughter, silently hugging her to his chest.

'Papa, why are you here?'

'My darling, thank God you're safe. Thank God,' his voice choked again. 'Will you ever forgive me?'

'There's nothing to forgive.'

'Indeed there is. I was the one intent on forcing you into marriage with that villain. You must believe me, Amelie, I had no idea what manner of man he was. I have only just discovered the evil he has practised against our family and I came immediately to warn you. But by then he had done his worst.'

'Not quite his worst, Papa', and she turned with a radiant face to her lover. 'I have my rescuer to thank for that. Grandmama, I believe you already know Gareth, but, Papa, let me introduce you. This is Gareth Wendover.'

The name made Lucas Avery's brows twitch, but Gareth signed to him to hold his peace.

'I don't think we've met before,' Miles was saying, 'but you have my most grateful thanks for what you've done this night. How can I ever repay you?'

'I wish to marry your daughter, Lord Silverdale. To have your consent will be ample repayment.'

Miles Silverdale looked taken aback. 'That will need some discussion, young man,' he began to bluster.

'Her father means that he'll be only too pleased that she is to marry a man of such courage and principle,' Brielle interrupted, giving Miles one of her basilisk stares.

'Is that what you wish, Amelie?' he asked his daughter mildly.

'More than anything, Papa.'

'But I had such hopes for you, my dear. Mr Wendover is obviously an honourable man who deserves the highest consideration. I would not wish you to think that I'm unappreciative of what I owe him. However, marriage is another matter and I'm sure he would agree himself that you could look a lot higher for a husband.'

Once more Brielle interrupted her son-in-law. 'Miles, we have already made the most dreadful mess of Amelie's life between us. Do you not think that she knows her own mind best?'

'I do,' said Amelie firmly. 'I'm going to marry Gareth and I hope you'll be happy for me. But I shall marry him even if you're not. He is the only man I will ever want and I intend to share the rest of my life with him.'

She looked mischievously around at the gathering. 'I shall make an excellent vagabond, I'm sure!'

'There will be no need for that,' her father rejoined hastily. 'Mr Wendover may not be the husband I had in mind, but he is a man of integrity and if he is your choice, I am happy to give my blessing. But not,' he added, 'to a life of vagabondage. I'm sure that between us—' and he glanced across at Brielle '—we can start this young man in a respectable profession and provide a home for you both.'

Brielle nodded her head vigorously. 'Naturally, Mr Wendover, it will be quite unnecessary for you to resume your former life.' Gareth smiled at the thought of the inward shudder she must be suppressing.

The presence of Lucas Avery had all but been forgotten, but now he was staring at them open-mouthed as though he could hardly believe what he was hearing. Then he began to laugh, amusement bubbling up in him, mixed with relief at his friend's safe return, until it exploded in a riot of noise that rang around the room. His companions turned to him in surprise. Gradually his mirth subsided and he whisked out a handkerchief to dab the tears from his eyes.

'I'm so sorry. Forgive my merriment. But to hear you talk about setting Gareth up in a profession…!'

He had all their attention, their eyes fixed on him in enquiry. Between laughs he managed to splutter, 'I think you'll find Gareth already has a profession. Meet the new Earl of Denville.'

Lord Silverdale and Brielle looked at first astounded, then their faces flooded with relief.

'But why are you travelling in this fashion?' Miles asked him in amazement.

The whole sorry story of Glyde's villainy had to be told and the signed confession passed around. Lord Silverdale read it and reread it, shaking his head, and muttering inaudibly from time to time. Then he looked up from the sheaf of papers and spoke with determination.

'Glyde is already widely discredited and I will make sure that everyone of my acquaintance, and their acquaintance, too, is aware of this confession. *You* may have promised him silence, but I have not. If I have any influence, the tale of his infamy will soon be known to every member of the *ton.*'

Reaching out to his future son-on-law, he clutched Gareth's hand. 'It's clear that you've suffered even greater harm from this devil. No one could be more worthy of my beautiful daughter.'

'Your beautiful daughter has something to say,' Amelie interrupted bitingly. She had kept silent until this moment, her lips firmly sealed, but now she turned a furious face to Gareth.

'Were you by chance ever going to tell me who you really were?'

Conscious of the seething indignation flooding her granddaughter's lovely face, Brielle made a decision. 'It is more than time that we all had some rest,' she said briskly and moved towards the doorway with surprising speed. In an instant she had shepherded her companions out of the room.

The door had barely closed behind them before Amelie repeated her question, her tone even more imperious.

'Well, were you ever going to tell me who you were? Or perhaps it just slipped your mind that you'd inherited a title?'

'Strangely enough, it did. Or at least has done these past few weeks.'

His blue eyes sparkled with an errant sweetness. She longed to reach out and feel him close again, but steeled herself against his charm.

'How could it slip your mind? It isn't possible. You vowed there would be no more secrets between us, yet the biggest secret has remained untold. How can I ever truly believe you?'

'Amelie, my darling, you must believe me when I say that I'd pushed the Earl of Denville out of my mind. You met me as

Gareth Wendover and I've loved you as he. The Earl of Denville is as foreign to me as to you. We must both get to know him.'

For a long minute she did not speak, her eyes scanning his face intently, searching and searching again, and knew he spoke the truth. Her anger drained away. This *was* the final deception, she thought, and the first brick in the bridge of trust they would build together.

He was by her side and looking directly into her eyes, wrapping her in stardust. She felt a wild, dancing joy surge headlong through her. His arms were back where they belonged, his lips close.

'I love you, Amelie Silverdale,' he whispered.

'I love you too, Gareth Wendover,' she replied.

HISTORICAL

Novels coming in December 2010

LADY ARABELLA'S SCANDALOUS MARRIAGE
Carole Mortimer

Sinister whispers may surround Darius Wynter, but one thing's for sure—marriage to the infamous Duke means that Arabella will soon discover the exquisite pleasures of the marriage bed…

DANGEROUS LORD, SEDUCTIVE MISS
Mary Brendan

Heiress Deborah Cleveland jilted an earl for her true love— then he disappeared! Now Lord Buckland has returned, as sinfully attractive as ever. Can Deborah resist the dark magnetism of the lawless lord?

BOUND TO THE BARBARIAN
Carol Townend

To settle a debt, Katerina must convince commanding warrior Ashfirth Saxon that *she* is her royal mistress. But the days— *and nights*—of deceit take their toll. How long before she is willingly bedded by this proud barbarian?

BOUGHT: THE PENNILESS LADY
Deborah Hale

Her new husband may be handsome—but his heart is black. Desperate to safeguard the future of her precious nephew, penniless Lady Artemis Dearing will do anything—even marry the man whose brother ruined her darling sister!

 MILLS & BOON

HISTORICAL

Another exciting novel available this month:

COURTING MISS VALLOIS

Gail Whitiker

From the fields of France...

Miss Sophie Vallois' looks and grace make her an instant hit with London Society. No one would know that the French beauty is a mere farmer's daughter, with no interest in marriage whatsoever...

...to the drawing rooms of London!

Except Robert Silverton, who has other reasons for staying away from Sophie. Yet her spirit and compassion intrigue him... Rather than keeping her at arm's length, Robert soon wants the delectable Miss Vallois well and truly *in* his arms!

HISTORICAL

**Another exciting novel available
this month:**

THE BRIDE
WORE SCANDAL

Helen Dickson

Virgin Lady…

From the moment Christina Atherton first saw the
notorious Lord Rockley she couldn't control her blushes.
She knew she could not hold out for long against
his dark and seductive ways.

…Scandalously Pregnant!

Lord Rockley only meant to protect Christina from a
dangerous highwayman, but she was oh, so beguiling. And
when Christina discovered that she was expecting, Lord Rockley
knew of just one way to restore her virtue. He must make
Christina his bride…before scandal ruined them both!